THE MAZE

A Thomas Pichon Novel

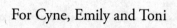

For Cyne, Emily and Toni

Cape Breton University Press recognizes the
support of the Canada Council for the Arts,
Block Grant program, and the Province of Nova
Scotia, through Film & Creative Industries
Nova Scotia, for our publishing program. We
are pleased to work in partnership with these
bodies to develop and promote our cultural resources.

Cover by Cathy MacLean, Chéticamp, NS
Layout by Mike R. Hunter, Port Hawkesbury and Sydney, NS
First printed in Canada

The font used in this manuscript is Garamond. It was familiar to all French
readers in the 18th century. Claude Garamond created the typeface in the 1540s
for the French king, François I. Over time, the Garamond fonts came to be used
throughout Europe. The Garamond typeface uses less ink than many other fonts.

Library and Archives Canada Cataloguing in Publication

Johnston, A. J. B., author
The maze : a Thomas Pichon novel / A.J.B. Johnston.

Issued in print and electronic formats.
ISBN 978-1-897009-76-5 (pbk.).--ISBN 978-1-927492-70-3 (pdf).--
ISBN 978-1-927492-71-0 (epub)

1. Pichon, Thomas, 1700-1781--Fiction. I. Title.

PS8619.O4843M39 2014 C813'.6 C2014-900512-1

C2014-900513-X

Cape Breton University Press
P.O. Box 5300, Sydney, Nova Scotia B1P 6L2 CA
www.cbupress.ca

THE MAZE

A Thomas Pichon Novel

by A. J. B. Johnston

**CAPE BRETON
UNIVERSITY
·P·R·E·S·S·**

Ambition can creep as well as soar.
Edmund Burke (1729-1797)

I
Perambulation

Château Le Mesnil, Brittany
June 1727

From the intersecting paths of golden flint, away from the eyes of any who might have been admiring his measured stroll, Thomas steps under the vine-covered wooden arch and into the garden maze. The walls on both sides rise green and dark, up to the height of the tricorne atop his head. He cannot help but wonder if Marguerite, his wife of several months, watched from one of the château windows as he disappeared. Better still, he'd like to think that her lady companion, the bewildering Hélène, was gazing out from her own room as he perambulated like a prince with a silver-handled cane. He likes the idea of that. Would that his elegance spurred her on to do what he wants, what they both want.

Thomas comes to a halt after the second turn. He reaches out to touch the interwoven branches of the yews. Their leaves of tiny needles are delicate to the touch. Yet poisonous, it's said. Bringing convulsions and collapse. He'll not ingest any needles to find out. He begins to move again, slowly inhaling the scent. He keeps his right hand extended so that his fingertips stay in contact with the green wall on that side. It's the first time he's stepped into a maze, but he shared a conversation with some gardeners at the Café Procope a few months back, and the subject of mazes came up. The gardeners spoke of the simple secret that lies behind each and every one. "A secret," Thomas thought to himself, when is there not? He leaned in to hear what it was. In the case of mazes, it seems that you have to keep your hand on the right-hand wall no matter what. The right hand takes you to the centre, no matter how many twists and turns. Disregard the obstructions. Don't think too much. Keep moving.

—

Hand to the pearl choker around her neck, Hélène sits in the window seat. It gives her a commanding view of the ornamental gardens directly below. Now that Marguerite's husband has stopped his posturing on the garden paths and gone under the arch that leads into the maze, she's lost sight of him. She stands to see if she can catch the top of his hat somewhere in the maze.

"There." She spots the dark grey tricorne a couple of rows in from the entrance to the maze. A deep breath comes out of her. She has a couple of hours before Marguerite needs her to help with her change of clothes and the rest of her toilette. So— so why not? Does she not deserve a little reward for being the dutiful servant for so long?

Affirmation brings a quickening patter in her chest.

Once outdoors, wearing her dress the colour of a robin's egg, Hélène advances as slowly as a person in a hurry can force herself. She knows she has to pretend to take her time. Madame Dufour, or even worse, Marguerite herself, could well be watching from somewhere inside the château. So, Hélène pauses wherever the empty garden paths intersect, seeming to study which lane of crushed flint between the plantings she should consider following next. Yet it's a ruse. She knows exactly where she's going and why. And, if anyone should ask, she has an answer primed. She'll tell them with a straight face that it was simply for a chat. A chat. The word makes Hélène smile.

—

As expected, Thomas finds a bench at the end of the twisting turning path, in the dead centre of the maze. Made of wood, it's painted the darkest of green, even darker than the yews. He takes

2

a seat, back stiffly upright, his left leg outstretched in his most pretentious pose.

Looking up, above the manicured top of the hedge, Thomas is able to make out a good portion of the vast roofline of Madame Dufour's château. The black slates tiling the roof and the windowed turrets jutting up here and there glint in the afternoon sun.

Thomas takes a long deep breath. He likes this world of green. He likes being out of sight of anyone and everyone.

There come to him a few lines of verse, the first he's heard in many months.

A beaten path,
A winding maze,
We journey on,
We journey long.

He comes to a halt. Waits. More words arrive.

The air it stirs,
There comes a blur,
We find ourselves.
Life is a maze.

He isn't sure if he wants to keep the lines or not. He tries them again, this time aloud, to see if they will hold up.

A beaten path, a winding maze
        We journey on, we—

Thomas hears his name break the spell of the verse. Then light footsteps on the gravel pathway.

—

Marguerite Salles takes in the grandeur of the suite of rooms her cousin Madame Dufour has given her for this stay in her Britan-

3

ny château. Marguerite's apartment in Paris cannot compete with this. The quality of the furnishings, especially the frieze above the wainscot, makes her eyes go wide. Still, which of the two of them has a new husband, one barely a third her age? Marguerite smiles. Dear cousin cannot match her there, can she now?

Yet where is her errant Thomas right now? He said he wanted to stroll upon the grounds. Marguerite wraps a pale green shawl around her shoulders and steps round the ottoman over to the turreted windows of the room. She scans the brick courtyard that defines the front of the house and peers into the darkness of the open stables across the way. Next, over to the garden with its diagonal paths. Marguerite wrinkles her brow. She shifts her gaze to where meticulously cropped yews stand as a maze.

—

With the day's light fading fast and the first of the château's candelabra and sconces lit, Thomas descends the stairs, heading for the salon. Along the length of the hall, with its half dozen tapestries of hunting scenes and the two coats of arms connected with the family of Madame Dufour's late husband, he feels his stride go a little longer and lighter than of late; his posture is definitely correct. He's not felt this good in weeks – nay, months.

The door to the salon is already ajar. Stepping in, Thomas glances at the small clock on the mantle above the roaring fire. It is as he thought: precisely seven o'clock. Tardiness is something he silently holds against those who arrive after him.

Two menservants stand erect as sentries at their posts. There is an angelic lad with tousled hair kneeling by the fire, tending to the grate. As for the people whose good fortune it is to be served by this staff, only their host, Madame Dufour, has arrived. Wide to begin with, she is seated in a vermilion chair as though it's a part of her, hands not resting but gripping the arms of the chair. And heavens, her expression. As glum as any Thomas has ever seen. Hers might be the face of an angry man rather than a woman of grand standing.

"Good evening, Cousin." Thomas offers a quick curling gesture with his right hand, followed by a tight bow. Then he presents what he is certain is one of the best of his smiles. He wants her to think that he feels honoured to be one of her guests.

Madame Dufour slowly cranes Thomas's way. She looks him up and down. "Good evening?"

Is this a question or a greeting? He understands she's never been overly fond of him – in fact, Marguerite has told him she tried to block the marriage – but she is the hostess here and he the guest.

Thomas twists toward the head male servant of the household, a pop-eyed fellow with a loose-fitting jacket. He's approaching with a decanter wrapped in a linen napkin cradled in one arm and a tray of stemware in the other. The glasses catch the light with their own glow.

With the elderly servant standing at attention, Thomas selects a glass off the tray. He takes his time undressing the carafe, then does the pour himself. He makes a point to stop at halfway up his bowl, glancing at Madame Dufour. "The others are not down yet I see."

"Your *wife* is not here yet, no." Thomas winces at the pointed emphasis in her voice.

Oh my. Why is this woman in such a sour mood? When their coach arrived at midday, Madame Dufour was at her best. She specifically mentioned how at seven in the evening the four of them would sample a much heralded rosé she had had sent up from Provence. Then they would move into the adjoining room and sit to dine. Where did that obliging hostess go? If this keeps up, he might suggest to Marguerite that they cut their visit short.

Thomas takes a tiny sip of the rosé.

"Fine, Madame, very fine." Thomas holds out his glass in acknowledgement of Madame Dufour's wise choice. "Flowery and with a lovely nose. And such a delightful pink. I've not been to Provence, you know. Not to the south at all."

Madame Dufour makes no return remark. She does not even glance his way.

5

"Last-minute touches, I suppose," Thomas says. "For my wife I mean, for your cousin. And her companion, of course. But then you know women better than I." He tries to manufacture a smile.

This time Madame Dufour does look over and up, to where he is standing a dozen feet away. When her gaze meets his, slowly, barely moving at all, eyebrows arched, she shakes her head.

The door opens at the far end of the salon and Thomas turns away from his sour hostess in relief. He takes a few quick steps toward the other end of the room but is brought up short at the appearance of his wife. She is wearing her new light green silk dress, purchased expressly so as to impress Madame Dufour. Yet Marguerite is walking stiffly, her usually rather handsome face drawn tight. The eyes, always so generous, hold no kindness. She is locked into a fixed, hard stare. And behind her, shoulders slumped, comes Hélène, in the same blue dress she was wearing earlier, only it looks unprepared, unrefreshed, almost battered. Her face empty, completely blank.

"Aha."

Thomas turns toward the voice, toward Madame Dufour. He sees something of a smile on her previously glum face. And it's not just any smile. It's a gloat. What is going on? His eyes scramble for an explanation from the faces in the room.

"What— how are we all this evening?" His gaze shifts back and forth, alighting even on the servants, who appear startled to have him notice them at all.

"Indeed," announces Madame Dufour.

Thomas gives his hostess the stiff shoulder she deserves. He focuses instead on Marguerite. But she gives neither nod nor blink, her steady stare making Thomas step back. His hands search the empty air. "Is something wrong, my Marguerite?" He takes a tentative half-step toward his wife.

Marguerites make a snorting sound, followed by a definitive shake of the head. Thomas has never heard or seen her do anything like that. At last she makes eye contact. It's a chilling gaze, a gaze she holds as she takes her seat. She lowers into a chair, grasping the arms in much the same heavy way as Madame Dufour is doing across the way.

A brittle silence descends. Thomas feels his head go a little light, as if the wig he put on a half hour ago up in his room is lifting off the top of his head. He widens his stance to make sure he is solidly in place. He turns away from Marguerite and scans the now bewildering room. He makes sure to avoid the gloating Madame Dufour. When he reaches the fireplace he allows his lids to close. How warm and good that feels. And what a comfort to hear the little clock on the mantle ticking on.

"Attention, sir." The servant boy by Thomas's knees is pointing at the fire he's tending.

"Of course."

Thomas slides his feet back and moves away. A spark might burn his pants or coat, and the boy was right to warn him away. Thomas watches the lad use his iron poker to stir the embers on the front of the grate. He wonders if he should tell the boy that the room is hot enough as it is. That he could and should leave the fire alone. But then, nothing in or about this château and its staff is his. He has to hold his tongue.

Thomas fills his chest with air as he shifts back to face the room. The first thing he notices in his en passant scan is that Hélène is no longer where she was. She has taken a chair, a bare wooden one positioned midway between his wife and Madame Dufour.

Thomas pretends to stretch, then to yawn. He risks taking a fleeting look squarely at Hélène. Her eyes are down. No, they are fully closed. The only movement she makes is with her hands. They are churning in her lap.

"Monsieur?"

Thomas nearly jumps. The elderly servant has come up beside him, come very close. He no longer has the tray of stemware, but he is holding out the linen-wrapped carafe for Thomas's consideration. It's practically under his nose.

"More rosé, Monsieur?"

Thomas shakes his head. "Go away," he says.

"Only doing his job," Madame Dufour intones.

The servant pulls quickly back. Madame Dufour gestures to Marguerite. "Sooner or later," she says, "one reveals who one really is. It comes out."

Thomas seeks out Madame Dufour with his angry gaze. She accepts the challenge; neither backs down.

"Just apologize, Thomas," says a weary Marguerite. "You, not the servant, are in the wrong."

Thomas breaks off the staring match with Madame Dufour, bowing first to his wife, then to the servant. The wide-eyed man is now ten feet away, standing well behind Marguerite's chair. Thomas redirects the reverence. "Please excuse me, my captain. As my wife has just said, I was in the wrong, not you. The rosé is excellent, as is your service."

"Enough, enough," comes from Madame Dufour. "Sit down, Monsieur Pichon. Will you sit down?"

"As you wish." Thomas adds a shrug.

He picks up one of the four bare wooden chairs in a line against the wall, farther down past the fireplace. He brings it back and places it so that he will be closest to Marguerite. As he lifts the chair it occurs to him that it's entirely possible that the sour mood in the room may have nothing to do with him. Maybe whatever it is – that which has made two women angry and the third subdued – concerns only the women. If he can simply remain apart from the passing storm he'll not likely be touched. Thomas brings his hands together in his lap. He presents his wife with what he is confident is a perfectly innocent face.

"Well, look at you." Marguerite shakes her head.

Thomas inclines his head but does not say a word. He will not take any bait. This has nothing to do with him, he is sure of it. He maintains his posture and his clasped hands.

Marguerite casts a tiny smile. The ends of her lips, only the tips, curl up. "You've not spoken to Hélène." Marguerite gestures toward her downcast lady companion seated to her left. "No greeting at all for your friend?"

Thomas feels his stomach pinch. Referring to Hélène as *his* friend does not sound good at all.

"You are correct. I am sorry." Thomas adjusts his posture. He turns slightly in his seat. "Good evening, Hélène."

"Butter would not melt," mutters Madame Dufour.

Hélène stops moving her hands and looks up. Thomas is startled to see a pair of dark watery eyes and is held, rapt. She sends him a long, slow blink, causing tears to flood her cheeks.

Thomas's eyes jerk down to his knees. How strange. He can make out the sound of his own breathing above the crackle and spit of the fire. He can hear the candles guttering to his left and right. Then there's that soft sobbing coming from sad-faced Hélène.

Thomas lifts his gaze to Marguerite. Is this what you want? he asks with his eyes. You want to punish your companion, the one you gladly accepted into your life a few months ago? Did Hélène steal something, is that it? Or say something rude? Thomas opens his mouth, but doesn't speak. His questions remain unasked.

"Something you want to say?" Marguerite's face loses some of its severity. She inclines forward. "I'm listening. Go ahead."

Thomas feels a racing pulse beating somewhere in his head. He leans forward in his seat. "I— I'm not sure I know what you mean."

"No?"

"No, Marguerite, I confess to feeling lost."

The sobbing stops. Thomas darts a glance at Hélène, who now has both hands covering her face. Yet he can still see her neck, her trembling neck. Thomas tries to draw a breath, but thinks better of it. He returns his gaze to Marguerite.

She is immobile. Her blue eyes say she is waiting him out. Where before Thomas was too warm, he's now chilled. He has the shivering sensation that he is somehow caught. A Latin phrase he learned at school as a boy comes into his head. *Iacta alea est.* The die is cast.

Marguerite glances at her cousin.

"Now?" Madame Dufour asks. She raises her right hand off the arm of the chair.

Thomas swings back to see his wife's reply. Marguerite shakes her head. What is going on? Thomas's eyes involuntarily well up. He looks beseechingly at Marguerite.

His wet eyes, an index finger lifted up to stem a possible tide, have an effect. Marguerite gives up her ceaseless stare. She blinks in sympathy and looks away from Thomas's youthful, penitent face. She pretends to examine her fingernails.

"Oh, please." A scowling Madame Dufour casts both hands into the air.

Thomas and Marguerite turn toward their hostess. Madame Dufour's complexion is dark, her chest puffed out. A thrusting hand punctuates the air. "If she won't tell you, Thomas, I will. We saw you. We saw you in the maze. Yes, *you*, with this one here." She jerks a thumb at Hélène.

"The maze?" Thomas feels his shoulders hunch. He wishes his words had not come out so high-pitched. He could have done better than that. He tries to find a quizzical expression for his face, but he's not sure that's the face he presents. He flutters his eyes at Madame Dufour, then at Marguerite.

Hélène lifts off her chair. She is off and running from the circle of chairs, heading for the door that leads to the stairs up to the rooms. She's out and gone, leaving a gaping void in the salon.

Instinctively, Thomas rises from his chair. He's dazed. Maybe he should ... because he wants.... Instead, he looks down at his seated wife.

Marguerite is shaking her head. Her face is once again as hard as it was when she first came into the salon. "You'd better not," she says quietly but determinedly.

Thomas hears the warning. Marguerite spoke it as calmly as if it were a mere statement of fact.

"She— Hélène," Thomas says, "your lady companion, she, she seems very upset." Thomas hears Madame Dufour bark a laugh, but he will not turn her way. It's Marguerite and only Marguerite who matters in this affair. Thomas puts a hand to his chin. He clenches his jaw, hoping that will help to steady all that's racing inside of him.

"So?" Marguerite opens her right hand to gesture her husband's way.

Thomas removes his hand from his chin. He leans back to press against the hardness of the chair. It feels good, good to hurt a bit. It should help him think. Yet no clear thinking comes. All he has are words. "Cousin said something about a maze?"

Thomas hears Madame Dufour vent some wind from her ass. Or maybe she has laughed. He refuses to even give her a glance.

Marguerite stares at her husband like she's trying to peer through a mist, a cloud. "What?" he hears her softly say. Then she turns toward the fire.

The latest log the servant boy has tossed in gives a hiss and pop. Thomas wonders why the lad will not go away and take the other servants with him. That would leave just him and Marguerite to work things out. Except for the dour Madame in whose château this terror is unfolding.

Thomas swings back to face Marguerite at the same moment as she does the same. He is struck by how tragically sad she now appears. Her anger appears to have slipped away. Thomas tilts his head, puzzled. What does this mean? Marguerite shrugs her heavy shoulders. She looks over to her cousin.

"Show him, Cousin. Show him what you have."

Thomas tips back his chair as he watches Madame Dufour lean to the far side of her vermilion seat. With a little smile, Madame returns his troubled gaze as she reaches downward and outward with a blind grasp, her hand and fingers searching for something on the floor.

Thomas steals a glance at Marguerite, whose face has no more colour and shows no more relief than it did a moment ago. Thomas lowers the front legs of his chair to the floor. He snaps back to see what it is that Madame Dufour is dramatizing.

And there it is, held aloft in Madame Dufour's slowly waving right hand. A telescope. Holding it up brings a cruel, hard smile to her mouth. Thomas winces. He pivots back to his wife.

Marguerite gives the slightest possible shrug. "That's right," she says. "A spyglass. We saw what happened in the maze. Her, that thing, in her blue dress."

Thomas's mouth goes dry. He gestures emptily with his hands, then makes the same pointless gesture a second time. He opens his mouth only to have it lock shut again. There was something he was going to say, but ... it's disappeared. He summons a not-guilty expression to his face, yet it fails to arrive. Maybe she would prefer bewilderment or surprise? Something or anything that allows for some kind of mistake and innocence. Normally, Thomas has a reservoir of appropriate faces, but he doesn't know where or how to summon them. So he sits here, cold as ice, and says nothing at all. He supposes that he looks as stupid as he feels, because all he can think to do is blow out a stifled breath.

"Nothing then?"

Thomas looks back to Marguerite. She's waiting for an answer, and she's waiting with one of the longest faces he has ever seen. It has lengthened by at least an inch, he thinks. Did he do this? Yes, he has to admit, he played a part. But he does not say so. He merely blinks at Marguerite. Then there comes a shrug. It wasn't really my fault, those shoulders are supposed to say on his behalf.

"Oh my," Thomas exhales. Then, like a flower that bends toward the light, he turns slowly toward the thing – twisting so he can take it in where it lies, across Madame Dufour's ample and triumphant lap. Thomas looks at the spyglass like it's a completely foreign object, a puzzle he's going to have to figure out.

—

As Thomas nods and maintains eye contact with Marguerite, it occurs to him that it's like being in a garden filled with bees, a maze. You hear the hum; it's all around, such an incessant song. Yet after you go inside, you cannot recall or describe what it is you've heard. It's just a hum. That's how it is with bees – and his wife's talking.

"Yes, of course," he says to his wife.

Marguerite's eyes are shining as she once again lays down the law. That he is a young and foolish husband. Thomas has lost count how many times, more or less, the same message has been offered up in the twenty-four hours since Hélène fled the salon. Yes, the very same salon with the very same cast, minus Hélène, of course. And without the telescope.

Thomas has not seen his lover since, though he did that morning keep himself hidden in the doorway of his room to catch two of Madame Dufour's servants whispering down the hall. They spoke about "that one" – no one since last night has dared to speak Hélène's name – who'd been sent to the attic the night before. There she lay still on her bed, silent, refusing to eat or drink or get up. The manservant added that he thought the fallen woman was to be taken into Vitré as soon as it could be arranged. "Cast into the street" was the phrase Thomas heard. "As is only right," a woman servant replied. "Where she belongs, is it not?" Then the servants went their separate ways, and Thomas took two steps back and closed the door.

"That's true enough," says Thomas very softly to Marguerite. It has to be his turn to say something to his wife.

"What's true enough? Are you even listening to me?"

"I misspoke. I meant I understand."

"Well, I hope so."

Thomas hears Madame Dufour clear her throat off to his right. He does not turn her way, but he understands the noise as some kind of coded comment – an injunction to Marguerite to not give him a second chance to make their marriage work.

"I do, Marguerite," affirms Thomas exclusively to his wife. He lifts his right shoulder and arches a portion of his back at Madame Dufour and her guttural sounds.

"Yes, well," says Marguerite. She adds an almost imperceptible tip of her head.

Thomas notices and thinks it a good sign. The resolute anger of yesterday evening is now spent, gone entirely from Marguerite's face. In its place, though, are dark circles under her eyes. Hers is a visage not of fury but fatigue.

Marguerite resumes her instructions. Thomas detects a hopeful cast to his wife's light-blue eyes. He sits farther back in his chair. He's not chosen one of the bitter wooden ones, with their hateful memories of a night gone wrong, but one with fiery-coloured stripes twisting in a weave, spreading out and intersecting against a beige background.

As Marguerite's voice modulates up and down – more like a brook than bees, Thomas thinks – he finds himself wondering what dinner might be. He's feeling peckish. A morning of the silent treatment followed by hectoring has taken its toll on him. Thank the heavens he was able to get away for the better part of an hour, out to the obelisk in the distant field. He did not dare perambulate in the brick courtyard or upon the garden paths. Not after yesterday. And God forbid he even so much as glance at the maze.

No, if he was to walk, and he was determined he would, it had to be somewhere else. And so he chose the obelisk, which apparently Madame Dufour's late husband's grandfather brought from distant India, or was it Egypt, and had erected on the spot. Thomas came back to the château along the road between the avenue of trees. The same route their coach passed down what seems like a lifetime ago.

Poor Hélène. She's done nothing but what nature ordains. Yet she has to pay the price and thereby lose the life of comfort she'd gained through cleverness. More than once since the incident in the salon, Thomas has wondered if he should slip away to the attic to see if she is all right. But each time, he weighed the impact of such a course and decided it best to leave matters as they lay.

"Harlots and trollops are just that, do you understand?" Marguerite is waiting for a reply.

"I do."

It's almost amusing, he thinks, to watch a person's mouth form the sounds they make. Cadence up, cadence down. Yes, Marguerite really is a brook.

"Thomas? Thomas?"

"Not even listening," Thomas hears Madame Dufour say. "Wasting your time. But I've said that before."

Thomas draws a bead on Madame Dufour. He still refuses to speak to her, but he can give her a glare. Then he offers two pronounced shakes of the head, to let the woman know that she is not worthy of conversation, hostess or not. Thomas is showing Marguerite that her husband is a gentleman. He will not stoop to making unkind remarks to her cousin, however justified he might be.

Thomas turns to Marguerite. He projects his most earnest listening face.

"Playing you for a fool," Madame Dufour mutters in a lower voice from her seat.

"On the contrary." Thomas addresses himself to Marguerite in a soft voice. He stiffens his back toward Madame Dufour. "I am one thing and one thing only, my wife. That is contrite. It is your forgiveness and only your forgiveness I request."

A groan issues from behind his back. Thomas gives his wife a shrug, along with a tolerant, understanding smile. Then he rises from his chair. He goes down on one knee in front of her.

"I make this pledge. It's all that I can do. I've wronged you, that I admit. I violated your trust. The sacrament of marriage was broken, but please understand it was not my intent.

"Yes, it happened and I was there. I was in the wrong, I now admit. A woman, your companion, she lost her way and tempted me to join her in a lusty whim. She was my Eve. Like Adam, I too failed the test. I committed a carnal sin. We both know I cannot go back and remove the stain.

"Know this: if I could, I would. Know that, my loving wife. The pledge I make is this. You have my word, Marguerite, my solemn vow. I will never again transgress against our marriage as I did yesterday with your former maid."

Thomas rises to his full height. He leans forward to place a hand on either side of Marguerite's head, touching firmly the bright white wig that goes round her ears on each side. Puffs of

powder fly up then snow down. Marguerite blinks in utter surprise as Thomas lightly kisses her on the forehead.

—

Thomas turns and strides across the room. Marguerite follows her
husband with her eyes as he goes out through the far door, the
door that leads to the foot of the stairs.

"You're not ... you're not accepting that?" sputters Madame
Dufour. "Please, Cousin, tell me that. Why he's—"

"Hush, woman. He's my husband, not yours. You've never understood that." Marguerite puts a finger to one of her eyes. She
has to stem a tear before it gets away. "Not one bit."

She notices that Madame Dufour rolls her eyes but then tightens her lips. So she should. Marguerite knows she is not the first
wife to turn the other cheek and two blind eyes to an errant man.
It is, alas, what wives must often do to preserve the sacred vow.

"All right then," says Madame Dufour standing up. She gives
two sharp claps of her hands. "Come now. Come here."

The two servants – the wide-eyed man Thomas had been rude
to the evening before and an attractive girl no more than sixteen
– come hurrying through the near door.

"There you are," sings out Madame Dufour. "To your stations,
my people. Bring up the platters from the kitchen, if you would.
Let's go then. To the table we go. Come on, Marguerite. We must
eat, I suppose."

Marguerite pushes herself slowly out of her chair. She hopes
there is no frown on her face, but she suspects there could be. She
does not much like her cousin barking commands. "I think I'll
go tell Thomas. He must be famished, I think."

"I see." Madame Dufour purses her lips. "You do that, Cousin, you do that."

"Thank you. I hoped you'd understand." Marguerite takes a
few steps toward the door that leads to the steps, then halts. She
turns back to Madame Dufour. "Thomas is more, I mean better,
than you think." She does not wait for any reply or comment.
Marguerite spins round and is gone from the salon.

———

"Is he now? We'll see, won't we?" whispers Madame Dufour to the empty salon after the door swings shut. "I'm afraid, dear Cousin," Madame keeps to herself, "that one actually does reap what one sows."

———

Ensconced in the library after a filling meal, Marguerite has a pensive look on her face. She's studying the wine in the bowl of her glass. Or rather, she is studying the image that the after-dinner wine reflects back at her. It does not bring a smile. If it's not a tired eye staring back, then it's an overly lined forehead. Thank God for the wig that covers her sadly aging hair. Where oh where did her youthful looks go?

She glances over at her husband. The nonchalant expression on his young, handsome face reassures Marguerite that he's oblivious to her misgivings about her advancing age in comparison to his. How fortunate that is. Yes, Thomas erred with that strumpet in the maze, but it was not entirely his fault. Men are like dogs following a scent, and that trollop was the one who led him astray. The man has been castigated long and loudly enough. It's time for Marguerite to move on, to compose the next chapter in the marriage. There is much to look forward to. She thinks of the silver motto ring she gave him when they wed. The Latin inscription along the outside band reads: *Crede quod habes, et habes.* Believe that you have it, and you do. Marguerite smiles at the recollection of that thought and at what she had inscribed on the inside of the band, not in Latin but in French: *Mon amour.*

Throughout this evening's dinner Thomas said nothing more than please and thank you. He continually presented a contrite face, at least to Marguerite. Sourness toward her cousin is something else again. She would like to see those two exchange at least a few civil words. In time, perhaps. The more important thing is that the lesson of fidelity Marguerite has been teaching her husband all day long seems to have been absorbed.

Thomas rises from his chair. He has a snifter of something strong and golden in one hand. He acknowledges his wife with a wink as he proceeds over to the bookshelves, where he scans the spines to read the short titles, occasionally giving an approving nod. He sips his drink then puts down the glass on a shelf. He pulls out one slim book and opens up the first few pages. Marguerite studies him as he reads the beginning of whatever it is. She cannot help but wonder what kind of husband Thomas Pichon will be for her in the years ahead. She already suffers from gout. There could be – no, there will be – worse ahead. Will he be attentive and kind? Marguerite takes a long drink. It finishes off her wine. There, that's better. There's no longer enough liquid for any reflection at all.

"Another, Cousin?"

Marguerite hears the disapproval in her cousin's voice. She supposes Madame Dufour has been counting how many glasses of wine Marguerite has had this evening, before, during and after dinner. By her count it's only three, but she supposes it could be four.

"Maybe I will." Marguerite sets her chin. She is not a child her cousin has to oversee and safeguard.

"Just recall, we only get old once."

Marguerite sighs at her cousin's pleasantry. It might be sarcasm, but it sounds like the truth.

"A taste of Armagnac?" asks Madame Dufour. Her face shows no sign of mockery or disapproval this time. "It will cheer you up. Look what it's done for your husband over there. A room full of books and a strong drink. You'd never know he ever had a care in the world."

—

Thomas looks up from book he's begun to read: *La surprise d'amour* by Marivaux. He did not see the play in Paris, but he's enjoying the read. He's curious to see how Marivaux's hero, Arlequin, fares. The comic character loves his women, does he not? Thomas closes the book. Arlequin will have to wait.

"An Armagnac for my dear wife. A good idea, Madame Dufour."

Marguerite's expression tells a tale. Thomas sees the surprise and relief she feels at his overture to the owner of the château where they both have to sleep for another two nights before returning to Paris.

Thomas gestures to the closest servant, the wide-eyed elderly one. "Good man. Madame Dufour wants my wife to have an Armagnac. If you would." Thomas dusts his hands like he's become the evening's host. "I'll have another touch as well." Thomas hands the man his glass. The servant pads to the buffet where the cut-glass carafe of Armagnac awaits.

Madame Dufour closes her eyes and turns away. Thomas hears her muttering under her breath, but what she's saying he cannot tell. If he can put his grievances to rest, why can she not try to do the same?

"All right," says Marguerite quietly. "Maybe I should. A deep sleep will do me good."

"And anything else?" Thomas asks Marguerite as he comes to sit down in the chair beside hers. He takes the two glasses of liqueur from the servant's tray. He sips one and holds the other out for his wife to take.

But Marguerite ignores the glass. She squeezes a focus on her husband. "What did you say?"

Thomas's brow wrinkles to see Marguerite's face go so askew. She looks like someone has just jabbed her with a pin.

"I asked if you wanted anything more than the Armagnac. Maybe a bite to eat?"

"You said, 'And anything else?'"

"All right." Thomas detects Madame Dufour leaning forward in her seat. She too hears something in Marguerite's voice. Doubt or menace, Thomas can't be sure. He leans forward and aims to speak as softly, as reassuringly as he can. "Something, anything, it doesn't matter. Here, take a sip."

Marguerite's shoulders shudder. She puts a hand up as if to silence what is already a silent room. There is only the scuff of the servant walking away with his tray to the far side of the library floor. And the crackle and spit of the fire. It is to that fire that Marguerite turns. She keeps her hand aloft as though freezing time, keeping her husband and the proffered drink at bay. The blazing hardwood crackles in the otherwise silent salon.

Thomas can see her mouthing. "And anything else." She repeats it three times. "Oh my God," she says in a ringing voice.

Marguerite stands and turns to face him. The look on her face is as if he has just killed someone. She jabs her finger into his chest.

"It was you." Marguerite bends over, moaning toward the floor as if to retch.

"What? What are you doing? Marguerite, are you all right?"

Thomas lays a hand lightly, carefully upon her back. Marguerite straightens up and bats his hand away.

"It was *you*. You were the thief." She lifts her hands and makes to strike his chest.

Thomas grabs her hands, holding them tight. Over her shoulder he sees that the elderly servant is standing especially taut. His large eyes are blinking hard at the scene unfolding.

"Don't you hurt her." Madame Dufour's voice is sharp.

"I— I'm not." Thomas lets his wife's hands go free. He steps back and shows the hostess just how innocent his hands are. "I don't know what she's talking about."

"No?" There's mockery in Madame Dufour's voice.

"No, she...." Thomas shakes his head at the hostess. She is not a friend. He turns back to his wife. "I don't know what's wrong. Maybe you've had too much to drink?" He steps toward Marguerite, two caring hands outstretched.

"Don't touch me, you."

"Come now, come." Madame Dufour's voice is businesslike. She herds her servants one by one. "Our guests require some time alone. Come. Right now, I say."

A skitter of hurried footfalls empties the room, except for Marguerite and Thomas.

Marguerite places both hands upon the back of the closest chair. Then she hauls herself around to the front of it, where she collapses onto the seat. "I remember, Thomas. I remember."

Thomas goes to the adjacent chair. He chooses to stand behind it rather than in front. "You remember? You remember what?"

Marguerite shakes her head. "My missing jewels. It was you, not Simone."

"Please," Thomas protests. He makes a beseeching gesture with his hands. "You're tired. You don't know what—"

"No. I do. It was you who took my things and hid them in poor Simone's room. It was."

Thomas gasps for air. He shakes his head. He hopes his face does not reveal his racing heart.

"I had to dismiss Simone because she had stolen my jewels. But *you* stole my jewels. That was when Hélène came to us.

"You just said: 'And anything else?' Isn't that funny? Here we are, months later, and you gave it away as innocently as that. When I first told you in our Paris apartment that I was missing jewellery, I named the pieces I could not find. And you said: 'And anything else?' I thought it odd. I couldn't imagine why you'd think there might be more than what I'd said. But there *was* another piece. So it was you who'd taken them, not Simone. You were the thief."

Thomas's eyes flee from contact with Marguerite's. They shoot to a sconce, its flickering candle dripping wax. To the fireplace. The logs are burning low now that the servants have been chased away. "You don't understand, Marguerite," is all Thomas can think to say.

A fresh realization sweeps across Marguerite's face. "Oh, Seigneur! It was for her. You did it for that tramp. You had to get me to dismiss Simone. Hélène. You wanted that woman under my roof. I bet you even gave her that foolish story she told me about being an orphaned aristocrat."

Thomas shakes his head. "No. I swear on my mother's grave. I did not."

Marguerite breathes in loudly through her nose, staring at her husband. "You would curse your mother's memory for that whore?"

"I had nothing to do with Hélène's story."

"Oh, Thomas, I don't know who you are. Leave me. Go." Marguerite buries her head in her hands.

Thomas takes a breath. Though she's not looking, he nonetheless bows. "Madame," he says. The walk to the doorway is brisk.

It's only when he's out of the room that the spinning inside his head stops. He comes to a halt at the foot of the stone staircase. With a hand atop the newel post, his ability to reason starts to return. This is not good. It could lead who knows where. His wife has connections. Madame Dufour, to begin with, but many more after her. His position with the magistrate, his life in Paris, it could all be lost.

Thomas puts a foot on the bottom step and finds his resolve. Much as he prefers to avoid rushed decisions, this matter requires exactly that. Hélène has already paid the price of Marguerite's wrath. Thomas could be next. There's only one thing to do.

II
Escape

Château Le Mesnil, Brittany
June 1727

It's a rush, a hurry of hand and eye. Thomas silently thanks Madame Dufour's staff for lighting the candles in the sconces of his room while he was downstairs. What he has to do would not be easily done in the darkness.

He flings open the double doors of the wardrobe and grabs his dark brown cloak from its hook. For an instant he recalls the kindly Russian tailor, Pierre, saying as he handed over the prized cloak, "This will keep you warm, mark my words, warm and safe." It had better, Thomas thinks.

Thomas spreads the great cloak on the floor beside his trunk. Only a day or two has passed since the elderly servant and a much younger one carefully placed this trunk in Thomas's room. It brings a trace of a smile to think how those servants would disapprove of Thomas's burrowing unceremoniously through the layers of carefully packed breeches, chemises, cravats and socks. He pulls out two of each and tosses them on to the outspread cloak. He spots a white silk mouchoir and takes that as well.

Down at the bottom of the trunk Thomas grasps a well-worn pair of shoes. Thrusting two fingers into the toe spaces, he pulls from each a small leather sack of coins. He brought the stash along on the journey into the hinterland just in case. Just in case. Thomas was thinking of highwaymen, but look. The unexpected happens much more often than people allow. Not in his wildest

23

imaginings could he conceive of what has happened over the past day and a half. One cannot take precautions enough against the many risks and dangers in life. Thomas tosses the shoes in the trunk and thrusts the sacks of coins into the pockets of his veston.

He removes his silver-grey wig and places it atop the pile of clothes, and then, going back to the wardrobe, he pulls down his two best hats. Stacking one inside the other as best he can, he stuffs the wig into the cavity, grabs opposite sides of his cloak and closes them over to make a great sack.

With the giant dark brown shape pressed to his chest with his left arm, Thomas goes to the closest sconce and pulls out a lit candle with his right hand. He's going to need some light. Using his foot to prop open the door, Thomas peeks out into the hall. He cannot go in the direction of the grand stone staircase, where he might encounter his wife, Marguerite, or their hostess, Madame Dufour, so he sets off the other way. He'd noticed servants coming and going through a slim door in the middle of the hall that must contain a set of stairs connecting all levels of the château.

Facing that door Thomas puts the candle between his teeth. Its melting wax spills onto his veston and the outside of the bundled cloak. The droppings matter not. What matters is that he keep the candle from going out. He tilts his head upward as best he can, to keep the flame from guttering out, a trickle of burning wax scorching his lower lip. He clenches his eyes and mutters a moan, but manages to open the door with his free hand and kick it wide with his foot. He grabs the candle out of his teeth. He spits, trying to rid his mouth of the taste of wax.

Yes, there are narrow stairs as he guessed. Both up and down. He lets drop his lump of clothes on the narrow landing and shuts the door behind him. He kicks off his shoes and leaves them beside the lump. Candle in hand Thomas pads down the wooden steps, his socked feet barely making a sound. He's sure no one knows where he is or what he is up to, but timing is everything and he has no idea how much time he is going to need.

At the bottom of the stairs the narrow door opens into a dimly lit corridor. The only light beyond the candle he is holding is a flickering glow at the far end of the hall. Thomas advances toward that other light. He finds a cul-de-sac. There, slouched on a wooden chair sipping a bottle of wine, is the wide-eyed servant from the salon. He no longer has on his livery coat. He has a blanket pulled up to his chin and appears to be half asleep.

"There you are." Thomas strikes a masterly tone of voice.

"Great God," the servant cries. "Why are you here?" He looks down at Thomas's socked feet. His eyes go even wider than they usually are.

"Up and about, come now. Let's go. Chore for you."

The servant looks Thomas up and down. He puckers his lips then shakes his head. He defiantly takes a nip from the bottle. "Don't think so. My day's done. Madame Dufour said as much not a quarter hour ago." The man allows his chair to come down slowly upon all four legs. The blanket falls off his chest, down to his lap. He has a firm grip on the bottle of wine.

"And does Madame Dufour know that you're hiding down here drinking her good wine? Which you have stolen from her cellar holdings?"

The domestic's eyes narrow. He takes a hurried sip.

"I thought not. Up you get. I'm in the law in Paris. I know a sly fellow when I see him."

The servant appraises Thomas from head to foot. The absence of shoes makes him tilt his head.

"Hear me out, my friend." Thomas lowers his voice. "You do something for me and I'll do something for you. How about it?"

The servant is impassive. That tells Thomas he is at least open to hearing what the proposition is.

"I'll give you a coin, a full écu."

The man puts down the bottle and stands his height. Out comes the hand, palm side up. "Let's see the coin. I don't trust your type."

Thomas shakes his head. "When you're done. Then it's yours."

"Done what?"

Thomas pulls the man close. Though they are the only ones in the dimly lit space, he will make sure no one else could possibly hear what he has to say.

"I'm not sure," says the servant, recoiling the instant Thomas's whispering is done. "It's not— I'm not supposed—"

"I'll double it. Two écus."

"It'll take me a few minutes."

"Be off then. I'll be there as soon as I can. Have it ready, do you understand?"

The man nods.

"Tell no one. Understood?"

The servant takes his time but nods again. He turns and hurries away.

—

Thomas retraces his steps back along the corridor. His candle is well melted down. The flame is only a couple of inches above his hand, but the wax is no longer burning him when it drops. What now spills builds up on the base of wax already laid down.

So far, so good. Things are in motion, yet there remains much to be done. Thomas climbs the servants' stairwell two steps at a time.

On the landing he has to take the candle between his teeth again, the flame now close to his nose. Yet what else can he do? He needs the cloak-wrapped bundle of clothes and requires both hands to get them up to his chest. It takes two tries but then he has everything in his arms and is off, climbing the next flight of stairs.

Ten steps up and he can see no landing or door looming above. Where the stairs come to an end is nothing but wide open, dark space. Oh, but now he can make out a dim flickering glow. Some of the beams that hold up the roof of the château are faintly visible way up overhead.

Thomas cannot risk giving away his advance. He has no idea who or how many might be up here in what he assumes is the servants' sleeping quarters. He places his bundle into the recess be-

26

tween two separate stairs and pushes hard. The bulky shape holds fast. He takes the candle out of his mouth. It takes two puffs to blow it out. He'll relight it or get a larger one from the quarters above. Thomas stretches out like a salamander might. Slowly, he peeks above the level of what he assumes is the attic floor.

A girl with upraised brows stares back. Thomas vaguely recalls her face. He saw her somewhere in the château, maybe this evening or yesterday. He sees the needle and thread in her hands. She's making repairs to a chemise, the lamp on the candle stand beside her wooden chair her source of light.

"Not supposed to be up here. This attic is just for us women and girls."

"Maybe so." Thomas clambers up to stand on the attic floor. He now towers over the seated girl. She shrugs. Thomas isn't sure if the shrug is meant for him or for the rules of the château.

He hears a tumbling on the dark stairwell from which he has just come. He cannot see but knows that his cloak and enclosed bundle of clothes must have taken off down the steps. He'll collect his things on his way down. Thomas turns back to the girl seated in the chair, who has gone back to repairing the chemise.

"Hélène." Thomas makes a questioning gesture with his hands.

The girl seems to think it over, then tilts her head sharply toward the darkness. Thomas squints to where she indicates; the other end of the servants' quarters is all black. He cannot see a thing down there.

"You're sure?"

"She is there."

"Thank you." He turns to head that way, then stops. "Take your lamp?"

"You have to bring it back."

"I shall."

Into the gloom of the far end Thomas goes, the lamp lighting the way. With each step the wobbling glow allows him to make out empty beds left and right. Yes, this is where the female staff of the château bed down for the night, after their chores are done.

The surrounds of the first few beds are tied back. There is no one in any of those beds. He continues on.

"Hélène?"

Thomas peers toward the bed on the left. His outstretched lamp reveals no one there. But he hears a low moan and the sound of fabric stirring from the other side.

"Hélène?" Thomas says softly as he goes to the bed on the right.

He sees a shape, a pale form. Lowering the lamp to waist high, he stretches out his hand. There is a woman lying on top, not beneath, the cover. She's dressed in a dark blue skirt and just a chemise. Her knees are pulled up, curled like a little girl. Thomas holds the candle closer to her face. She blinks at the light. He recognizes those eyes, but, uncharacteristically, there are tracks of tears on her cheeks.

"Come on, get up, we have to go." He sets down the lamp on the floor. He takes both her hands in a single clasp.

"What are you doing here?" Hélène's voice is distant and throaty. She is stirring out of sleep, or deep sadness.

"Come on." He pulls her up. She doesn't resist, but she doesn't help. It's a strain to get her to her feet.

Hélène reclaims her hands. "I'm ruined because of you. Because of that." She points at his groin as he bends down to get the lamp.

Thomas has to smile. "Just get your things."

Hélène shakes her head like she disagrees. But then she runs her fingers through her hair and adjusts the waist of her skirt. She slips on the shoes her feet find beneath the bed. She starts to set off toward the steps. Thomas lays a hand on her shoulder.

"Your things."

"This ... this is all I own. Marguerite took back everything I had."

"Oh." Thomas puts an arm round her waist and presses her to his side. They come to the servant girl seated in the dark. In the light of the lamp he carries Thomas sees she is still waiting where she was, needle and thread in her hands, chemise across her lap, waiting for the return of the light.

Thomas sets the lamp back on her table. "Thank you."

The girl looks at the lamp, then at Thomas and Hélène. "Need it more than me." She hands the lamp to Hélène. "I can finish this tomorrow."

"Thank you Suzette." Hélène blinks at the girl. "It's Suzette, isn't it?"

"It is. I won't tell anyone you've left. I won't. But where do you go? It's night and we're in the woods."

Hélène shrugs. She is tugged along by Thomas who is already one step down.

"The lamp," he says.

"You carry it then."

The couple halts at the bottom of the steps and Thomas hands the lamp back to Hélène. He bends to rebundle his strewn clothes inside his great Parisian cape.

—

Lamp extinguished and set down on the wooden floor beside the doorway, Thomas and Hélène peek out. They can see that there's a bit of light from the moon overhead, even though it's behind a giant cloud. The darker the better at this point. All that's illuminating the brick courtyard are two torches in their brackets. They make the bricks appear orange in their dim, flickering light.

The flight across the courtyard is a soft slap of hurrying shoes, two bodies trying to run as one. Between them both sets of arms hold up the bundle of Thomas's things.

"Where to?" she whispers close to his ear.

"Shush."

A small door beside the large double stable doors opens a crack. A hand beckons Thomas and Hélène. The wide-eyed servant is holding a beaming lantern aloft. The man shakes his head as he quickly closes the door. He takes a step toward Thomas and presents an angry face. "You didn't say anything about her."

29

"Be silent." Thomas snaps his fingers. "Is it ready or not?"

"What's this about? I cannot—"

"Not your worry. Where is it?"

"Through there." The servant points at an interior wooden door. "I'm taking a big risk. I want my money. Now."

"What's he saying, Thomas?"

Thomas gives Hélène a tiny shake of his head. He turns to the servant. "Show us first. Nothing until we're set."

The servant strikes a pose, chin upraised, a hand on each hip. "I'll not be taken."

"Enough!" Thomas shouts. "Bastard," he mutters under his breath.

"Here," he says to Hélène, pressing the bundle against her chest. She's startled, but gets her arms around it.

Thomas goes to the servant, whose wide eyes narrow to a squint when Thomas places a single finger only inches from his face.

"First, we make sure there really *is* a carriage waiting."

A second finger shoots up. "She and I get in."

A third finger. "*You* open the stable doors."

The fourth finger. "That's when you get your coin."

"*Coinssss*. You promised two écus."

"Yes, two. It will be two."

The servant hesitates before he makes a quick nod. His expression suggests he's been duped before. He leads Thomas and Hélène over to the door that connects with the main part of the stables. He pulls it open and stands back. Thomas takes the lantern from the man's hand as he steps by.

The smell of hay and horses is strong. The animals are clearly disturbed by the coming of people and the light. There are four wooden stalls, with horses standing and craning over their gates in two of them. They are whinnying and tossing their long necks up and down in the excitement.

Thomas hoists the lantern high to see what else is in this structure. It's a building of rustic stone, not smooth-cut limestone like the main part of the château. Wooden pillars support the upper

30

level, which is overflowing with hay. A dropped lantern, or an errant flame of any kind, would send the whole thing up. Thomas casts a glance at the candle burning inside the lantern's glass. He goes to the nearest post and hangs the lantern on a hook.

There are three coaches in the stables. It's the farthest one, a small, open, two-wheeled black carriage that has a horse harnessed up, a single horse. The horse is chestnut brown. It's pawing the ground, sniffing the air.

"It'll do."

"Do? That's a fine calèche. Do you understand the risk I'm taking here?"

"Not really." Thomas puts a hand on the servant's chest and gives him a light push out of the way, then takes the cloaked bundle from Hélène. He pulls down the little iron step for her. "Up you get."

Hélène puts a foot on the step and pulls herself up by grasping the side of the calèche. Thomas tosses the bundle up to her. She wedges it into the narrow space behind the bench seat. Thomas climbs up and reaches for the reins. He shakes them up and down. He's not sure what comes next. He's never in his life ridden a horse, let alone been a coachman handling reins.

"You don't know horses, do you?" Hélène is shaking her head.

"Not yet."

"Not yet?" Hélène grins and laughs. She takes the lines out of Thomas's hands and at once tightens the tension between her and the horse. The harnessed horse whinnies at the tightening. Hélène utters soothing coos and chucks. The horse settles down. "I grew up in a coaching inn, remember?"

"I do." Thomas winks at her. He feels better without the responsibility of the reins. He taps the pockets of his veston just to reassure himself that he still has the leather pouches of coins. "We're set."

The ancient servant steps up on the iron foothold. He's seen Thomas tap his pockets. "I'll have my due."

"Doors first." Thomas points at the two wide doors beyond the horse's snorting nose.

31

"And watch you take off? No. The money now or I'll wake the night."

"Give it to him." Hélène gives Thomas a push. "We have to go."

"Step off," Thomas directs.

The man does as he is told. Thomas brings out one pouch and searches its coins with his longest fingers. He pulls out a single one. "Your écu." He tosses it through the air.

The servant catches it and studies it in the dim light. "And the other?"

"When the doors are opened and we roll."

"Your word?"

"Of course." Under his breath, Thomas mutters, "And what word is that?"

This time, Hélène elbows Thomas in the ribs. "Give it to him. We have to go."

"All right." Thomas feels for another écu. "Here." He throws it to the servant. "The doors." Thomas makes a widening movement with his two hands.

"If you're caught, I did not help at all. Agreed?"

"Agreed," Thomas says.

"Agreed," Hélène repeats.

The man goes to the double doors. He shows his age, for the opening of the doors proves to be not a simple task. He lifts the long plank that bars both doors from the inside. He carries it with wavering difficulty over to the wall on the left. Hobbling now he retraces his steps and lifts the iron latch.

"Hurry up," Thomas calls out.

"Hold on. Nearly done."

The servant pulls the first door open wide, and pushes it all the way to the left. He trudges back to pull and push the other one. Thomas measures the half-opening with his eyes. He compares it to the width of the calèche they're in.

"That's enough," he whispers to Hélène.

"Not yet," she says.

The servant jerks the second door partway open. He bends and puts his shoulder to it. The opening widens with each staggered step, though there are still a half dozen more feet until the second door is pushed as far as it could go.

"Now," says Thomas.

Hélène cracks the reins and yells. The horse startles and rears. Hélène snaps the reins again and gives a whistle. The carriage jerks and starts to roll. The aged servant leaps out of the way. "Hey!" he shouts.

The calèche jumps into the opened space. The horse strides out of the stables with ease, but the coach does not. It catches on both sides. There's an awful scraping sound. The little carriage wedges to a halt.

"You've wrecked Madame's calèche," the servant shouts. He tries to grab Thomas.

Thomas thrusts out a leg. He kicks at the servant to move him back. "Away," he yells. The old man grabs hold of Thomas's leg.

Hélène cracks the whip and screams some new guttural sound at the horse. The horse whinnies as it rears. There's a loud creak, a metallic scrape. Then a crack. But the calèche begins to move. Thomas reaches out and undoes the servant's grip upon his leg. The old man tumbles to the ground.

The carriage is all the way through. With building speed the horse's hooves hit the bricks of the courtyard. It's a clattering, swelling sound. Hélène holds the reins taut to steer the horse on a sweeping turn. The calèche straightens out. They are heading for the portcullised gate.

Behind them the servant cries out, "Thieves! Stop, thieves!"

Thomas glances back. The old fellow is now standing in the centre of the brick courtyard brandishing an upraised fist. He's yelling at the top of his voice.

"Have to give him his due," Thomas says to Hélène. "He earned his coins."

"Him? What about me?" She makes as if to hand the reins over to Thomas.

"Maybe later." He half stands and grabs her by the shoulders. He kisses her hard on the mouth.

"Can't see." She pushes him away.

Thomas beams back. Always a surprise, is she not?

—

At the sudden shouting and the clatter of hooves on the bricks, Madame Dufour and Marguerite go to the windows of their respective rooms. Madame Dufour parts the curtains and opens a window a moment before Marguerite does the same. Two flickering torches and a shaft of moonlight light the courtyard.

"Gilles!" cries out Madame Dufour. "Gilles, our calèche!"

The elderly servant stops waving his fist. The coach is now under the portcullis and barely visible at all. Gilles cranes up to speak to his mistress.

"He's a scoundrel, Madame. He tricked me. I didn't know that he—" Gilles stops when he notices Marguerite at her window. She is leaning out and evidently listening to every word. The servant sends a deferential nod in Marguerite's direction. "Madame," he says with a bow.

"Keep on," yells Madame Dufour.

Gilles places a hand beside his mouth. He pretends he is speaking only to her, that Marguerite in the next window cannot listen in. "Might I come up and explain what I know? It's delicate."

"Of course. But hurry, will you please."

—

Gilles takes his time. He knows he has to get the story straight before he opens his mouth. He has a laughably easy life at Le Mesnil, except for the few weeks when Madame Dufour comes down from Paris. His future depends on how well he'll be able to explain this unfortunate incident away. It comes to him that it would be best to say he encountered the two house guests in the stables readying the horse to the calèche. He did everything he could to stop them from getting away, from stealing the coach. He even placed his very body, frail as it is, in harm's way.

Alas, Marguerite's unscrupulous husband Thomas – with his harlot, the servant called Hélène – they shoved him down. They kicked him and threatened to pierce out his eyes. No, that might be a bit too far. They kicked him and spat in his face.

Gilles stops on the first landing and kicks off his shoes. He puts one of his new coins in each, then slips the shoes back on.

———

Still leaning out their windows overlooking the silent courtyard, now bathed in the moon's sickly glow, Madame Dufour and Marguerite exchange dour looks. Neither woman dares to say aloud, at least not across a public space, whom she thinks she spied riding away in the calèche. Each is certain who those two people are.

"I will speak with my man Gilles." Madame Dufour looks to Marguerite as if to seek approval.

The woman whose husband has just ridden off with a whore steps back, making no reply. She latches the windows shut, then yanks the curtains closed.

Marguerite grabs a candle out of a sconce. She goes at once down the hall and into her husband's room. She sees the open trunk, everything within it all stirred up. The wardrobe, doors ajar and gaping, stands nearly empty. So it's true. It is. It really was Thomas, her Thomas, in the calèche. He was looking back over his shoulder while a slender-figured woman held the reins. That thieving slut.

Marguerite staggers over to a chair. Once again, she has learned that this man, the man she married barely seven months ago, practises deceit. She brings her hands up to cover her face.

"Aha. There you are. Not surprised, I bet."

Marguerite splays her fingers. She peeks through her hands at Madame Dufour in the doorway to Thomas's room.

"I thought you'd be in here. Just to confirm, I suppose."

Madame Dufour pauses and tips her head back just a bit. To Marguerite it looks like her cousin is weighing the consequences of what she might say next.

"I was right all along, you know. I told you from the start, before you wed, that man was no good."

Marguerite removes her hands from her face and rises swiftly from her chair. She meets Marie-France Dufour at the foot of the bed and grabs her by the sleeves of her nightdress. She spins her cousin round and pushes her toward the door.

"What— what are you doing?"

With a push and fling, Marguerite shoves her cousin out into the hall. She closes the door and locks it before Madame can come back in.

"Marguerite," implores the voice through the door. "I'm on your side. I am."

"Leave me, will you please?" Marguerite's voice is a plaintive appeal.

She hears a mumbling from Madame out in the hall. She can't make out the words, but she is relieved to hear the sound of re-treating footsteps.

"Thank you," Marguerite says quietly, briefly closing her eyes. She goes back to the chair she was in a moment before. She has to figure this out.

Yes, she's hurt and seething mad, but she knows those senti-ments always pass. Unbridled emotions accomplish nothing in the end. To be sure, her first husband had his lapses and distrac-tions too. Yet she was always able to overcome the various pre-dicaments he put her in. Marriage is a sacrament sworn before God. It is a promise and a vow. An oath. Are not oaths the basis of everything in the world? Of course they are. Otherwise it would be every man and woman out only for themselves. Obligations given and observed are a check and a balance in such a world. Since marriage is the path she has chosen, the real question is: Is it still possible, after these past two days, for her to find some way to work things out with this Thomas Pichon as it was with her first? Marguerite inhales as deeply as she can, then empties her lungs as though firing up her resolution.

She rises from the chair, goes to the wardrobe and closes its doors. Next it's the trunk, whose lid she closes as well.

What's wrong with Thomas, it comes to Marguerite as she returns to her chair, is that woman he has fled with. She has him bewitched. There is likely nothing for her he would not do. For her, the wench, alas, not for his wife. Her husband is young. That makes him easily led. What he's done on this trip ... these actions are not really who and what he is. No. What Marguerite has to figure out is how she can liberate her young man from that woman's spell. Before it's too late. Too late for him, too late for Marguerite, and too late for the union they made seven months ago before God. They both have immortal souls to be saved.

Marguerite moves off the chair and toward the door. The errant couple is undoubtedly heading back to Paris. Where else? A determined wife would be wise to do the same. She'll speak with Madame Dufour and ask if she will make the arrangements.

—

Hélène slows the pace of the horse once the calèche is well beyond the château gate and climbing the road that leads up the hill through the avenue of trees. Though she saw no other coach in the stables ready to come after them, she glances over her shoulder just the same. It is reassuring to see that she's right, at least for now. But pursuit is only a matter of time. Most likely it will be tomorrow. She and Thomas should have the night to get a considerable distance ahead.

"Thank you, Thomas. Thank you for getting me out of there."

"I just wanted you instead of her," he says to her, with a shrug.

—

Relieved to be off the resounding bricks of the courtyard and onto the dirt road, Thomas looks to the sky. The moon is up high and enough to see where they are going. "It's enough light, is it not?"

"Should be," Hélène replies, eyes straight ahead. "So long as the horse remembers the road." She sends Thomas a quick smile. Then she makes the sign of the cross.

"Think that helps?"

"I do. And you'd better hope as well."

Thomas looks away, off to the darkness of what could be a field of flax. There are no blue flowers visible in the night, but it does look like flax just the same.

He and his Paris friends have been mocking religious believers for so long that he's always surprised when Hélène evokes her Catholic heart. Marguerite, he knows, lives her faith. But Hélène, well, Hélène is his own age and otherwise seems so smart. Thomas looks around at where they are: two people in flight from a château on a dark road in the middle of the night. He hunches his shoulders. Who knows? Maybe Hélène is right. What harm could there be in hoping that the Blessed Virgin and the Seigneur might be watching out for them as they head into the unknown?

His thoughts turn to what they have just given up. Well, not *they* but *him*. Hélène already lost all she had the day before. But Thomas has just left behind a life of considerable comfort and went through a tiresome interrogation to keep it. Not to mention some noble promises to his wife. Oh my. He was higher up and better off in the world with Marguerite than he had ever been before. Yet here he is, with a woman who has not a thing. And neither of them a clue as to what comes next. What sense is there in that, in the path they are choosing?

"What's wrong with you?" Hélène is looking Thomas's way.

"Nothing."

"You should tell your face."

Thomas stares into her eyes. "I ... I'm ... well, we're leaving a lot behind. It'll be a long time before we're back to that level again."

"You want me to turn the horse around?"

"No, but it was a Rubicon. That's all."

Hélène tilts her head quizzically. "I don't know what that means. But I do know it doesn't do much good to mope."

"Mope? Who was that in the attic just now?"

"You want another thanks?"

"I guess I do."

"Thank you."

They are silent for a while. The lull is broken by a laugh from Hélène.

"Why did you say *we're* leaving a lot behind? Me, I've already lost it all. But you, you're still all right."

Thomas stares at her, eyes wide. He waits for her to explain.

"I was a lady, or nearly so. Steady meals, fine clothes. *I* lost everything because of the damned maze. I fucked my life by fucking you. In front of a telescope."

Thomas purses his lips. "I've just fled from my wife. My entire Paris life – maybe even my position with the magistrate judge – is lost."

Hélène is silent while she makes sure the horse rounds the bend in the road. As they progress along a straight section between tall, slender trees, she turns back to Thomas. "Do you know how many husbands stray from their wives in this world?"

Thomas shrugs.

"Lots. I've probably been with a hundred all by myself. Oh, grimace all you want, but do the sums. Trust me, Thomas, you're not lost. You're in trouble, yes, but you're still married to Marguerite."

Thomas hesitates.

"You two were married in the eyes of God. That can't be altered by running away with me."

"And she has no children," mumbles Thomas. Silently he goes over what this means. He is indeed Marguerite Salles's husband, and she has no heirs. So he is linked to her estate, unless she takes action in the courts to lock him out. Modest though it is in the great scheme of things, her estate is much more than he has by himself. Much more. Hélène could be right. He may not, necessarily, have burned all his bridges.

"Well, look at that little grin. So you agree? You might yet reconcile with Marguerite?"

"You're not just any woman, are you, Hélène?"

"Who is?" Hélène gives her attention back to the road.

"You know," she says, eyes peering forward, "you could tell Marguerite that it was me who planned this escape. That I made you come along because of my ... allure and charms." Hélène snorts at that. "Your wife would probably believe that."

Hélène turns to make eye contact. "She detests me because she had given me a place in her heart and then I let her down. To her, my betrayal was worse than yours."

"I don't know."

"No, you're a man. Women expect more from women than they ever do from men."

They hold eye contact, and then Hélène lets loose a sputtering laugh. Thomas hunches his shoulders, shakes his head and turns back to stare off into the darkness of the night. With Hélène guiding the horse along the moonlit road, Thomas reaches behind his seat. He pulls up the large cloak that carries everything he took from his room. He shakes it out then places the cloak around Hélène's shoulders.

"My tailor in Paris, a Russian, he said this cloak would keep me warm and safe. It'll do the same for you."

"It *is* warm." Hélène blinks her appreciation.

"You want me to take over?"

Hélène tilts back. "I think we need to get further away first. Maybe I'll give you the reins later."

Thomas shrugs and looks up at the sky. Though there's no wind at ground level, the thin clouds are whirling like they have somewhere to go. The canopy of stars is much more visible now than when they left the château. One by one Thomas locates the constellations he knows.

"What happened to you back at the château?" asks Hélène.

"What do you mean?"

"You were someone else."

"I was, wasn't I?"

"For a moment I thought you were going to beat the old man."

Thomas bites his lower lip. "Marguerite found out it was me behind the missing jewellery, the theft I blamed on Simone."

"The little servant I replaced?"

"Yes. When I saw the look on Marguerite's face, I panicked I guess. That's when I went looking for you."

Hélène turns away from Thomas. She seems to study the horse's bouncing tail. But when Thomas leans forward to see her profile, he sees she is squeezing her eyes tight shut. When she turns back to face Thomas again, her eyes are shining like they are wet.

"Good then." There's a tremolo in her voice. "I have another chance."

She leans into Thomas and kisses him lightly on the lips. He is taken aback.

"You know," he says, "I don't know what happens next."

Hélène straightens up, turning to set her eyes back on the road. "Who does? If we knew all the disappointments and setbacks that lie ahead, we'd probably all give up."

"You really think everything's in vain?"

Hélène shrugs. "Yes. No. I seem to keep hoping that it's not."

The road takes a long curve as it climbs slowly to high ground. At the top of the hill the trees thin out so that Thomas and Hélène can see down into a valley below.

"Look, that's it." Hélène prods Thomas with her elbow. "The château."

Thomas sees the sharply contoured slate roof. The light of the moon has it shining almost white. The turrets stand out and there is a faint glow from a few windows where lamps are lit.

"Think they're talking about us?" Hélène's eyes and smile are especially wide and saucy.

"How could they not?" Thomas gives her shoulder a gentle push. "We have notoriety, if not renown."

"Is that what you really want, Thomas, renown?"

"Don't we all?"

"Not me." Hélène gives him a steely glance. "Not sure what I want, other than a bit of comfort and a place that's safe to sleep. Speaking of which, my friend, you look spent. Here." She pats her lap.

"For a bit?" Thomas asks.

"Go on."

41

As the horse begins its descent from the hilltop, picking up speed as the forest re-establishes itself, Thomas shifts to lower his head onto Hélène's lap. She places her free hand gently upon the side of his head, while holding the reins in the other.

"You know," says Hélène, "this ride, this may be the freest I've ever felt."

"Me too."

Thomas fills his eyes with a field of stars and his ears with the soft tapping of the horse's hooves on the dirt. He can hear his breath go out and come back in. "I like you, Hélène."

"Shush. Have a nap."

"But I do."

"Shush, I said." Hélène takes her finger and traces a line along his now sealed lips.

Thomas closes his eyes. He knows he should be thinking about what he and Hélène are going to do next, when they get to Paris. But he can't. As long as they can keep rolling on, that will have to be enough until he's had a nap. The call of sleep. The trembling of his eyes are beyond his control.

—

Hélène presses her back against the seat. The moon and stars are so bright at the moment that she no longer has to peer to find the road, a gently rutted track that goes through the woods and down this hill. Funny to think that this road was made no one could say when, some time long before she was born. And it'll still be right here after she is gone. Yet all she and the horse have to do on this night is to follow where it leads.

Hélène feels Thomas's entire body shudder. She can tell he's gone, deep into his sleep. She'll take her turn later on. Right now, she is content to have the horse as her only company along a sky-lit forest road.

III
Arrangements

Paris
June to October 1727

With the horse and calèche housed in the closest Paris stables, Thomas and Hélène hurry toward the building that
houses Marguerite Salles's apartment. It's been raining for a day
and a half, ever since they left Alençon. Neither has dared suggest
to the other that the constant downpour is somehow a judgement
on what they've done. Silently and secretly, however, each has
been having exactly that thought.

"At least it's a warm rain," Thomas said once along the way.
Hélène's baleful look told him not to try that again. In fact, for
the last stretch of the journey, once Paris came into sight, they
hardly spoke at all. There were too many unknowns lying in wait.
They both resolved, independently, that no talk at all was better
than sharing worries.

The heavy cloak they share has long since become sopping
wet. It is more weight than comfort round their shoulders as they
scurry toward the building where less than a week ago they lived
in harmony with Marguerite.

"You remember?" asks Thomas. He reaches out and stops Hélène from rushing directly in. "The lines we rehearsed last night?"

"Stay out here and rehearse if you want. I'm getting out of this
rain."

Hélène jumps out from beneath the cape. She pulls open the
door and goes in, Thomas following behind.

Two floors up, standing outside the door to Marguerite's suite
of rooms, Thomas and Hélène shake the great cape. Droplets
sprinkle and pool on the wooden floor. They flap their arms,
swing their hats and wiggle their legs, trying to dismiss as much

of their bedraggled appearance as they can. Yet their efforts don't change a thing – both are soaked to the skin. Hélène is not wearing much at all. She is still dressed as she was when Thomas found her in the attic three nights ago. Like the lowest servant of any house, in clothes already tattered and stained before they became thoroughly wet.

"We need to get you into some new clothes," Thomas says.

"Really?" Hélène shakes her head. She straightens her shoulders and once more flutters and flaps her wet blue skirt and adjusts her chemise. She tucks her sopping hair under her soaking wet servant's cap.

Thomas smiles at the preparations she is making before opening the door. Then he puts a silencing finger to his lips. They agreed that once they are inside the building they will not know who might be listening on the other side of any wall or door. They will speak only when prudent. Once inside Marguerite's suite of rooms, they will be doubly careful of what they say and do. Marguerite's servants must not suspect a thing about what happened on the short stay at Le Mesnil. Of course they will notice Hélène's tattered state, but they have come up with a ready explanation for that.

Thomas puts the key in the lock and turns. He pushes the door open carefully. None of Marguerite's long-time household servants are in sight. The place is as quiet as he and Hélène hoped. She should be able to get in and changed before anyone sees her in these lowly clothes.

Hélène taps him lightly on the arm. She asks with a gesture if they should begin their practised exchange. He nods that they likely should.

"Well, that was one trip I'll not care to repeat, Monsieur Pichon."

"Right you are, Mademoiselle. Dreadful."

They share grimaces. They sound like they're in some terrible play. In their rehearsal in the inn last night, this patter sounded fine. Pronounced in the empty foyer of Marguerite's residence, with the hall table and engravings and prints staring back, it sounds contrived.

Thomas forces a cough. He whirls a hand in the air. Hélène's brow wrinkles, but then she understands. They will start again.

"My wife made the right decision, don't you think? To stay behind and ask us to return on our own."

"I do, Monsieur. I just hope her journey, delayed as it is, will be better than ours was in all the rain."

Thomas beams at Hélène. "Best I get out of these clothes. You'll want to do the same. I wonder if any of the servants are about."

Then, with a broad grin, Thomas sends his two hands to grab Hélène's breasts. She bats his hands away. She pushes him into the wall, knocking a framed map of the siege of La Rochelle off its hook. Thomas catches it before it hits the floor. He winks at Hélène and rehangs the map.

"Perhaps we'll have dinner together later. Would you like to join me in that, Mademoiselle?" Thomas holds up both hands. He pokes the index finger of his right hand through a circle he makes with his left.

"We'll see." Hélène gives a wide, deliberate shake of her head as she walks past Thomas, heading for her room. She reaches out for the door handle, but before she turns it she pivots Thomas's way. He is following her every move. She makes as if to blow a kiss. Then she makes the same hand gesture Thomas did and mouths: "Two times."

"As you wish, Mademoiselle," says Thomas aloud before he crosses the hall to his room. The instant he opens the door there emerges the sound of panting and the slap of skin on skin.

"What?" Thomas shouts.

It's Charles, Marguerite's sad-faced lackey from Brive, and Sébastien, the plump little Gascon cook. They're wrestling front to back, or something like, atop Thomas's bed in Thomas's room. The lackey's breeches are down and he's on top of the cook. The cook has nothing on but a pulled-up chemise.

"What are you two doing in here? And on my bed?"

The two men separate and jump off the bed. Their stunned faces announce their guilt. Sébastien retrieves a corner of the blanket to cover his hairy groin.

"Weren't expecting you, Monsieur." Charles pulls up and buttons his breeches fast.

"What is it?" Hélène is at the doorway. She steps in to stand beside Thomas. Her eyes go wide at what she sees. Thomas asks her with a look if the two servants were doing what he thinks. She tells him with a couple of blinks that, yes, that's exactly what it was. Thomas feels warm air rush out his mouth and nose.

"In *here*," he cries. He is speaking to Charles and Sébastien but he's waving at the whole room. "And on my bed. Get out. Out." Thomas's voice is deep, like he's the commander of a ship. He's pointing at the door.

"Monsieur, you were away and we were— trying on some of your things." The cook suddenly studies first Thomas then Hélène. "But, but why are you so wet? And in those clothes? Where is Madame Salles?"

"We'll ask the questions." Thomas puts a hand on his hip. He does not like the look of the cook's bare, fat ass.

Sébastien tries to fold the blanket that's covering him as he sidles by.

"Whoa." Thomas grabs Sébastien by his wrist. The fellow has on one of Thomas's chemises, a silk one at that. "That is *my* shirt."

Thomas turns to examine Charles, half hidden behind the cook. And are those not Thomas's long-lost scarlet breeches the lackey just buttoned up? They went missing from Thomas's wardrobe at least two months ago. "My pants. My shirt. You two are thieves. As well as...." Thomas waves at the tumult of bedclothes on the bed.

"How were we to know you'd be back?" Charles assumes an indignant pose. "As soon as this?"

"It's *my* fault?" Thomas glances toward Hélène, as if to ask if she has ever heard the like of that. Hélène, however, has her gaze lifted on high. It seems she does not want to see another thing in the room.

Thomas curls his lips at each servant in turn then points at the half-open door. Charles and Sébastien scamper off. Thomas cannot resist shouting a parting shot. "When Madame Salles returns, in a few days, I may have to speak to her about this. Buggery's a crime. Not to mention a sin."

Thomas smirks at Hélène. He has no intention of telling anything to anyone. But catching the servants the way he did might just buy Thomas an extra portion of compliance from them. One cannot get too much of that.

Hélène tugs on Thomas's sleeve. There's amusement and relief on her face. "Won't be seeing them for a while, I bet."

"Not if they have good sense." He shrugs. "Which maybe they don't."

Hélène tilts her head toward the tangle of bedclothes on Thomas's bed. She says in a hushed voice close to his ear: "I didn't know those two were so close, did you?"

Thomas likes the feel of her warm breath in his ear. He rolls his neck round and brings his lips close to hers, ready to see where this feeling might lead. Hélène gives him a quick peck and steps away.

Thomas steps over to close the door. "How about that proposition you made in the hall?" he whispers. He puts his hands around her waist and draws her close. "Something about two times."

Hélène uses a hand to intercept the face descending for her lips. She pushes back and steps away, out of his grasp. "I think it was a joke."

"A joke? That is no subject for a joke."

Hélène covers her mouth and whispers, "Marie-Claude."

Thomas nods. That's right, he had forgotten about the long, lean maid from Marlotte. Marie-Claude is a woman of few words and ever-darting, always doubting eyes. She could be lurking somewhere close at hand, waiting to overhear something that could ruin Thomas's slowly forming plan. Marie-Claude would never hesitate to tell Marguerite any little thing she sees or hears, especially if it might harm Hélène. Ever since Hélène arrived, Marie-Claude has resented her as the should-be servant who does not do servant chores. She'll be delighted to learn that Hélène was caught out by the mistress and put into the street.

Hélène uses a loud speaking voice, just in case the unseen Marie-Claude is near. "You'll be wanting to change out of your wet clothes, Monsieur. As I must change out of mine. After that, we must make sure the apartment is perfect for the return of our dear Marguerite in a few days."

"To be sure," says Thomas in his stage voice. He closes the door after Hélène steps out of his room. He begins to strip everything off the bed.

—

Tomorrow he'll help Hélène find a place over on the left bank. That will greatly diminish the likelihood of Marguerite ever seeing her again. The right side of the Seine is his wife's world. She rarely travels over to the left. So when Marguerite returns to the apartment, he will quietly explain how the harlot in her employ charmed and confused him. That they met in a chance encounter a month before the unfortunate incident with Simone. He'll make a point not to use Hélène's name. He'll refer to her only by one or more of the many epithets that exist for women of her kind. In any case, Thomas will tell Marguerite that his first meeting with that one was after a night of excessive drinking with his writer friends. One among them – Thomas will use Jean Gallatin if Marguerite presses for a name – convinced him to try a courtesan. It was a mistake Thomas will swear he'll never make again.

The courtesan had her tricks, and so placed him under some kind of spell. For the second time he'll say that he was Adam to her sultry and sneaky Eve. Marguerite likes to cite Christian parables, so why not reinforce the earliest Bible story of all?

Yes, Thomas sees logic in what Hélène suggested, to blame everything on her. He'll assert that he now recognizes how wrong and sinful his actions were. He'll swear that he is going to make a full confession of his wrongdoings at church.

As for the midnight flight from Le Mesnil, Thomas will point out he did that strictly for Marguerite. He felt deep remorse for his betrayal and knew that Marguerite could not stand the sight of the duplicitous whore. So he took it upon himself to get that woman out of there. As quickly as he could. Back to lusty Paris where she belongs. Yes, Thomas knows now he could have and should have waited until the next morning and explained what he was about, but he wanted to make immediate amends. The calèche and horse he borrowed from Madame Dufour are well and safely stabled a few minutes away from the apartment. A few scratches, it's true, but he trusts that her cousin will understand the haste. Most of all, he hopes Marguerite will give him another chance to be the husband he still longs to be.

Oh yes, he'll likely have to explain why he brought the harlot back into Marguerite's for one last night. It was charity, nothing else. He could not cast the whore out with no place to stay. He did not want to abet an immediate return to her life of shame. So he asked himself, what would Marguerite do? She would let the poor woman have one more sleep in a decent bed and one more fulsome meal. The next day, however, Thomas took the strumpet out of the apartment as soon as it was light.

Yes, it's a pretty good explanation if he does say so himself. He'll go over it again tomorrow to see if there are any rough spots he needs to smooth. The time of Marguerite's return to Paris is unknown, but he wants to be ready. The important thing will be contrition. He has to head off any intention Marguerite might have to take him to a court of justice over what happened with the dismissed Simone. Or to spread tales of his alleged wrongdoing among her friends. Careers rise and fall on gossip, and Thomas cannot afford any blackening of his name.

A rapprochement with Marguerite is possible, Thomas is convinced. The trick, as Hélène told him more than once in the calèche, is to admit as quickly as he can to Marguerite that he was wrong. There are many shakier marriages in Paris than theirs. He genuinely likes the woman with affection and respect. The secret will lie in keeping Hélène and Marguerite far apart. It was naive of him to think he could have them under the same roof.

—

Warm and dry in new clothes, Thomas and Hélène's evening unfolds as they thought it would. The lackey Charles and the cook Sébastien keep mostly out of sight. When they come and go in Thomas and Hélène's presence they say only "Yes, Monsieur" and "Yes, Mademoiselle." Not once do they ask why they are back from Brittany earlier than expected and without Marguerite. They keep their lips tightly drawn and go about their tasks.

As for the inscrutable Marie-Claude, she is no problem at all. Her brooding eyes register only the thinnest hint of doubt when Hélène states in a loud clear voice that Marguerite was unfortunately delayed at Madame Dufour's château. Hélène says nothing more than that Marguerite will be along in a day or two. A quick curtsey is Marie-Claude's entire reply. It's further proof that the truth or falsehood of a story is less important than how the story is told. After that, Hélène gives Marie-Claude a long list of chores. The gangly servant spends the rest of the evening after dinner in either the scullery or the *cabinet*.

Dinner itself tastes not too bad to Thomas and wonderful to Hélène, who savours every bite. She knows it's the last meal she's going to enjoy that she does not prepare herself or purchase at a cabaret.

The meal begins with escargots in butter then moves on to a platter of braised rabbit, with two individual Chinese porcelain bowls overstuffed with saffron-coloured scented rice. Next comes the celadon bowl filled with a combination of bright green lettuce wedges and freshly steamed green peas. A couple of cheeses Hélène does not recognize come at the end. Flecks of blue in one and a gentle almond taste to the other. Then a pastry that brims with cream and slivered strawberries. A tiny cup of coffee and, for Thomas, a snifter of cognac.

It is only after the candles in the main rooms are extinguished and Sébastien, Charles and Marie-Claude are completing their tidying and cleaning before they go to their respective beds, that Thomas and Hélène allow themselves to retire from the public space. For the sake of appearances, Hélène pretends to go by herself to her separate room. Only after a safe interval has passed will she creep up the hall and into Thomas's room.

—

For a quarter hour Thomas lies atop his bed, clothed in only his chemise. His legs are bare but the fire is giving off sufficient heat as he waits for Hélène. He's reading a book his friend Jean Gallatin sent him from London more than a month ago. It's a novel, a genre Thomas does not often turn to. And it's in English, a language he's only casually acquainted with. It's now two years since Jean crossed the Manche to London, attracted as he was by the political ideas of that nearby land. What prompts Thomas to pick up the book he's not read in all the weeks he's had it, is its title, *Fantomina, or Love in a Maze*. Love in a maze! Gallatin, you prescient bastard, laughed Thomas when he came in the room and spied the unread book lying on the table beside the bed. However did he know? Before starting to read the story, however, Thomas rereads the short note that Gallatin sent with it.

Mon cher Thomas,

Vous êtes souvent dans mes pensées, je vous assure. Un jour, j'espère, vous viendrez à Londres pour me rendre une visite. Maybe you'll even consider moving here as I did? And to help you start the process, you note already, I switch to English. Practice makes perfect we say in both languages, in our different ways. Vive la différence, n'est-ce pas? I've added a painter to my circle of friends. Most are writers, but this man tells stories with his paintings. His name is William Hogarth. When you see what he produces on his canvases and in his engravings, you'll understand.

Meanwhile, I think you'll like this little book I'm sending along. Love in a Maze. Yes, I know, you think fiction is a junior discipline in the writing arts. Not up to the standard of the older forms. Nonetheless, I urge you to give this one a try. It has caused quite a stir over here. I confess that I fear its subject matter might whet your already ravenous appetite for love-making with different women. Such is the world, it seems. Here in London it is just the same and I still stand apart, looking for a single woman to be with me. I thought of you often when I read it and could not resist sending it your way. My friend Henry Fielding calls its author, Eliza Haywood, "Mrs. Novel." The woman is prolific. I wonder, Thomas, if this might not be a genre you would someday want to try yourself, given your many encounters and adventures on the battlefield of love.

Please know, cher ami, that I think of you often. I hope that one day our paths will cross again. London welcomes the world, my friend.

Au plaisir de recevoir une lettre de vous avec toutes vos nouvelles.

Jean

P.S. My English is pretty good, n'est-ce pas? Yours could be as well. It's like anything else in these passing lives of ours, it only takes a little time.

Thomas smiles as he refolds the letter into the small square it was. Turning to the title page of the book, he sees it was published in 1725, two years ago. Not red-hot, perhaps, but still warm. Eliza Haywood is a name he's heard before, though this is the first work of hers he's held in his hands. *Love in a maze.* Is she referring to something literal or something more figurative? And how will love be described in a story coming off a woman's quill?

As he turns the pages Thomas learns that the central character, Fantomina, is a woman of quality without experience with men. She decides to dress and act like a prostitute to see what all the fuss is about. It's Hélène's recent adventures in reverse, is it not? Thomas stops reading and looks at the candle flickering on the little table by his bed. It's true, anyone can get away with whatever role one wants, as long as one can dress and act the part.

There's a sound of movement at the door. Thomas places the letter from Gallatin into the book to mark his spot. He must tell Hélène about the book and its ingenious plot. Too bad she cannot read it for herself.

—

She enters swiftly, closing the door behind her in a rush. All she has on is a chemise. Thomas yields a delicious smile as he recalls the first time they met. They were just fifteen. He was expecting her to come fully dressed tonight, in case one of the servants happened to glimpse her in the hall. But this is better. He likes the boldness. And he can see that her eyes are excited. Keen is the word.

Hélène holds up a cautionary finger as she climbs upon the narrow canopy bed to join him atop the covers.

Thomas speaks as softly as he can. "I've just started this book, and its heroine—"

"Shhh," Hélène says. "No noise." She has a stern look.

"Everything all right?"

"I'm chilled." Hélène snuggles close, pressing against Thomas's frame. Her cold brow burrows into the warmth of his throat. "Warm me, will you?"

"I will," Thomas whispers in her ear. He inhales her scent. Strangely, it reminds him of Marguerite. He begins to stroke Hélène's back. His breathing ticks at a faster pace.

"That's good." Hélène closes her eyes.

Thomas increases the pressure of his hands on her back. Then he lengthens the strokes. It's not long before his hands are making contact, still through the chemise, with the upper contours of her buttocks.

Hélène's eyes lift open. She leans back to take in the whole of Thomas's face. "Are you thinking what I'm thinking, Thomas?"

"Definitely." He allows a laugh, and slides his caressing hand down to grasp the hem of Hélène's chemise. He pulls it up above her knees.

"Not that." Hélène pinches her knees shut, pinning Thomas's hand. She shakes her head.

"Stop," Thomas protests.

"Stop yourself."

"But—"

"But nothing. We have to talk."

"Talk?" Thomas's eyes and lips shift from arousal to disappointment to frustration. The rise he was feeling starts to drain away.

"Come on, you're not a child. You can wait. What about tomorrow and the days after that?" Hélène catches her voice rising louder than she wants. She wiggles close. "Voices down, all right?"

Thomas shrugs, his expression long.

"Tomorrow," Hélène begins, "we leave as soon as we get up. Or I do at least. I have to be gone before Marguerite gets here. I do. Otherwise— Well, you know what could happen to me. Are you going to help me find a place on the left bank or just put me out in the street? Sorry if that makes you frown, but I have to know. I also have to find some work. Maybe you know someone who is looking for—"

"Whoa." Thomas places his hand across Hélène's mouth.

She bats his hand away. "This is what's on my mind."

"May I speak?"

Hélène indicates with her eyes that he may.

"All right then. What I think is—"

"Start with Marguerite. Will she be here in the morning?"

"No, I don't think. She'd have to have left shortly after us and pushed the pace like we did."

"So, we're safe?"

"I wouldn't say *safe*, but surely we can have something to eat before we look for your new place."

"Over on the other side?"

"Yes, around the university, or perhaps the Fauxbourg Saint-Victor or Saint-Marceau."

"I know those areas. They're good. You'll visit once in a while?"

"I'm not abandoning you, Hélène."

Hélène smiles, then studies Thomas's earnest face. He's more handsome now than he was when they first met. He was almost pretty back then. He looks better with a bit of age on his face. A bit like a priest. Well, not a priest. He would consume her like she's the staff of life if she let him have his way. But priest-like in some other way she does not fully grasp.

"So, maybe you know someone who could give me work?"

"Me? Can't think of anyone."

Hélène makes a deliberate sour face.

"Sorry, but I only know law offices. Well, and writers who gather at night."

There is a long silence. Each is lost in thought.

"I'll have to be careful with you for a while, Hélène. Marguerite will be on the lookout for any sign I've strayed off the path."

"I know." She nudges her body closer to his. They are now in contact the entire length of their two frames. "You're married. You have to look out for yourself."

Hélène rolls away and lies on her back. She is staring up at the canopy top.

Thomas watches her deep brown eyes. It looks to him like she's figuring something out.

Thomas gets up on an elbow. "What?" he asks.

Hélène rolls back into full contact with Thomas. This time she kisses him roughly on the lips. It's more a bite than a kiss. "A few thoughts is all. Mine, not yours, my friend Thomas."

"Your friend Thomas? Is that the best I can be?"

"What more do you want?" Hélène tilts her head. There's a sparkle in her eyes.

"This?" Thomas reaches down and lifts her chemise.

This time Hélène does not make him stop. His hand goes where it wants. She gives a little gasp. "Right to the pudding, is it?" she asks.

"The pudendum," Thomas corrects.

"Oh, I know."

"You know the Latin term?"

"Voltaire was like you in that regard."

"Oh."

"Not so clever after all, is it?"

"It's not."

"More talk?" Hélène asks. "Or something else?"

"The something else."

They put themselves together, as close as they can get. The air is a mix of musky scents. But there is also a hint of sweeter smells, from the sprinklings each has applied. Thomas sniffs the air inches from Hélène's chin.

"You like?" she says.

"I do. It's familiar. What is it?"

"Lavender and jasmine, I think. I stopped in Marguerite's room before I came in here. Gave myself a little splash. Do you think it wrong for me to take what belongs to her?"

"The perfume or me?" Thomas smiles as if that were clever. "Either way, she isn't here to complain." He begins to get to work. He starts with light kisses on her neck.

Hélène twists her neck to allow Thomas to get at the back side. It always makes her shiver. "I need to take some of her clothes as well. So I can start as a lady, or near enough."

"Take what you need," Thomas mutters. "Just nothing recent. Or any of her favourites. I'll make up some story to cover it when she gets back."

"What I hoped you'd say. But then you'd say near anything to get what you want from me, is that not right?"

"Maybe." He reaches out to tweak the nipple of one then the other breast. "You should be pleased to know you have such a hold on me."

"You're the one with the hold, not me." She looks down at what he's doing with her breasts.

Thomas reddens just a bit and removes his hands. "Now?" he asks.

Hélène nods, and pushes herself up into a sitting position. She grabs hold of her chemise from its hem and pulls it off over her head. It goes to the floor. Thomas puts a hand to his chin. He pretends to study a perplexing work of art, a work that is the contours of her naked body.

"Jack in the box?" she asks.

"The toy?" Thomas is perplexed. "Where the smiling devil pops up?"

56

"Something like that. Only I get to box the devil in this game."
She swings a leg over Thomas and is soon straddling the centre of
his body. The necessary adjustment is made.

"Ah, funny girl."

"Sometimes. Enough talk, all right?"

—

Hélène reaches out and runs a finger along the faint, barely no-
ticeable scar line beside Thomas's nose. "Want to know what I
was thinking before?"

"Sure. Then I'll tell you about the book Gallatin sent me. *Love
in a Maze*, it's called."

"What?" Hélène blinks repeatedly.

"It's true. But you first. What were you thinking before?"

"That I need to take a leaf out of your book."

"What book is that?"

"To marry. To marry up, I mean."

Thomas's expression changes from smiling expectantly to bewilderment. "That's your plan?"

"It is. And I can and I will." She punches him hard on the
shoulder.

"That hurts."

"Not as much as it could. Yes, me. I too deserve an arrangement like you have with Marguerite. To wed someone who can
lift me up. I've got a lot to offer."

Thomas glances down to some of her charms.

"Not just that."

"Of course not. But, marrying up is not as easy as you think.
It's not always possible to find—"

"Shhh. Shhh." She runs a finger along his lips. "I'm going
to marry someone above me, that's it. And you, you're going to
help." She jumps out of bed and pulls on her chemise.

"But you—" Thomas sputters.

"No buts, all right?" Hélène sends a kiss across the room. "Tomorrow, I start by finding a place to live. Then the rest."

She is out the door. Thomas does not even hear her footsteps padding down the hall to her room. He shakes his head. What she aspires to sounds so simple, yet it is not. Hélène has to understand that aspirations are just that. They're not always the way things end up.

———

The day dawns fine, and each of them takes it as a good sign. The world begins again.

The Pont Neuf is its usual concert of rough voices. Each hawker has his or her cry. A few intone, their voices deep, but most yell as loudly as they can. Cheese or ribbons, whisks and brooms, hot buns, fresh fish, roofing slates, toys for boys and girls, a lotto ticket. Hélène can even make out one of the comic poets beginning his latest rant. Then way off to the left she spots a juggler, five cascading balls making a circle in the air. It's as if there's an invisible string.

Hélène reaches out and grasps Thomas by the sleeve. She tugs him close. "Thomas, the things I took from Marguerite, they don't make me a thief, do they?"

Thomas gapes at her. Apparently he thinks her foolish to even breathe the word "thief" where anyone might overhear. He shifts his eyes away from her to focus for an instant on the bas-relief on a huge hydraulic pump. It's a biblical scene that depicts the Samaritan woman drawing water for Jesus at a well. Thomas sucks in a breath before he returns to face Hélène. "Not here," he says. He flashes a glance in the direction he wants them to go, over to the much less crowded far side of the bridge, beyond the open seam where the coaches roll.

Thomas maintains the stern face as he waves to let the many sellers in his and Hélène's way know that they have to give ground. Thank the heavens he has a walking stick in his right hand. He brandishes it like a sword.

Their advance is slow. The man with the tray of oranges, who sings out "Portugals" at the top of his voice, will not cede an inch. No matter which way Thomas and Hélène turn, the seller matches their move. He is insistent, an orange thrust out and a leering grin on his face. At last, Hélène feints left and goes right while Thomas does the reverse. They are both past.

Thomas scurries around a bent-over seller of old clothes while Hélène has to deal with a scrap-iron vendor whose head is constantly swivelling. "Oh my, the poor thing," she says. The man's head goes left then right then left again. Next it's a water carrier in her path. With the big metal container on his back, the little man does not move fast. Hélène hears him breathing heavily as he shuffles by. She cannot help but wonder how soon it will be before she's on the bridge again, not as a lady but as a seller like all the rest.

———

"Careful," Thomas calls out from her left, a half-dozen feet away. Though sometimes she cannot see him, he can always tell where she is. Her rose-coloured parasol, taken from Marguerite's wardrobe, rides gently up and down above every other head nearby. And from time to time he can even make out her pretty profile as she pushes through the crowd. Hélène nods vaguely in Thomas's direction. "Careful, yes," he hears her mutter back.

Yet Thomas sees that she is not being nearly cautious enough. She's glancing sideways at the water carrier more than she is keeping a vigilant regard straight ahead. The open cobbles, left open for the wheeled conveyances that rumble by, are not far from where she is.

"Careful," Thomas calls out. He stands up on his toes in an attempt to make himself both seen and heard.

But Hélène is not looking his way. He sees her bite her lip and make her shoulders taut. It's because she is now confronted by a shaky old woman selling brooms. The humpback has her wares held up high for all to see. To get away from the cluster of brooms being waved in her face, Hélène spins away. She pushes off the seller's held-up brooms and strides out into the only place where no one is, the open space in the middle of the bridge.

"Hélène!" Thomas yells. Heads turn his way up and down the bridge, Hélène's gaze as well. She swings round to find where Thomas is. She makes eye contact with him and smiles back. "I'm all right. It's open here," she calls back.

"No, no!" he shouts. "Look out! A fiacre!"

He points at the two horses pulling a hired coach coming across the bridge. The chopping sound of their advancing hooves on the cobbles is a terrible noise. The snorting muzzles and frightened eyes of the horses have frozen Hélène where she stands. She does not jump or run, she does not move. The parasol she's been holding up collapses and drops from her hand.

"Mother of shit!" Thomas flails at those in his way. He pushes through the crowd, sending the water carrier falling, spilling his tank. He pushes the broom-selling woman to the ground. He hurtles out into the open and tackles Hélène. He takes the two of them across the bridge toward the far side. They tumble down in a puddle, a pool of rain from the past two days. The horses and the steel-clad wooden wheels of the fiacre miss the couple sprawling on the cobbles by no more than half a foot. The spray spit up further soils Thomas's and Hélène's clothes.

"Idiots!" the driver of the fiacre shouts back. He's standing up, a fist clenched. "Next time, death." He snaps the whip to get the slowing horses of his coach rolling again.

"You all right?" Thomas asks. He's on his knees, his pants soaked.

"Me? I'm fine, but...." She shakes her head as she too goes up on her knees. "I— I've ruined my dress." She's pointing at the wet stains. "And lost my parasol."

"No, not quite." Thomas reaches behind her and picks up the parasol. Still on his knees, like her, he opens it up and gives it a spin above their heads. "Look, none the worse."

A crowd of gawkers comes round, wide-eyed and shaking their heads. "Should be hanged, 'e should," announces a woman with a tray of fish. "Driver of that fiacre."

"Hanged," repeats the man with jowly face standing beside her. "Hanged" is picked up by others. It becomes a chant.

A dozen arms reach out to lift the stricken couple up from their knees. Among the helpers Thomas is surprised to see three waifs with dirty faces. They have sly looks but he has to admit they are enthusiastic about getting the two of them to their feet.

"Fine, I'm fine," Thomas says. He wishes he did not sound so annoyed, but in truth he is. It's not like he or Hélène were actually struck by the horses or wheels. Yet their clothes are soiled and—

"Thank you. You're very kind," he hears Hélène saying over and again to everyone who gives her a hand or offers a word of sympathy.

"That's it. Enough. Move away." Thomas gives a stern look to the tallest of the waifs. The scruffy lad is going so far as to straighten out Thomas's justaucorps and veston. "Shoo!"

The boy presents a startled face. Despite his size, he begins to cry. He beckons his two friends to come near to comfort him, then just like that the three of them are off, running toward the far end of the bridge.

"Hold on," says the jowly man who was the first to call for the fiacre driver to be hanged. The man thrusts a finger an inch from Thomas's nose. "Got no right to do that. Boy was only trying to help and your type made him cry. Maybe the driver was right. Maybe he shoulda run you down."

"That's it." The woman with the tray of fish is shaking her head. There's a scornful scowl on her lips. "Imagine, hurting a lad who was only trying to help."

"But," Thomas begins, then throws up his hands. What's the use? He bends down to pick up his silver-handled walking stick. "Come on," he says to Hélène, taking her by the hand. He drags her away from the small crowd, over to the stone rail. "We need to figure this out."

"You sure you're all right?" she whispers in his ear. "Everyone was only trying—"

"I know," he says, "but I didn't like it. I didn't—" Thomas feels for the pouch in the pocket of his veston. He doesn't feel the lump where it should be. It contains the coins he brought with him to give to Hélène, to cover her rent and food for the first month. He slaps his hands across his chest and abdomen.

"What?" Hélène asks.

Thomas looks at Hélène, then tips back his head and closes his eyes.

"What?" she whispers. "Your purse?"

"Seigneur," Thomas hears himself say, quiet as a prayer. He feels a little dizzy. One shoulder and one knee are sore where they must have made first contact with the cobbles as he dove. Thomas opens his eyes and gives Hélène a long, sad look.

"It's gone, isn't it?" she asks.

"It is."

Thomas scans the crowd up and down the length of the Pont Neuf. There, at the far end, standing on one leg atop the distant stone rail, waving at Thomas, is one of the boys. He's holding up something in his hand. It's too small to see yet Thomas knows exactly what it is. He shakes his head.

"Do we have to go back?" Hélène asks.

Thomas exhales long and loud, then nods. "Not just the money. We need to clean up. Find you another dress."

Hélène makes the sign of the cross. "Marguerite won't be there yet, will she?"

Thomas shrugs and turns to begin the walk back. Hélène sighs and does the same. "I don't want to face her again, I don't."

"Then let's be quick," is all Thomas can say to that.

Hélène loops an arm in Thomas's and together they pick up the pace. "I don't really want to see her servants either, you know."

"Oh, fuck the servants." Thomas turns to face Hélène to see what she says to that.

Her face brightens into a broad smile. "Isn't that how we got into this mess?"

Thomas feels his grin. "I suppose it is." He halts her progress and steps in front of her. "Would you rather we'd not gone into the maze? Have things back as they were?"

"I do." Hélène tries to soften her admission with a beseeching kindness in her eyes.

"Me too, though it was good, was it not?" Thomas asks for her agreement with his eyes.

"It's not the pleasure, I regret, Thomas. It's the consequences."

"Ah, yes. Such is life. Well, the quicker we get there and are changed, the quicker you'll start your new life." He grabs her hand and tugs it to get them walking again.

—

"I think I should accompany you to your apartment," says Madame Dufour. "Just in case."

Marguerite watches her cousin incline her head meaningfully forward. She's clearly waiting for Marguerite's reply. It's been a good hour since the two cousins last spoke. The rocking and swaying motion of the coach has lulled each into something like a trance. Each has closed her book and is sitting with heavy-lidded eyes. The trip back from Brittany has been long, stretched out over three and a half days, despite Marguerite's request that they go faster. Madame Dufour has had to explain repeatedly that the horses, and the poor driver, need to rest along the way.

"What I mean," Madame Dufour elaborates when Marguerite chooses not to reply, "is that suppose you find the two of them there? Suppose that's the situation, my dear? Who knows what those two might do. They're fornicators and cold-hearted thieves as well."

"So you repeat every hour," Marguerite mutters to herself. Louder she says: "Yes, dear cousin, I know."

Marguerite glances out the window of the carriage. She thinks she recognizes the shape of Montmartre off to the left. She squints to make sure. Yes, she can see the windmills that stand upon the hill. "Montmartre," she says, with a flick of the hand.

"Yes," replies Madame Dufour, leaning back in her seat. "The Fauxbourg Saint-Honoré will be just ahead. After that it's straight on past Louis Le Grand and—"

"I know, Marie-France, I've lived in Paris all my life."

"I'm just trying to point out that we could be at your place within a quarter hour."

"That's right." Marguerite vents a weary exhale. Will this interminable coach ride never end? What happened at the château was bad enough. But she's been forced by her cousin to relive it and dissect it over and again. This ride from Brittany must be what the Church means when it teaches purgatory is almost as unpleasant as hell.

Marguerite looks again at Madame Dufour. "The journey has been long. So I would prefer it, Cousin, if your coachman took you to your place first. I would rather go into my apartment by myself. Just in case."

"Just in case what? Oh, never mind. You have your stubborn side, my dear. Yes you do." Madame Dufour turns toward the window and the scenery of Paris rolling by. Though her cousin keeps her eyes out the window, Marguerite hears the woman continue to speak. "Only trying to look out for your interest is all. Once a criminal begins, it's impossible for him to stop. And what we have here are two criminals, not just the one."

"Really, Cousin? Thomas is still my husband. I will hear him out. I cannot imagine I'm in danger returning to my place. You do not know him as I do. You'll grant me that."

Madame Dufour turns fully toward Marguerite. Her cheeks are enflamed. "Forgive all you want, but it is foolish, very foolish, I say. You are not the Mother of Christ. Nor his wife."

Marguerite's eyes go wide. Is that not a sacrilege? What can she possibly say to such a thing?

Madame Dufour wags her finger. "They stole my calèche and that *I* do not forgive. I'm seeing a greffier and laying charges, I am. I'll see justice done. And he stole it, by the way, that husband of yours, to run away with a whore. That's who your Thomas is."

"Is it?" Marguerite feels she is biting her lips. She knows her face has to be flushed.

"Is it? Is it? Those are simple facts, Marguerite."

Marguerite forces a shrug. She will give the woman, her busybody cousin, no more satisfaction than that. Marguerite swivels in her seat, tilting a shoulder to Madame Dufour. But then, an instant later, Marguerite swivels back. She will speak her mind

"You know, Cousin, I will not be surprised if Thomas did not steal that calèche at all. That you will find it safe and sound in a Paris stable. My guess is that Thomas borrowed it, that is all. In his haste to get that woman away from me, away from your precious Le Mesnil. It could have been an act of consideration, not theft. I for one will wait to hear what he has to say."

Madame Dufour snorts. She puts a hand to her mouth to keep herself from replying at all. With a show of lifting her legs and hips, she turns to gaze out the window on her side.

Relieved, Marguerite turns to the opposite window. She spies an opening between two buildings. It is the Place Louis Le Grand. She acknowledges with a habitual nod the bronze equestrian statue of Louis XIV in the centre of the square. She admired the late king, she did. The Sun King. Twice they attended the same ball. They didn't meet, but she saw him glance her way. He was the epitome of what a king should be.

Marguerite hears a rustle as Madame Dufour swings her legs back to face Marguerite's way. Marguerite turns to make eye contact.

"I hope you'll not be disappointed, Cousin," says Madame Dufour. "If things are not as you expect."

"How kind you are." The words barely squeeze out through Marguerite's lips. "I think it best if we say not another word."

"On that we agree."

—

"What's in that?"

Thomas is pointing at the large cotton sack Hélène is carrying. Whatever is inside, it has a lot of volume but not much weight, judging by the way she has it slung over her shoulder.

"And why are you dressed like—" He lowers his voice in case Marie-Claude, Charles or Sébastien might be nearby. "Like you're nothing but a servant?"

They've been back in the apartment only a few minutes. While he was changing his sullied clothes in his room, Hélène, apparently, has decided to leave any pretense of being a lady far behind.

"I have a dress in the sack." Hélène's eyes are darting, not focusing on Thomas at all. She appears to be more distraught now than when they returned to the apartment. "I've taken the lemon-coloured one with white panels. It's linen, not silk. Marguerite hasn't worn it once. Not since I've been here. And a pair of shoes and a hat that almost match. It's enough. I'll get a tailor to make adjustments if it's too large."

Thomas takes her hands in his and whispers in her ear. "Slow down. You look like someone is coming to hunt you down. Take the time. Try on the dress." He's pointing at the sack.

"No, I have to go. I'm shivering. Feel." She reaches out and puts an icy hand on his cheek.

"My God, you're freezing."

"I know. I can't warm up. It's this apartment. I thought I was gone, but here I am, back. Back at Marguerite's."

"Please, Hélène." He draws her to his chest and presses hard.

"I don't want to end up in a pillory, Thomas. People taunting and throwing rotten food. Me branded with the V."

"Lower your voice. Why are you talking like this? Marguerite is in Brittany, or at best somewhere on the road."

"I have to get away." She pushes him back. "Let me go."

"But I'm going with you, to help you find a place."

"No. No, you're not." She shakes her head.

"Yes, I will." He stands as stiff as a plank, his feet glued to the floor. His hands reach out.

"No, I've decided. You've been generous, but from here on, I look after myself." Her eyes are fierce.

"Well." Thomas uses a hand to cover his mouth. "Marie-Claude did give me a cunning look at our return. Maybe I should—"

"Yes, you should," Hélène says to him, her chin jutting up. But then she begins to shiver. She lowers the sack to the floor and begins to sway.

"You don't look good, Hélène." Thomas sees an immense sadness on her face.

—

Hélène's thoughts swirl. She sees now that the incidents on the Pont Neuf are signs from above. She's been laid low by a vengeful God. The soiling of the silk dress she took from Marguerite was His judgement, nothing less. She has to accept that she's not fit for any reward in this earthly life. Her dream of marrying someone who could raise her up society's ladder is gone. She will still try for honest work for one week, she will. But she knows it's for nought. She will end up paying her bills the way she used to. She only hopes the dress she's taking will let her pass as a courtesan. She does not want to end up in tattered rags and no perfume at all. She doesn't want to share her body with stinking men in some stinking stall.

"Good bye," she says, finally looking Thomas in the eyes. She knows her eyes are wet, so she squeezes them dry. Then she stoops to hoist the sack.

"Oh, Hélène." Thomas takes her in his arms. "It will be all right. I'll come to you soon."

She pushes him away. "I— I— have— to— go."

Thomas holds out two helpless hands. Hélène takes hold of the handle to the door.

"Wait." Thomas grabs her elbow. "Where will we meet?"

—

Hélène's expression is one Thomas cannot place. It's much more than sad. She looks resigned to some horrible fate.

Hélène starts to shake her head, but then she lets go of the door handle and leans forward. Close to his ear she breathes, "I don't know. Saint-Médard? I like it there. I like rue Mouffetard."

"Saint-Médard," Thomas repeats. "Yes, Saint-Médard is a good choice."

Neither Marguerite nor any of her circle would be caught dead in that part of the city. It's named after the church where in a time gone by he met with Collier from the Paris police to pass on secrets about his old writer friends. More recently the crazy shoeless Jansenist beggar priest used the Saint-Médard church as his base.

No, he was only a deacon, not a priest. Yet since his death his tomb at the church has become a shrine. People took clippings of his fingernails and snippets of his hair and splinters off his coffin before they buried him in the ground. The cardinal archbishop even came to the funeral. Hélène has selected wisely such a place to meet. The crowd of pilgrims at the deacon's shrine will provide a cover when they meet.

"What, why the little smile?" Thomas asks of Hélène.

"Doesn't take much to make you happy. Just the thought of a secret rendezvous."

Thomas shrugs. "But when? Tomorrow? Or should we make it a week from today?"

Hélène gives him a hard kiss, half biting his lips. "Don't know," she says.

Thomas is startled. He steps back.

Hélène turns. She swings the cotton sack over her shoulder and reaches for the door. But before she can grab the handle, the door opens. It comes at her fast, nearly striking her on the chin. She stumbles out of the way.

"No!" Hélène cries. "God be merciful." Thomas sees her legs wobble and then she falls to her knees.

Thomas grabs hold of the door and pulls it open all the way. "Shit," he mumbles under his breath.

It's Marguerite. The look of shock on his wife's face doesn't last long. It switches to disappointment then to scorn. "Well, well. So my doubting cousin was right. Here you are, the two of you. Together, right in my home."

"A minute, Marguerite," Thomas begins, but the look Marguerite gives him prevents him from saying any more.

"I'll have you know, Thomas, I was trying to give you the benefit of doubt. But I was wrong. You insist on being with her and so it is. And look at her. Carrying off whatever of mine she wants. And you abetting her theft."

"No, that is not it." Thomas finds his legs taking a half stride away from Hélène. "What you think you see, my wife—"

"Don't call me your wife. It's a vow. It's something earned and kept. Can you even understand that?"

"Here." Hélène is up off her knees. She holds out the sack, its mouth opened wide. She thrusts the opened sack against the front of Marguerite's dress. "Look. I say look. That's all it is, Madame. A gift of charity, an old dress, from your husband to a poor reformed whore. Nothing more than that."

Hélène lets go of the sack and it spills to the floor. She clutches her hands together like she's in prayer. "To start my life anew, Madame, that's all I want. A better path. Please do not deny me that."

Thomas feels his chest clench. "Hélène—"

"Not a word, man," Hélène says, eyes fixed on Marguerite. "This is between me and your blessed wife."

Marguerite stoops to take up the sack. She looks inside, and stirs things up with her free hand. An annoyed expression sweeps across her face. She casts the sack back to the floor. "Take it, woman. Take it and go. And never ever come back to my door."

"Oh, Madame, thank you." Hélène rises up.

"Go. Just go."

Sack tossed over her shoulder, Hélène is through the doorway and down the stairs.

—

"As for you," Marguerite scans Thomas from head to toe. "The only word that comes to mind is 'weak.' Do you know why I say that?"

"I'm afraid I do."

"Well, this is it, Thomas. I've had three long days to mull it over. I'm going to explain to you how this marriage of ours is going to work. You will listen and agree. I'll have your solemn word or else, or else you might as well go after that tramp." Marguerite points a single finger at the still open door.

Thomas inclines his head and bends a knee in contrition. He chooses to not say a thing.

Marguerite grabs hold of the door to the hall and stairwell and sends it shut. "In there," she says to Thomas, pointing at the interior door painted a pewter grey. It leads into the salon. "Now, if you please."

"Of course, Madame," her husband says, as meekly as a child.

No sooner does Marguerite take two steps toward the salon door but that door opens wide. Marie-Claude gazes admiringly at her mistress. She steps into the doorway and makes a curtsey as deep as if Marguerite were the queen. Clearly, the little woman has been listening on the inside of the room, waiting for some kind of cue.

"Welcome home, Madame. Your return brings me joy. We had no idea when you would return. Your husband and the other one told us only you'd been delayed in Brittany."

Marguerite catches a smirk Marie-Claude aims at Thomas. It makes her smile to see such support and sympathy. But wait, Marie-Claude is a servant and that makes any smirk toward her husband insolence. Marguerite will have a word with Marie-Claude about that after she has straightened Thomas out.

Marguerite chooses the divan. After she has adjusted the folds of fabric of her dress, she gives Thomas the disdainful glance he deserves. Maintaining a frown she waves him to sit nearby, on the bright green chair whose seat is an inch or two lower than the divan.

———

Thomas flexes warning eyebrows at Marie-Claude as he walks past her on his way to the chair to which he's been summoned. The servant inflates her chest as her reply, then exits the room.

Thomas slows his racing thoughts. This is the moment he's been preparing for ever since he and Hélène left Le Mesnil. If there's one thing he's learned over and again in this life, it's that an easy confidence counts the most in a situation like this. And earnestness.

Yes, he's ready, he's ready to listen to Marguerite. He will reply only if and when he must. He is prepared. He has a story to tell her and a vraisemblance of contrition that should serve him well.

—

Not that evening, nor the next, nor any time before a week and a day have elapsed, does Thomas feel it's safe enough to go looking for Hélène. Marguerite's stern lecture upon her return shook him of any inclination to make his way over to the left bank.

It's only now, a Monday evening in late June, before he goes home to Marguerite, that he's heading across the river after a day of clerking in the magistrate judge's office. He cannot take long, it's too soon to be errant. Yet he wants to have an initial contact with Hélène. He wants to know that she is all right. Then they can make arrangements for later on. But he has no specific address, only the choked suggestion of Saint-Médard. A preliminary walkabout, he tells himself, a refamiliarizing reconnoitre of the church and its neighbourhood, no more than that. He's allowing a half hour, three quarters at most. Then it'll be back to Marguerite's so as not to raise any suspicions or doubts.

Marguerite made it clear that she is willing to give her young husband another chance, but only if he follows the rules she has clearly laid down. There may have been a dozen rules, Thomas isn't sure. His mind wandered after the first few. They all seemed to be about not seeing Hélène, albeit worded slightly differently: trollop, tart, wench, strumpet, whore. Oh, and pretender, yes, that was said as well.

Thomas's ears reconnected with Marguerite when she told him she was going to see if she could somehow locate poor wronged Simone. The servant would be welcomed back, if she could be found.

—

If Thomas had to put down the conclusion of Marguerite's lecture on the page, let's say for a character in a play, he would have to say that it went something like this.

"If ever you stray – I'm not naive, Thomas, I know men sometimes do – make sure you wrap yourself in one of those English gloves for your base carnal pleasures. Don't bring any maladies to me. And under no circumstances will you see that one again, do you hear? Do you understand?"

Seated in the centre of the stage, a character somewhat like Thomas would nod to the audience that yes, he understood.

"The best way to resist temptation, dear husband," says the wife as she circles his chair, "is to not go near its source. Have you not learned that yet?"

The poor fellow would nod once more that he had. Would the audience applaud or laugh out loud?

"Because if ever I catch you two together, you and that tart, who once shared these rooms and pretended to be my friend, if I catch you with her, on a street, in a room, anywhere at all, in any kind of public arena where others can see my embarrassment, then understand this: it's you who will pay. You, Thomas, no one else. Understood? Your standing in society, your work with the magistrate, it and everything else will end. Is that understood?"

The character in the play would suck in a breath. Standing at last, still facing the audience, the man would say aloud, "Yes, Madame, I do, I understand." Then he would wink at the crowd and they would laugh again.

The scene in Thomas's head brings a smile. If only he had been as brash as the man in his imagined play.

A foul smell fills his nostrils. He looks down at the gutter of the cobbled street. A mound of dead cats – there must be a dozen – has attracted a thousand humming flies.

"Not again," Thomas mutters. Why do certain types in this city amuse themselves by killing cats? He turns abruptly down a narrow lane to go another way to the church of Saint-Médard. As he reaches out to make contact with the walls on either side, a few lines descend.

Sadness, sadness sublime, you test our measure.

What good, oh what good comes if there is no pleasure?

—

"There it is," mumbles Thomas aloud.

The spire of what he believes is the Saint-Médard church has come into view at the alley's end. He has arrived atop the counterscarp in less time than he thought. He hurries on.

"Yes, that's it."

Even at this distance, Thomas can see a line of people queuing up at the main entrance of the church. Each one appears to be in a state of reverie. That much he expected, given the still mounting popularity of the cult over the late deceased deacon. But what surprises Thomas is that the devotees are not all poor, as he would have thought. No, there are some well-dressed individuals in the mix. Even a few ladies and gentlemen, judging by the fortune they are showing in their clothes. The pilgrims' heads are all bowed low or else swaying, gently gazing at the sky. Each no doubt has come to pray for a miracle at the tomb. Thomas shakes his head, but then who is he to judge? He likely has blind spots and foolish beliefs of his own. Then again, maybe not.

He walks up and down the mumbling queue looking for Hélène. Alas, she is nowhere to be seen. So Thomas hurries to the door on the far side of the church and goes in. He takes off his tricorne and carries it by his hip. He pads up the nave then off into the short transepts left and right. Still no sign of Hélène. Back outside, she's still not there. But what did he expect? That she'd be waiting at the church round the clock? Each day for a week? Of course not.

On this first attempt, Hélène is nowhere to be seen, but it is just a first look. He'll be back another day. They'll reconnect. He just hopes she's not living in some horrible room and forced back into wrapping her legs around strangers for a few coins.

—

Thomas returns to the Saint-Médard church a few days later, then again and again over the days and weeks that follow. He is always a little surprised to see how many are still drawn to the shrine. Not once does he so much as glimpse any woman who even looks like Hélène.

One day it dawns on him that of course she did not say the church building, only the name. The entire parish bears the name. So he begins to pound the cobbles along a much wider, twisting path, as if in a maze. He does so twice a week. Sometimes he circulates after work, but his preference is to come on a Sunday or on a feast day of the church, for on those days he does not have to work and has more daylight hours to spend on his quest. The evening before a holy day of obligation he tells Marguerite that the next day he is going to reinvigorate his somewhat lapsed faith by going to church. He adds that he has decided to visit as many different churches of the Roman Catholic and apostolic faith as he can.

Marguerite didn't look like she believed him the first time he made his pledge, but as his feast day disappearances add up, they have a cumulative effect. She has told him that she is greatly pleased. "Contrition and devotion, husband, they are marvelous, are they not?"

"You are right," was his modest reply, made with lowered eyes.

Thomas supposes Marguerite credits her stern lectures for having made him more alert to his need to restore his faith. So she should, Thomas admits. Nothing like the fear of losing his position to make him inventive. He has asked Marguerite to join him on his pretend spiritual quest, knowing that her aging feet and legs are not up to any such test. She has developed what her physician says is gout. So he wins twice: he does his search for Hélène all by himself yet proves himself a loving, penitent husband to Marguerite.

Each holy day when Thomas comes home from a half-day ramble, Marguerite asks about the church he has worshipped in that day. How fortunate for Thomas that he spent several years working as a fly for the Paris police. He could not count how many nights he spent rendezvousing with Collier in the dark recesses of one church or another. He is able to recall well enough the details of each one to convince and satisfy Marguerite's queries. Though she did ask the last time, "Why are they all on the left bank? We have churches over here, you know. You do know that?" He replied that he would eventually be done with the left side of the Seine and then he'll start on the right. He is a man of reason. He likes to be systematic about these things.

And so the late June feast day of Saint-Pierre and Saint-Paul goes by. A month later it's the feasts of Saint-Jacques and Sainte-Anne. All four holy days in August – Saint-Laurent, the Assumption, Saint-Barthélmey and Saint-Louis – come and go. Still no sign of Hélène. As the disappointments add up, the prospect of reuniting with Hélène begins to slip. Certainty becomes probability, then a possibility at best. As September begins in rain he finds himself beneath a cloak going through the motions without any expectation of a result. He begins to stride more quickly in and out of the Saint-Médard church and all around its parish. He looks left and right as he goes, but sometimes after he's gone up a street he cannot recall what he might have taken in.

Hélène could have moved out of Paris altogether. That's true. Or she could be dead. The Nativity of the Holy Virgin comes on September 8. Thomas goes to all the usual places even faster than before. The hunt for Hélène has become a chore. So at the end of that day he sets a deadline. If he's not found Hélène by the Saint-Mathieu, he will search no more. No, how about the Saint-Michel, the day before the end of the month? That will give the quest a few more days. But then the Saint-Michel comes and goes and Thomas finds himself deciding that, all right, he'll look for just one more month. He'll keep returning to Saint-Médard off and on throughout October. The last day of his searching, the last day for his hunt for Hélène, will be November 1. The Feast of All Souls.

———

It's the last Sunday of October. Thomas is coming over to the left bank for what he recognizes is his penultimate search for Hélène. This time, however, because it's unseasonably warm, he's not in an eager rush. It's a slow saunter across the Pont Neuf – past the usual collection of charlatans and quacks, the jugglers and fortune tellers, the food peddlers and the sellers of flimsy parasols.

Thomas chides himself for having been duped by Hélène and for having wasted five months of his life. He squints to recall that when she said "Saint-Médard," he should have been able to see something hidden in those dark eyes. She was giving him the slip. Thomas scuffs the packed dirt road as he steps off the bridge. Is this the wiser view of what has transpired, or is he just being like La Fontaine's fox, finding a reason to walk away when he cannot grasp the sour grapes? Well, he has only this day's search and one more after that. Then he's done. He'll be all right. He and Marguerite have come to an agreeable arrangement of a marriage. It is working well enough. It's just that he wanted Hélène back in his life, at least now and again.

Today, his walk around the church and neighbourhood of Saint-Médard will not be without at least a small reward. He intends to descend rue Mouffetard to visit his tailor for the first time since before the ill-fated trip to Brittany. He is going to order a new outfit: veston, justaucorps and breeches to match. Maybe a chocolate brown. It'll be a gift to himself, nothing more than that. Something to mark his dedication to pursuing a lost cause these past few months.

No, the new clothes are not really about Hélène. Things are going extremely well at his work in the magistrate judge's office. There's a hint of another position, a promotion, in the days ahead. For that he has to dress the part. A more expensive fabric than he currently wears and a superior cut. In anticipation of his climb up another rung, he needs to be measured by his Russian tailor, Pierre, to make sure his numbers have not changed. But first, he makes the obligatory spin through the parish of Saint-Médard.

As he strolls along, looking neither left nor right, Thomas mulls how things are going with Marguerite of late. He really cannot complain. If Marguerite has smelled upon him the women he occasionally visits in the stalls – it's been only a few times – she has not said a word. One night, after he and Marguerite had a congress of their own, she took his chin in her grasp and looked deep into his eyes.

"The truth, Thomas, the truth. Have you seen that one again? That scheming former servant of mine?"

"No," he said, in complete truthfulness, "I have not. I gave my word and I give it again here and now."

It was only after he'd returned to his room and his own bed that he felt bad for swearing such an oath. Yes, he'd spoken the truth about not seeing Hélène, but it was not for want of trying. Avoidance of the truth is always better than a flat-out lie. Hairsplitting, yes, nothing wrong with that. It doesn't put his honour on the line.

Self-satisfied with his reasoning, Thomas decides he must write on the subject one of these nights. Perhaps he will share it with Gallatin, who would warm to such a discussion. In fact, Thomas will compose a letter this very night once he gets back to Marguerite's.

The spire of the church of Saint-Médard makes its first appearance up ahead. His tailor's shop is not far now, about halfway down rue Mouffetard. There is a crowd of people beside the church, in a circle, each of them wearing a dumbfounded look and staring at the ground. Of late he ignores the pilgrims and their cult, but this is too much of an oddity for him to resist. He goes up on tiptoes. He sees a woman writhing on the ground.

"What's wrong with her?" Thomas taps the man beside him on the upper arm.

"Holy Spirit." The man's eyes are glazed.

"Is she shivering or too hot?"

"Holy Spirit," is once again the reply.

"Right." Thomas resists shaking his head. He turns and walks away.

Because of the commotion surrounding the woman on the cobbled ground, Thomas finds he can enter the church anywhere he wants. For the moment, the woman outside is the show. He goes in the door closest to the tomb of the deacon Antoine Paris. There are only a handful of believers at the tomb, but Thomas is taken aback by the sight of so many bouquets of flowers. And then there are all the crutches left behind by people who have been cured. It must be nice, Thomas thinks, to have so strong a faith. As though one were still in the time of Jeanne d'Arc. It's a faith he has not had since he was a boy in Vire.

Thomas's tour of the church earns him the same result as every time before. Back outside, into air that does not taste of ancient dust, Thomas sees that the crowd encircling the woman on the ground has doubled in size. There are loud shouts of exultation and cries of joy. Thomas beckons to the glazed man he spoke with a few minutes earlier, a well-dressed merchant type.

"What now?" Thomas asks.

"Two more," the man shouts over his shoulder, not wanting to miss a thing. "Two more convulsers. The Holy Spirit is all around. Join us, friend. You could be next."

Thomas smiles. "Maybe later."

Walking away, he speaks softly to himself. "Or, maybe a reinette."

He picks up his pace to select his apple at one of the fruit stands on rue Mouffetard. He inspects its rusty orange skin. First with his eyes then with his nose. It's an important part of the pleasure, before the all-important first bite. As with a sip of wine or a gulp of beer, or anything else in life, it's the first taste that's best.

As he raises the apple to his mouth, he senses movement above his head. He jumps back and aside. A cascade of waste water narrowly misses his head. It splatters on the street. Thomas scowls up whence it came, but all he catches is a hand closing a shutter as quickly as it can. He looks down to see what the damage is. Not as bad as he feared. Only a few splashes reached his socks and shoes. He'll put his apple in his pocket for now.

He hears a distant church bell sound the hour. He had not realized it was so late. He needs to go see Pierre and place his order, then get back to Marguerite before the light of day is all gone.

Round the corner, a dozen strides ahead, Thomas spies a woman with a basket at her hip. Her gait and the little side-to-side swing of her head are familiar. Yes, the woman reminds him of no one else but Hélène. Thomas hurries closer.

Behind her now, nearly close enough to touch, Thomas is not so sure. With her hair tucked in her bonnet and from the back, it could be any woman. He sees her glance sideways. His hurrying footsteps must have given her a slight alarm. He allows his pace to fall off. No, though he wants it to be Hélène, it makes no sense that he would come across her now, after all these months. She's likely dead, or moved out of Paris, back to Évreux or somewhere else.

The woman, dressed in middling clothes, is clearly not a servant. Nor is she a lady of Marguerite's rank. She is from the vast grey area in between. She is or has been shopping. Even from his distance he can see what her basket contains: a cabbage, a bunch of carrots and a cloth-wrapped wedge that must be cheese. To watch her moving down the street, Thomas has to admit again that this woman has the walk and shape of Hélène.

"Why not?" Thomas mutters. He regains the quick pace. He comes alongside the woman and risks a touch upon her shoulder.

"Hé— Hélène."

The woman stops. She turns to face the voice.

"Thomas!" Hélène beams the instant smile of someone who has just found a long lost friend. But almost as quickly a shadow crosses her face. The smile disappears. She glances up and down the street.

"My God, Hélène. Where have you been? So long I've searched these streets and all around the church. You are ... you were nowhere to be seen."

Hélène gestures for him to quiet down. She begins to walk again, and at a quick pace.

"You're safe? You're fine?" Thomas is undeterred as he matches her stride. He reaches out to stop her by the shoulder. When she halts, he opens his arms, ready for a great embrace.

"No." Her voice is firm. A hand comes up in defence. Her eyes warn him to step back. "Not here, not now." She starts to move again, even more quickly than before.

"But I've found you. If you only knew how long I've—"

Hélène pauses momentarily. She places her basket between them and whispers. "Walk beside me if you wish. But I live around here. People know me. You're a stranger who in their eyes could do me harm." She sets off at a brisk pace.

"A stranger? Harm?"

Thomas scans up and down the street as he walks at her side. Rue Mouffetard is crowded with people going about their day. No one is paying the least attention to him or to Hélène. No, that's not so. He spies a woman up ahead, a fishmonger with a cart, and she's staring with what looks like suspicion at Hélène as the distance between them closes. Oh, and there's a man with bread in his back carrier. He's doing the same, squinting first at him then at Hélène. Thomas moves farther away and shows no more interest in Hélène than in any other stranger on the street.

"Why are we doing this?" Thomas mutters through his teeth.

Hélène comes to a halt before a butcher shop. She pretends to examine a pig's head and its trotters on the cart in front of the shop. Thomas makes the same stop and comes to stand a few feet away from her. They take turns sniffing the air above the cart, and bending to examine the head and feet.

"You owe me some kind of explanation," Thomas says at last.

Hélène glances up from the pig's head but keeps her eyes straight ahead. She adjusts her bonnet in the reflection of the shop glass. "Do I?"

"You do."

"All right." Hélène turns to face Thomas. She clutches her basket firmly to her chest. She inhales. "I'm married." Her eyebrows arch up.

Thomas twitches to hear such a word come off Hélène's lips. "I see."

Hélène turns back to the beheaded pig. This time she's inspecting the snout. But with a gesture of her hand, she sends Thomas a message to come a little closer to where she stands.

"My husband's shop is nearby," she whispers. "Just down the street. We live upstairs."

Thomas stretches to his full height. He makes a face of displeasure and at first fools himself into thinking it's an act he's putting on in response to the smelly pig. But if it's an act, he wonders, why is there a tightness in his chest? And a weakness in his arms and legs?

"Don't follow me." Hélène sets off down the street.

Thomas's eyes burn into the back of her head. He will do as he pleases, as he must. He comes alongside. "Married? How can that be?"

Hélène stops. "A ceremony. With a priest."

Thomas's chest feels squeezed, like it's down to half its normal size. He steals a breath. "But who, Hélène, who'd—"

"Who'd marry me?" She shakes her head in disgust.

"No, who did you marry? Who is he?"

Hélène adjusts the basket on her hip. With her free hand she takes hold of the handle to a dark-green door where she has stopped. It's the entrance to a shop. She says nothing but with her eyes she directs Thomas to look up.

He does, and takes in a hanging wooden sign he knows very well. A painting of a giant pair of scissors spread open with a man's coat in the space above and a pair of breeches in the open space below. His tailor.

"You ... you live here?"

"That's right." She's not turned the handle to the door, but neither has she let it go.

"Near Pierre?"

"*With*, Thomas, *with*. I'm Madame Kharlamov." There comes a smile.

Thomas cannot control his eyes, nor his jaw. "But he's at least three times your age."

Hélène shakes her head. "And your Marguerite, is she not twice yours?"

The door of the shop suddenly opens wide. Hélène half stumbles in.

"Caution, my love," says the man in the doorway. It's the tailor, Pierre. As always, the man wears no wig. He still has no hesitation about showing his thinning white hair to the world. There's a kindly smile upon his face as he grabs hold of his young wife to keep her from tumbling into the shop.

"Thank you, my husband."

Pierre places a hand on each side of her face and transfers his affection for her with a touch of nose on nose. Then he turns to Thomas. With each word the tailor speaks, his Russian accent becomes more pronounced.

"So it is you, Monsieur. I thought so through the window. And how are you, my friend? It's been a long while, has it not?"

"It has, Pierre, it has. I— I— A great pleasure to see you."

Thomas makes a tight upper-body bow, which the tailor returns. The two men enter into a protracted handshake. Then Pierre clasps Thomas like a long-lost customer he's glad to see again.

"Tell me, my friend, what brings you to my shop?"

Thomas blinks. His lips open but for the moment no words come.

"I'm going in." Hélène touches her husband lightly on the arm as she slips by. She turns to Thomas once she has her husband between the two of them. "A pleasure to meet you, sir. You are, by the sound of it, a customer of the finest tailor in Paris, is that not so?" Hélène winks at Pierre.

"Yes, he is," says Pierre. "His name is Thomas Pichon. Does an old man still have his memory or not?"

"That you do," says Thomas. "And yes, Madame," he offers to Hélène. But she is no longer where she was. She is somewhere in the darkness of the shop, out of sight.

"Very pretty, is she not?" Pierre's eyes are asking for only one reply.

"Yes, very." Thomas takes in a tight breath.

"She has for name Hélène," the tailor confides. "Like one in Troy."

Thomas frowns.

Pierre explains. "She who launched the thousand ships? You not know that tale? It's Greek." The tailor laughs.

"I do. Homer. And yes, you are right. Your Hélène is as pretty as that."

"The widow of naval officer, she is. A storm at sea. Off Brest, I think. Still waiting her widow's pension, she is. It will come, it will. Eventually from the King. Down on her luck was Hélène when we met. But not her fault, no it was not. But maybe you don't want to hear her story, my friend."

"No, please, Pierre, go on. I have the time."

"She came to Paris some months back, looking for a room. And work to be had. Back in June that was. Well, at my age, my friend, I still know a pretty woman. Much younger than me, I suppose you'd say."

Thomas hopes his expression suggests he had not noticed.

"I played my cards. Job and room. But soon, I propose. And Hélène accept. Now, Madame Kharlamov. And me sixty-three." Pierre's chest puffs out. There is a broad smile on his face.

"Lucky you, Pierre, lucky you."

Thomas seeks out the tailor's hand for what will be the second time. He clasps it hard, like he's delighted to hear the news. But then Pierre squints at Thomas.

"Excuse me." The tailor takes his hand back. "You come only for talk? No, I think not. How about we step inside my shop." Pierre gestures for Thomas to go in ahead of him.

"Right you are. I came ... to be measured for a new suit."

"You come right place. We have new fabric. Best in all Paris for you to select."

"Yes, I hope. Tell me, Pierre, does your wife – Hélène, you said? – does she help you in the shop?"

IV
Appearance

Paris
March to October 1731

It's not just that it's Easter Sunday, and a warm sunny afternoon
at that, with all Paris out for a stroll. Nor is it that his thirty-
first birthday is a mere five days away. Those factors contribute,
of course, but there are two other elements that make Thomas's
chest swell as he perambulates along the Seine.

The first is his promotion. He's now the senior overseeing dis-
tinguished clerk in the magistrate judge's office. That position
comes with a significant rise in status and in pay. To be sure, it's
not a job he'd select if allowed to pick anything in this world. He
would be a writer of poetry, or essays, or history. Or maybe even
try the new novel form if it were up to him. But no one's going to
pay him to use his quill for any of those. So he takes pride instead
in being good at using his ambition and his talents in the service
of someone else, someone willing to pay for what he can do.

The second reason for Thomas's glowing mood is that today
is a feast day across the land. That means he gets to spend an
hour or two of intimacy with the woman whose company he
enjoys the most. The complications of the first few months of his
marriage to Marguerite and the fallout from the incident at the
château in Brittany are now dim memories. That was four years
ago – no, three and a half. Since then everything has worked out
more or less the way he hoped.

So Thomas is a little light-headed and has a spring in his step as he takes in all the other feast day cavorters swirling about him as he comes to the Pont Neuf. With a full hour to fill before the rendezvous, he will meander back and forth across many of the city's bridges, stopping when and where he chooses. He can savour Paris in a way he's not done in a while.

His first stop is to listen to a street singer standing atop his moveable step. Wearing a giant paper hat and with a fiddle in one hand and a pointer in the other, the brightly dressed fellow points to the images on the canvas he has strung up and sings out naughty couplets to the rhythm of a catchy tune. It's an air Thomas recognizes yet cannot name. He winces and the crowd in front of him groans to hear the pun about the great cardinal and an unnamed courtesan playing mortar and pestle in the kitchen at Versailles. Thomas takes a step back. It's best not to be associated too closely with humour like that. The kingdom has it spies, as he well knows, having once practised that trade. It would not do for him to be seen laughing at the court. He does not want to do anything to jeopardize his new position with the magistrate judge.

Yet Thomas does not distance himself too much. There's a definite pleasure in lingering near something taboo. He glances at all the smiling faces laughing at the singer's barbs. Nonetheless, he would be willing to make a small bet there's a tell-tale taking mental notes. How can there not be? The stability of the realm is everything to those on the upper rungs. Thomas would be the same, if ever he had the chance. So, he understands, if the king and his ministers are too often mocked and maligned, they will be undermined. Chaos will reign instead.

His gaze goes to the singer's assistant. While not exactly pretty, she is good at what she's there to do. Her low-cut chemise and bright smiling eyes are helping to sell trinkets and booklets of the singer's songs. Thomas crooks his head. Wouldn't it be funny if it was her, the singer's assistant, who was the spy? She's someone the singer would never expect. Who better to betray than someone as close as one can get to the source? God knows, they'd be privy to near everything. What do women not know, and better and deeper than any man? We men are easily duped, Thomas concludes, once a woman lifts her jupe and puts her delightful body in play.

Thomas sighs. He looks to the blue sky overhead then pulls out his pocket watch. Three quarters of an hour until the rendezvous. This time they are to meet on the garden paths of the Tuileries – her choice. He has more than enough time to get there, but he'd better move along in that general direction.

With the sun on his face and warming his chest and legs, Thomas feels content. The arrangement – that's what the two of them have taken to calling it – is good for all involved. Well, less for the two who do not know about it, but the lift it gives the two principals undoubtedly has a positive impact on the other two as well. How could his wife and her husband not be pleased to see what better moods they're in when they get back home from their Sunday and feast day walks? Thomas chooses to think that even if the other two were now to find out, they'd likely shrug. They'd have to admit, would they not, that the little rendezvous does no one any real harm? Besides, with their deteriorating health, don't his wife and her husband have bigger things to worry about than what their spouses are doing out of their sight?

Ah, poor Marguerite. Where her gout was bad for a couple of years, it's now much worse. No longer does Thomas hear her boast about having a royal malady, one that saves and protects her from getting any other disease. That perspective on her illness faded as the gout spread. There are days when she can hardly walk. It started with a single toe, large and inflamed. Now it's an ankle and a knee, both on the left side. She hardly ever leaves the apartment. Only occasionally will she agree to go with her cousin to a concert or a play. That's when the left leg allows, and when the two ladies are not having some kind of spat.

As a result of the gout, Thomas and Marguerite do not often share the same bed for sport at all. Sex between them is a little like the snow that only occasionally dusts the city. It doesn't happen often, nor last very long. Nonetheless, Thomas tries to do his best, once a month or so. He is beginning to think that maybe she'll soon want to give that up as well. Besides the gout, Marguerite is showing her age in other ways. She complains occasionally of a racing heartbeat. Sometimes there are sudden flashes of heat. Though at other times she's chilled to the bone.

As a boy, he used to hear his mother make similar complaints. He would sometimes sit with her in the kitchen and listen. Now he makes a point to sit and talk with Marguerite in the salon. Not every evening, but several times a week. He sits in a chair while Marguerite prefers the divan, her left leg propped up and a blanket pulled up to her chin. Sometimes she asks him to read aloud. Her preference is for the latest novels. She loves a world where the good are good and the bad so clearly bad, and love triumphs in the end. Thomas supposes that must be fiction's edge. Unlike people's real lives, everything has a chance of working out in the end. Though, truth be told, he has no complaints – at the moment.

Thomas studies the contour of the roof of the Louvre. Surely his husbandly duties with Marguerite should grant him credit. She must see how relatively young he still is, compared to her. She must have mellowed when it comes to whom he might seek for a tryst, no? No, maybe not. Marguerite does seem to know how to hold on to a grudge.

As for his lover's husband in this *situation double*, well, Thomas knows how he might feel. He would not be pleased. Men are so possessive of their wives. To wear the antlers, as it were, is judged a great shame.

Thomas looks away from the Louvre. It's especially delicate, is it not, that his lover's husband is someone Thomas likes and respects, someone he counts as a friend?

"Here."

A young man hurrying by thrusts a square of parchment paper into Thomas's hand.

"Read it, Pichon. Read it, memorize it and pass it on. It's a good laugh."

Thomas frowns. "Happy Easter yourself," he calls out after the disappearing figure of the young man. He folds over the paper and stuffs it deep into the pocket of his veston.

Where a few moments ago Thomas was worried about being seen laughing at a rude song, now Mathieu-François Mairobert is giving him something even riskier to pass along – in public. Oh, the man is a talent, to be sure, younger than Thomas and active in the writers' crowd. But Mairobert makes Thomas nervous with his enthusiasms, not to mention his penchant for composing riddles and rhymes that make fun of everyone on the rungs above.

Thomas moves over to the stone railing so he can pretend to study the Seine. He takes notice of a half dozen small boats and barges plying up and down. He can smell the water, and there's also the smell of fresh-cut cordwood coming from the barge immediately below. A hurdy-gurdy is tuning somewhere he cannot see. He hears its wail and groan. It'll be some woman from Savoy, as it almost always is. He associates the sound with the group of tightrope walkers he often sees along the riverbank on days like this. Thomas wonders where they are. He inhales as he takes a peek at the piece of paper Mairobert handed him a moment ago. He unfolds it slowly.

O bastard of the whore

Thomas quickly refolds the paper and shoves it away. He'll read the rest, the whole poem, when he's back in his room at Marguerite's. There is only risk in reading something that begins like that in front of any observing eyes. If it has any merit, which he doubts, Thomas will pass it on. More likely, he'll watch it go ablaze upon his grate.

Thomas pulls out his watch. Less than a half hour to go. He slips the watch back into his pocket and picks up the pace. Perhaps she'll be early for a change. He can always hope. The plan is to meet along the boulevard beside the river then stroll upon the garden paths of the Tuileries. After they've done enough promenading, they'll repair to the room he has rented for two hours.

Meeting in a busy public park as they now do, and on the right bank, is a recent twist. But given the age and maladies of their spouses, it is surely safe. Though, as Thomas knows all too well, his wife has friends with eyes. And a most formidable snoop in the form of her cousin.

"Thomas. Thomas."

He hears his name being called from somewhere to his left. A woman's voice.

—

Hélène is under a parasol the colour of the flax flower. It's a colour she thinks draws out the blue tones in her dress. Blue is a colour she thinks looks especially good on her. She is making sure she holds up the dress as well as she can with her free hand, to keep it from brushing the sandy surface of the boulevard. Her cheeks feel flushed. Her face must be even redder than when she applied the touch of rouge before she left her home and Pierre.

She sees Thomas coming toward her, closing the distance fast. She slows to a halt and turns to gaze out over the Seine. It's important they give the right appearance, that of strangers who accidently arrive at the same place at the same time. The boulevard is crowded, as it always is, and there remains a chance, a risk, that someone might see the two of them and pass it on to either Marguerite or Pierre.

"You're early," he softly says.

Thomas is standing beside her but not too close. He too is pretending to study the slow movement of boats and barges on the water. He's good at this.

"Thomas," Hélène says as quietly as she can. She allows a quick glance his way, then it's back to the boats. "I— I don't think I can. No, I can't."

"Can't? Can't what?"

Hélène glances his way. She sees that his form has gone tense and there's confusion in the profile of his face. Yet surely he can guess what she's trying to tell him. Oh, maybe not. Maybe she has to spell it out. "I, I think he knows."

"Pierre?"

Hélène turns to stare at the man beside her. "No, Mathieu, Marc, Luc et Jean."

"All right, all right. What did he say?"

Hélène's eyes swing back to the river. She makes sure her voice is controlled and as low as it can be and still be heard. "He asked if I would consider staying home, just *once*. That's what he said. He asked if I'd help him go for a short stroll on *our* street for a change. As if I have been abandoning him. Which I have, Thomas, I have."

"I see."

Hélène turns to see if he really does see what this means. Thomas's head has sagged forward as though it has suddenly become a great weight.

She will allow herself only a few minutes more standing beside Thomas, watching the river traffic, before she heads home to Pierre. It will be a long and quiet afternoon, but it will be correct. More correct than having this man she's known since he was a boy, admiring her by pressing his body against her like she's the one for him. Hélène takes a breath. Best not to dwell on what she's giving up. Think too long about anything and you can find a way in or out of it.

Hélène makes herself recall the other reason she's deciding not to go with Thomas today to their rendezvous. In the confessional last week, the nosy priest pressed her for details when she mentioned she sometimes had "conversations" with a man who was not her husband, on the feast days of the church. The priest would not let it go. She never admitted anything more than inappropriate talk, but the priest implied there was more going on than just words being exchanged. She wondered if he could hear, in the wavering of her voice, the truth about her carnal relations with a man not her husband. Hélène had always thought – no, hoped – that the fact that she and Thomas were sinning equally at the same time, that the two sins might somehow balance each other off. A rough justice of sorts. Contrary to what people like to say, maybe two wrongs could actually make a right – the right to feel as fully alive as she can. Now, however, it seems that God, through the nosy priest, is telling her she was only fooling herself. Pleasure must not come before duty to God and her marriage to Pierre.

———

Thomas's thoughts race over the past few years. How often over the first twelve months after finding Hélène along rue Mouffetard had he been to his Russian tailor? Measurements, fittings, more measurements and fittings. Once a month he made the trek to the shop to order something and to have a fleeting glimpse or a fragment of polite conversation with Hélène. The number of items he purchased added up. Marguerite never complained, though once she did wonder aloud as to how many coats, jackets and breeches Thomas required. He explained it was for his new position. Variety was required. That made Marguerite smile. She never questioned again why he was acquiring a wardrobe far beyond what he might reasonably wear.

"So then," Thomas breaks the long silence and rubs his hands, "you don't know exactly what Pierre knows? He made no specific mention of me? He does not suspect who it is?"

Hélène turns to face him. Her eyes look as if they want to burn holes. "As long as your relationship with your tailor is safe, is that it?"

"No, but—"

"Try thinking of how this is for me. I took a vow. Before God."

Thomas manages to turn away before his face reacts. *A vow?* he mouths. Oh my.

"As you did with Marguerite. Turn around, Thomas. Let me see your face. Your vow may not mean much to you, but mine does to me."

Thomas cannot help but flex his eyebrows. How many times have the two of them lain together? "Our vows have not stopped us before," he says as softly as he can.

Hélène pushes Thomas on the chest then glares at him. "I have to go."

"No, don't. I'm sorry."

"Sorry? About what?"

"I'm sorry ... I'm sorry for ... I don't know. I'm not sorry for wanting to be with you. I love our time."

Hélène allows a momentary smile. She closes her eyes. She takes in a deep breath. "Come here," she says, though she keeps her face straight ahead, facing the river and its barges and boats.

Thomas slides along the rail to brush against Hélène's hip.

"Pierre is not well. I don't know how long he has."

"Yes, but—"

Hélène holds up a hand. She steps decisively away from any appearance of closeness between two chance strollers who have come to two separate stops along the path. She readies her shoulders. She takes in a breath. She lifts her parasol higher than it was and composes her face. When she turns back to Thomas he sees by her expression that he has become merely an acquaintance she has enjoyed conversing with along the boulevard.

"You should drop by the shop, Monsieur Pichon. My husband would love to see you. He values your friendship as much as he does the business you bring."

"As I do his." Thomas has no choice but to go along with the play Hélène is composing as they walk.

The couple moves at the same slow pace as the other strollers along the Gallerie du Louvre heading back toward the Pont Neuf. Hélène acknowledges with a smile and an incline of her head and a dip of her parasol two women passing by. They are gaily dressed in pinks and pale greens. They interrupt their sing-song conversation to consider whether or not they should reply to Hélène. They allow that they will. There come two cautious smiles and shallow dips.

"I don't want to lose this again, Thomas, I do not."

"What's that?"

"Respectability."

"Ah, no. It's the first step. You're as good as those women, Hélène. Better in bed, I'll bet."

"Shush." Her lips are firmly set, but Thomas sees a glimmer
of amusement in her eyes. "Oh, look." Hélène is pointing over
toward a crowd of people. "Look at them. The boy with his toy
sword, the girl with her little boat. Are they not cute?"

"I suppose."

"Not wanting to father descendants of your own?"

Thomas shrugs. "It's too late for Marguerite."

"Ah yes, please forgive me for not asking sooner," Hélène says
in a sweetly innocent voice. "How is your wife? Well, I trust?"

Thomas looks her squarely in the eyes. "Well enough. Usual
complaints of age. Which as you know with your husband—"

"We will speak of something else."

"Last week's Treaty of Vienna?"

Hélène gives him a cold look.

"The latest rumours from court?"

Hélène shakes her head.

"Well, how about ... La Camargo? You've heard of her?"

Hélène's face shines like Thomas has just spoken a magic word.
She halts their promenade and turns to face him.

"La Camargo! They say she can leap like a man. Yet light upon
her feet. 'Dazzling' is the term people use."

"So they say. The talk of the town."

"Only twenty-one and known by a single name." Hélène
seems to toss back her head. "La Camargo," she breathes.

"L'Hélène?"

"Sadly, no."

"Well, what if," Thomas halts their progress along the path.
"What if I were to try and get tickets to see her dance? The judge
sometimes goes to the Opéra. I could ask. Would that please
you?" Thomas unrolls a courtier's hand.

Hélène smiles like it's all she can do not to laugh. "Seriously?"

"Why not?"

They begin their promenade again, now holding each other's hand above their waists, as is the style for real gentry. Each time Thomas takes a peek, he sees that Hélène is smiling at the world.

—

Thomas steps over to the mirror in his room to take the measure of his appearance. He's a little startled to see the image reflected back looking so stern. He tries to tender a smile, but it looks forced. So he rolls his shoulders and rolls his head from side to side and up and down to relax. It brings a better result.

He hesitates to think it, but there it is in the mirror. This may be the best he's ever looked. It is the blackest justaucorps he owns, made of the finest cloth, and with breeches that match perfectly. Another fine piece of tailoring by Pierre Kharlamov. His last, as it has turned out. Yet what better outfit to wear for a day such as this? A tribute to the man. A true craftsman to the end.

Thomas takes the brush to his short brown hair. He'll soon need to have it trimmed again. Today's wig will be the silver one with the dozens of tight little curls on either side. He thinks it his most elegant, especially with the black silk bag at the back and the solitaire to complete it in front. It suits the formal occasion, as do the new shoes with the silver buckles. The lace ruffle of his chemise, however, may be too much. No, Thomas decides, it'll do after all. He'll select his hat after he's paid his dues to Marguerite.

He reaches for the small bottle of orange water. He gives himself a couple of squirts, one on each side. Back to the mirror, Thomas looks into his own brown eyes. Yes, he knows there will have to be a period of mourning, of course there will. But that's for the public realm. The private world can and should be something else. Thomas winks at his reflection, which sends the wink right back.

He opens the door and steps into the hall.

"Monsieur," says the maid, stopping to curtsey to her mistress's husband as he passes her in the hall.

"Ah, Simone." It is getting easier to meet her in the apartment. And well it should, after the nearly four years the little woman has been back in Marguerite's service. But Simone is still a reminder from Marguerite that Thomas's past actions haunt him yet. "Good day, little one."

"And to you, Monsieur." Simone curtseys once more.

Thomas finds another smile. He supposes he should not have said "little one." Oh well, it's done. He knows little Simone would like nothing better than to even the score between them, but he's not going to give her that opportunity.

—

Marguerite sees Thomas come into the salon with an especially pleased look on his face. He's wearing the black outfit his wife knows he adores, even though she is not overly fond of it herself. She prefers almost any other colour in the world to black. And look at those shoes! The silver buckle is huge. She sometimes thinks her husband would wear the red heels of the royal family if he could.

"Where are you off to today, my husband?"

"The left bank, Marguerite. It's the funeral for my tailor."

"Oh yes, so you told me I think. But a funeral for a tailor? Do you really have to go?"

Thomas's face remains gravely serious. "The man was a skilled artisan. Best tailor in the city, or one of them. He's the one who has made all my best clothes these past few years. I owe him this final respect."

"Oh, of course you're right. Well done, my husband. It often strikes me that there's not enough respect given to the many artisans upon whom we all rely. Very good. A Russian, was he not, your tailor?"

"He was. Pierre. Pierre Kharlamov. I'll offer my condolences to the widow Kharlamov after the service at Saint-Médard."

"Why, of course. That is correct. And do you think you should make a donation to the church? For masses to be said for the repose of the man's immortal soul?"

"I hadn't thought of that."

"I think you should. It would be a comfort to the widow. I know that for a fact. It was for me, some years ago."

"Well then, I shall."

"Is she Russian?"

"Who's that?"

"The widow."

"Oh no. I mean, I don't think so. She does not have the same accent."

"As aged as the tailor?"

"The widow?"

"Quite."

"No, but a certain age just the same."

Marguerite nods. It's a sombre truth that sooner or later everyone ends up in the same place. "Do tell me about the service, Thomas, when you get back. Will you do that for me?"

"Of course, I will. Did you ... do you want to come along?"

"You're sweet to ask, but no, as you can see, my leg is not good today."

"I understand."

"But it's a good thing you're doing here. Showing respect for the old tailor and his widow." She feels emotion welling into her voice. She raises a hand to her cheek, near the eye, just in case.

"I thought it was correct. I must go if I'm not to be late." Thomas bows deeply to his wife and leaves the salon.

Marguerite nods at the door after it closes. Yes, she thinks, she was right to give her man another chance. He is becoming the good man she thought he might be back when she married him, despite the naysayers who said he was too young. She just had to give him some time, enough to put the selfishness of youth behind him. Wouldn't her cousin Madame Dufour be surprised to see how Thomas has matured?

—

By the time Thomas arrives outside the tailor's shop on rue Mouffetard, the area in front of the building is already crowded with mourners. He sees it will be impossible to get anywhere close to

Hélène before, during or after the service. The grieving widow will still be inside, upstairs, where the coffin holding Pierre's remains will have spent the past two nights. Had it not been for the folded-over handwritten note a Saint-Médard neighbourhood boy brought to Thomas at the magistrate judge's office two days ago – a mere three words, *Pierre est mort*, printed in Hélène's child-like hand – he would not have known about the death at all.

Thomas looks down at his appearance. His new shoes are soiled and his fine black breeches have absorbed a few splatters from passing carriages and carts. Nothing he can do about that. Thinking back to the note, it occurs to Thomas that he really should teach Hélène how to write better than she does. And, for that matter, to read. If only they were not so pressed for time. It seems it's not reading and writing on his mind when they are together. He feels the smile his wit brings.

He presses closer to the crowd of mourners in the street. Everyone is waiting for the bells of Saint-Médard to ring, signalling the start of the sequence of events. Thomas cannot but listen in on two old fellows as they whisper back and forth only inches from his ears. They are artisans, he can see, but he cannot judge their particular trade from their grizzled faces.

"Has it made, she does."

"Who's that?"

"Widow woman."

"Why say you that?"

"A widow!"

"True enough. Widows are the luckiest of all."

"There's the church bell," the older of the two says in a loud voice. He lifts his chin. "Silence please. Here they come."

All eyes go to the large crucifix coming out the door of the tailor shop. It's carried by a young man. He must be an assistant to the local parish priest. Next comes the coffin carried by a half dozen men. All strangers to Thomas, burly types, faces serious about their task. They maintain the wooden box containing Pierre's cadaver at shoulder height. A few drops of water are coming from the box. That would be from the ice required to keep the body cold over the past two days.

After the coffin comes the priest. A sad-looking man casting blessings left and right. Next, at last, is Hélène. Her face is shrouded with a veil, and she's slightly stooped. Despite the sag in her shoulders, she's walking with a dignity that brings a smile of quiet pride to Thomas's face.

"That's her, isn't it?" A fresh round of whispers begins between the two artisans.

"Can't see the face, but must be. Canny, that one."

"How so?"

"Marry old Pierre? Gets the shop. No one else."

"Right you are."

"Know I am. Another canny widow, I say."

Thomas pulls back. He's tempted to speak up in Hélène's defence, but steps away instead. This is not the time or place, or the kind of people one argues with. As he stands apart from the crowd and watches the procession take its slow turn toward the church of Saint-Médard, he mulls over what he just overheard. It had not occurred to him that as Pierre Kharlamov's widow and only surviving heir, Hélène is now the owner of one of the better – and perhaps profitable – tailor shops on the Left Bank.

—

Thomas is no sooner through the door than Marguerite comes out of the salon into the foyer. It's a halting advance, given the condition of her leg. Yet her face is expectant in a way he has not seen in a while. She reverently clasps her hands before her chest.

"Was it a comfort? To the widow?"

Thomas blinks to recall their earlier conversation. Oh yes, he was to purchase masses for the repose of Pierre's soul. Marguerite's interest in the funeral for a man she never met comes from her imagining the predicament of the widow left behind. It touches some part of her heart. Thomas assumes a disappointed face.

"It was very crowded, too crowded to speak directly with the widow. Nor to buy the masses. I'll have to go back, I guess."

"You must. And don't just speak with the priest. Express your condolences to the old Russian widow. Would you do that?"

Thomas cannot resist the tiniest of smiles. "You're very kind-hearted, my wife." He bestows a soft kiss upon her brow. "Now, can I help you back into the salon? You really should keep off that leg."

"I know I've been a burden to you lately, Thomas. I'm sorry. But do go see the widow. I know she'll appreciate it. She will."

"As you suggest, Marguerite."

—

With his index finger made wet by his tongue, Thomas traces a circle twice round the closer of Hélène's nipples. Then he pushes gently off the nipple's tip, wets the finger again and moves on to do the same on the other one.

"Still finding them fascinating after all this time?" She gives a bemused eyebrow raise.

"Little raspberries."

"You have raspberries of your own, but I bet you don't give them so much attention."

"No, I don't."

Thomas props himself up on an elbow. It looks like he intends to lean over and do with his lips what he's just done with his finger.

"I think that's enough." Hélène gently pushes his face away from her chest. She's had enough. They've accomplished what they came to do and that is that.

She sits up and places two firm hands upon his bare shoulders. She directs him to lie all the way down. She wants them side by side, shoulder to shoulder on the narrow bed.

"You're not much for play for the sake of play, are you, woman? You know, there's a sublime pleasure in touching, kissing, smelling the one you love. Why, another bit of time and I just might be able—" He sends a hand sliding down the flat of her belly toward her most tender spot.

"No." Hélène coils away from his hand and stands up beside the bed. She gives him what she hopes is a stern look. But it gives way to a chuckle. "Look, I have to go. I don't want any of the neighbours, or my journeyman tailor, talking about how long I take for lunch."

"They understand a person needs a couple of hours to rest and digest."

"Is that what we just did? Rest and digest?"

"We have more than one appetite."

"It seems we do. Where's my chemise? I have to get dressed."

Thomas locates her chemise in the bedclothes and tosses it to her. She sees his disappointment as she pulls it over her head. It's nice to be admired, though she knows she no longer has the slender figure of the girl she once was. Then again, neither does he. Eating three meals a day every day and sitting in an office as he does has started to add a softness the younger Thomas would easily have walked off.

She likes the feel of her chemise. It's the finest linen she's ever treated herself to. She feels like she can afford such quality since she has come into Pierre's modest inheritance.

Hélène walks over the window, stocking in her hand. "I like being able to see the top of Notre-Dame from our room."

Thomas pulls on his chemise and comes over to where she stands. He makes contact with her as he looks out as well. The twin towers are glowing in the sun.

"It's why I chose the room."

"Really? You surprise me. Well done."

Thomas shakes his head. "I didn't check the window view. Though I did ask for a top floor room. And since all the top floors in this city have fine views, I guess I deserve some credit after all."

Hélène reaches up under his chemise and gives him a squeeze. "Your credit is good with me."

"All right then." Thomas reaches out to pull her close.

"No, no." Hélène scuttles away. "A joke. Help me with my things, will you?"

Thomas snorts, but gives a nod.

The next few minutes are spent putting on the clothes they were wearing when they arrived. Thomas helps her with whatever she asks. He laces the strings and pulls her stays tight. It's only after all is done – and the mirror consulted to make sure wigs and accoutrements are straight and Hélène's cheeks suitably rouged – that she touches Thomas on the forearm. They are standing near the door.

"There's something I've been meaning to tell you."

"By that long face I'd say it's serious. You know we're too far from your parish for anyone around here to know who you are or that you're meeting with me. Remember, I have to be careful to keep it from my side as well."

Hélène laughs. "Your side? You mean Marguerite?"

"And Simone and Marie-Claude. And anyone else who would tell. There would be disappointment if I were found out."

"I don't think disappointment is the word. But no, that's not it." She takes a breath. "I— I'm selling the shop."

Thomas leans back, apparently startled. "The tailor shop?"

Hélène nods that yes, that's the one – the one and only shop she owns.

"I guess that makes sense. A full-fledged tailor might want to buy the place. Or maybe even your journeyman. Maybe he's ready to move up. Location's good."

"That's what I thought. But Thomas...."

Mumbling to himself, Thomas does not catch that Hélène has not finished yet.

"Three months since the funeral," he mutters, hunching his shoulders, "no one will think ill of you for taking this step. It'll be all right. Someone will come along."

"Well, that's just it. It's done, Thomas. A tailor from a few streets over approached me a few days ago. Yesterday I agreed. He takes possession in a month."

"The sale? It's done?"

"It is."

"And you kept this ... you did this by yourself?"

Hélène covers her mouth with her hand to hide her smile.

"I could have helped." Thomas holds out a hand.

"I didn't want to involve you, given our ... situations."

"No, of course." Thomas walks around in a tight circle, coming back to stand before Hélène. "So, we need to find you a new place."

Hélène hears herself send a jet of air out her nose. "That's the other thing, Thomas." She reaches out and lays a hand lightly upon his cheek. "I ... I'm leaving."

"You're leaving?" Thomas's cheeks ride high. There are laugh wrinkles, yet it's not laughter she sees in his eyes. It's bewilderment. "Leaving what? Leaving where?"

Hélène tries to shrug, without success. She might as well just say it. "Thomas, I'm leaving Paris."

"But ... but Paris is the centre. The centre of everything."

Thomas makes the shape of a ball with his hands. But when he sees Hélène smile, a near laugh at what he's done, he flattens his hands together like he's just crushed something.

Hélène reaches out for the handle to the door. "Who's that friend of yours? The one you write to in Londres? Gaillardin?"

"Gallatin, Jean Gallatin."

"That's the one. I'm going to do what he did. Once I get the money from the sale of the shop, I'm going to Londres."

"Londres," Thomas repeats in what he hears is a small voice. He stares at the floor. He didn't notice how narrow and worn the boards are until now. He looks up at Hélène. "The English pronounce it Lon-*don*, not *Londres*."

"Lon-don. I see. Without the *r*."

"That's right. Listen, Gallatin is my friend, not yours, Hélène." Thomas wonders why his voice is sounding so weak. It's like it's coming from someone other than himself.

"I know that. I'm not going especially to find your friend. People say there are thousands of French in England. Even our old friend Voltaire lived there for a long while."

Thomas makes a face at the mention of Voltaire.

"I do ... speak ... their English," Hélène says haltingly.

Thomas leans back. His eyes go wide. "I am a surprise," he says, trying out some English of his own. He has read some English books, including those sent him by Gallatin, but rarely does he speak the language out loud. "How do you do ... how did you do?" he asks.

"Un garçon ... an English boy and his père," Hélène continues in a mix of English and French. "At the auberge in Évreux. We— vous savez. Later, à Paris, when I was ... accepting men ... il y avait un particulier, a regular he call himself. In the ambassade d'Angleterre he was."

Thomas takes in a breath. "I see," he says in English.

Hélène laughs. "We not just—" She glances toward the bed. "He like talk almost as much." She shrugs. "Un beau smile. That's how my English learns."

Thomas rolls his eyes.

Hélène switches back to French. "Look, I have to leave." She turns the handle and pulls. The door comes open half a foot. "It'll be after two by the time I get back. My journeyman never asks, but I know he wonders where I go when I come here. The neighbours as well, I'm sure. I have my loyal widow's reputation to protect."

Thomas reaches out and grabs Hélène by the wrist as she is halfway out the door. "About England, I don't know what to do."

"So I see. Well, you've got a few weeks, maybe a bit more." She turns toward the hall and its dark, narrow stairs.

"Londres," mutters Thomas. "London," he repeats, following Hélène down the stairs.

—

The first week goes by as slowly as seven ticking days can do. Instead of having their get-together once a week, Thomas has insisted that they rendezvous every second day in the little upstairs room that looks across at the towers of Notre-Dame. He saw the reluctance on Hélène's face when he made the request and was relieved when after a moment of long silence she agreed. But the three sessions of that first week came with little joy. What was a delightful, secret pleasure is now a chore. An obligation. Apparently even worse on Hélène's part. Thomas feels he's getting charity from a woman he'll soon be seeing no more. It makes him study the beams overhead for a long time after they've gone through the usual motions on the first day of the second week.

Thomas sits up and pulls on his chemise. He watches Hélène pull on her stockings. She notices his attention and acknowledges it with a curt nod.

"You don't— we don't have to do this anymore," Thomas says haltingly.

"It's all right." Hélène does not glance his way. She is attaching her garter belt. "A few more days is all we have. Then...." She does not complete the thought.

Then you're gone? Then I'm left alone? Then I go back to reading to my invalid wife in the evenings and fucking whores from time to time? "Then what?" Thomas finally says aloud.

"Would you tie me up?" Hélène makes fleeting eye contact before she turns her back to him. "Please?"

"You said: we have only a few more days and then. Then what?"

"I don't know, Thomas. That's right, pull the laces tight like that."

Thomas does as she requests. And he decides not to repeat his question. He does not see any point in coming to this room again with her. Where once there had been nothing more that he craved than the feel of the curves of her body and a certain look in her eyes, he no longer feels that way.

"Better end it," are the words his lips mouth. Better end it. That's what his father said to him back in Vire. They were in the shop and his father was gesturing at the cat. She was lying on its blanket on the floor making an awful noise. Thomas knew exactly what those words meant. At twelve, he was apparently old enough to manage the task all by himself. The last time, six or seven years before that, he'd gone with his father to the river with a kicking, screaming sack. He'd watched the man, twice his size at the time, hurl the sack out into the water. It splashed and disappeared from sight. "Showing its age," his father said. "No mice in a month. I'll get a new one this afternoon." Thomas's face must have betrayed sad surprise, because his father put a hand on his shoulder and explained. "It's what we do before our animals get too old. We don't eat them, so—" The man glanced at the water. "Better early than late."

"Better early than late," Thomas says aloud.

Hélène turns around, her brow furrowed. "What's better early than late?"

Thomas finds a grim smile. "Most things in life, it seems."

Hélène gives him a puzzled look. "I'm almost set. What's keeping you?"

There is an order to things, thinks Thomas as he steps into his breeches and hoists them up. The trick is to be a part of the order, somewhere near the top. Like where he is, on the ascendant, in the office of the magistrate judge.

"Oh," Thomas says, glancing at Hélène waiting by the door. She cannot hide the look of impatience on her face. It makes him smile. He's going to miss her, he is. "Do you remember you once said you'd like to see La Camargo?"

Hélène gives Thomas her full attention. "I do."

"The judge told me this morning that she's at the Opéra for the next two weeks. But he has to be in Rouen for a case. He asked if I wanted his tickets." Thomas holds up two fingers. "Two tickets."

"Don't tell me that if it's not so."

"But it is. Are you pleased or not?"

"Of course I am." Hélène's expression shifts from a broad smile to trying to be coy. "As long as—."

"As long as—?" Thomas finishes buttoning up his veston and reaches for his justaucorps. "As long as *you* are the one I take? Is that it?"

"If you insist." Hélène's eyes sparkle in a way they have not for quite a while.

"It'll be something to remember Paris by," says Thomas with a shrug.

"You're sweet." Hélène pulls him to her and kisses him hard on the mouth.

—

"Thomas."

Marguerite thinks her voice especially soft as it floats across the table. She and her husband are about to begin their evening meal. She has something to confide in Thomas that she does not want any of the servants to hear. She's not sure how he will react. "I'm going to be out with my dear cousin tomorrow night. I'm afraid that means I'll be leaving you here all alone."

"I see." Thomas's face shows mild surprise, nothing more than that. "And what do you and Madame Dufour have planned?"

"A play, I think. Something satirical, no doubt. It always is with her. You know the type. Supposed to be witty and clever when it's nothing of the sort. Cousin has a box for the evening and she insists I go along."

"The Opéra or the Opéra Comique?"

Marguerite wonders if she sees his left eye twitch. "The Comique, I presume. That's where Marie-France's taste runs. I'd rather stay home, but I really have no excuse. Cousin knows my leg is at the moment not swollen or acting up."

Thomas leans back in his seat with what Marguerite recognizes as a kind and generous expression on his face. "That should be fun for you, my wife."

Marguerite is delighted to see how pleased Thomas is that she is going out. She had wondered if he would resent her doing anything with Madame Dufour, who never tires of disparaging him. Yet, clearly, he does not. He has a forgiving heart.

"Yes," replies Marguerite. "I just hope it's not like those shows they put on at the fairs of Saint-Laurent and Saint-Germain. Dreadful. Madame Dufour pretends they make her laugh. The pantomimes, the grimacing. They so tire me."

Thomas smiles again. "Well, it's good of you to keep her company. And your leg?"

"It has been good this past week, knock wood. I'm taking Simone along, just in case. She can help the two of us, the old girls, in and out of the coach. Run errands. That sort of thing."

"Well, my wife, I predict the play will be better than you fear. With your expectations so low, you can only be pleasantly surprised."

"Aren't you sweet."

———

Back in his room after dinner, Thomas's chest feels like it might swell to bursting. He can release the grin he has kept reined in throughout the meal. So Marguerite is going to the Opéra Comique with Madame Dufour! Now he does not have to make any excuse at all about where he's going. How fortune smiles on him!

Maybe seeing La Camargo will convince Hélène to not leave Paris after all. That the city is the centre of the world and that she should stay connected to someone as fortune-favoured as Thomas Pichon.

———

"Well, this should be fun, should it not?" asks a smiling Madame Dufour.

Marguerite waits until Simone is settled in the seat beside her before she replies. "Yes, of course. Thank you, Cousin, for taking me, for taking both of us along. Right, Simone?"

Simone curtseys as best she can toward Madame Dufour from her seated position.

"My Thomas sends his regards."

"Does he now? Pity he was not able to come along with us this evening."

Marguerite maintains what she hopes is an agreeable expression. At no point, at no time at all, did Marie-France ever so much as hint at inviting him. Does Madame really think she did? Or is this her way of reminding Marguerite that Thomas is not of sufficient rank to go with them to a social setting? Marguerite controls her breath. She feels a throb in her gouty leg. Thomas really is good to forgive her cousin for being the ill-natured woman she is.

Marguerite turns to Simone. Her servant's gaze looks to be locked at something out the window, out upon the street.

The coach shifts, then begins to roll.

"Here we go," says Madame Dufour.

"To our pleasant evening." Marguerite addresses her kindly words to Madame Dufour. "Thank you again, Cousin dear."

—

By the time the women are seated in their box the musicians in the orchestra in front of the stage are all tuned up. They're ready for the conductor to raise his baton and start the opening music.

"A lovely box, Marie-France," whispers Marguerite.

"Except it's too far back." Madame Dufour does not lower her voice at all. "Especially considering what I paid. We're nearly at the rear."

"Still, the seats are comfortable. And we have a good view of the stage. Oh, look, the curtain's going up. I hope it's amusing."

The orchestra begins to play. "I believe the music is by Rebel," announces Madame Dufour.

Marguerite nods. She does not want to be one of those many patrons who talk loudly and disturb the show for everyone nearby. It seems as if the box already has one of those. She gives her cousin a disapproving glance.

From the first few notes, Marguerite's attention is more on the orchestra than on the stage. From time to time she follows the dancers, led by a young woman who spins and swirls and jumps. Marguerite hears appreciative remarks from Madame Dufour and a few whispers from Simone. She, however, is more captivated by the violinists in the orchestra. How they lean into the music as they play. Their bodies arch and sway while their bow hands stir the air. It's as if there's a life force in the music that they are trying to capture and absorb within their chests. As a girl Marguerite learned to play a few simple tunes on the harpsichord. It was never anything like this. Maybe if she'd been encouraged. Maybe she could have learned the violin. It must be wonderful to be part of something larger than oneself.

The descent of the curtain for the intermission arrives suddenly, or so it seems to Marguerite. But then she'd not been following the dramatic exit of the principal dancer on the stage. Her eyes had moved from player to player in the orchestra. Most recently, she'd settled on the young man with long hair that had fallen out of its queue. He had a cello tucked tightly between his legs as he bowed the strings. His head swayed with abandon from side to side with every note he played.

Marguerite turns to her cousin. "Thank you again, Cousin. I am enjoying myself. If you had not insisted on me coming along, I'd likely be home with a book."

Madame Dufour tilts her head and places a particularly knowledgeable expression on her face. "Are not her entrechats à quatre and cabrioles well done? I think La Camargo may indeed be the best."

"Oh, that's who it is. I've heard that name before. La Camargo." Marguerite glances down at the orchestra area, now empty of its players. Only their instruments are left behind. She brings her gaze back to Madame Dufour. "It's such a relief to come to something with real music. I'm afraid I find most comedies a bore."

"That's the second time you've spoken of comedy. This is the Opéra, Marguerite, not the Opéra Comique."

"Oh."

"Madame. Madame."

Simone is tugging gently on Marguerite's sleeve. "Yes, Simone."

The servant looks like she's just had a shock. Her face and frame are stiff.

"Madame." Simone gestures for Marguerite to lean her way, away from Madame Dufour on the other side. Simone turns so as to not make eye contact with Marguerite. She whispers out of the side of her mouth. "Madame, I ... I think I see your husband down there."

"You what?"

Simone points at the rail. Marguerite gets up out of her seat.

"What is it, you two?" calls out Madame Dufour.

"A minute," hisses Marguerite to her cousin. "Just a minute please."

Marguerite goes to the rail. She follows where Simone's trembling finger leads.

"Blessed Seigneur."

Marguerite grabs the rail with both hands. It is. It is Thomas. He's wearing the black outfit he likes so much, and he has on the silver wig Marguerite always tells him makes him as handsome as a prince. "But—"

"Madame," Simone whispers in Marguerite's ear, "I thought I saw him leaving our building in a hurry as our coach was pulling away."

Marguerite stares at her servant. There comes a low nod. Now Marguerite returns her gaze to Thomas. He is caught up in an animated conversation almost directly below. Why and what is he doing here? Why didn't he just say? Oh, she sees. It's a little surprise that he's planned. This means he'll be coming up to the box for the second half.

Marguerite turns to Madame Dufour. "Marie-France, did you know this? Did you know he'd be here?"

"Whatever is it?" Madame Dufour lifts herself out of her seat and bustles in between Marguerite and Simone. "Marguerite, whatever are you talking about?"

Getting no response from her blinking cousin, Madame Dufour turns to Simone. "Show me, little one."

Simone does as she is told. She points to a particular man in the noisy throng below.

It takes Madame Dufour a moment.

"Why, that's him, your husband. And whoever is he with? Some deep, dark conversation, it seems."

"What?" gasps Marguerite.

In her chest it feels like something is taking away her air. She takes hold of the sleeve of Marie-France's dress and peers down below. Yes, there is a woman sitting beside Thomas. She had not noticed her before. And yes, Thomas is chatting away with her, a broad smile upon his face. But who is she? She's wearing a dark green dress. It looks like the sort of thing a merchant's wife might wear. Alas, Marguerite cannot see her face. It's obscured by the ruffle and the barbe on the woman's white cap. And at the back, the lace lappets hide her hair and neck. All that Marguerite can make out is that the woman in the green dress is more slender than herself. That means younger, does it not?

A hot sensation, like the tip of a red-hot poker, makes its presence felt in her gut.

"There is an explanation, I'm sure," offers Marguerite. Even as she says it, she hears the wobble in her voice. "Dear Simone, would you please go down and speak with my husband? Perhaps he does not know exactly which box we're in. Please let him know. I expect he'll be joining us for the second half."

"Do you think that's wise?" There's a warning look in Madame Dufour's eyes.

"Why ever not?" Marguerite hopes her thin, rigid lips do not betray any doubt.

"As you wish." Madame Dufour exhales loudly, and makes a show of looking up to the ceiling for help.

—

It's the way it used to be. The knowing looks, the smiles, the laughs. Their conversation is moving like a brook. Thomas can't get over how delighted Hélène looks to be, and this only the midpoint of the programme. Surely she'll reconsider leaving Paris after this.

"Tell me again," he says, pretending to be serious, "do you really think that that woman knows how to dance?"

"Oh, isn't she wonderful, Thomas? I'm so glad you were—"

Hélène halts when a woman from the aisle, a short woman in servant's attire, makes her presence felt. Thomas refuses to look around, though he can see at the corner of his eye that the servant is reaching out tentatively to touch him on the shoulder. Best to ignore such people, he thinks. Yet with a beseeching gaze, Hélène is asking Thomas to turn around and see what the woman wants.

"Excuse me, Monsieur," Thomas hears the woman say. Then comes the tap he knew was on its way.

So he must turn and tell her to go away.

Thomas sees who it is. "Oh, shit" comes muffled off his lips. He tries to smile at the servant yet cannot. Instead he casts frantic looks to the servant's left and right. No one else, no Marguerite. Thomas takes a breath. "Simone, whatever are you doing here?"

"Simone?" he hears Hélène say. "Simone."

Simone presents a faint smile to each in turn. The smile widens as the diminutive servant raises her right arm and points above their heads. Thomas follows Simone's gesture up to the row of boxes where the wealthiest patrons are. He scans one then another. He sees faces he does not know chatting among themselves. When his gaze comes to the third box, however, he finds two women staring down. Each seems to be pointing at him. He blinks at their wide-eyed faces. It takes him what feels like forever, two, maybe three, seconds, to recognize Marguerite and Madame Dufour.

Thomas feels the refusal of the muscles in his neck to tip further back. He is dimly aware that one of his hands has come up near his chin. He watches it make a small wave at Marguerite. His eyes close of their own volition before he turns away.

"Monsieur?"

"Yes, Simone." Thomas stares into her eyes.

"Monsieur, will you be joining your wife and her cousin in their box? They've sent me to ask."

"I think not."

Thomas sees and hears Simone snort. "No?" The servant then points at Hélène. "We've not been introduced."

"I am the widow Kharlamov," Hélène says in a near whisper.

"Sorry, what's that?"

"Widow Kharlamov," repeats Hélène. Her expression is that of someone resigned to her fate.

"Ah," Simone nods then shrugs. The name does not seem to mean a thing.

But it will, Thomas knows, when it's repeated to Marguerite. "If you'll excuse us," he says, stepping out into the aisle. With his outstretched arm he moves Simone back. He takes hold of Hélène's hand. She moves out to join him where he stands. They turn at once toward the back of the Opéra, wanting nothing more than to get out to the street. As they push through the crowd of theatre-goers coming the other way, coming back to take their seats, Thomas notices the great roaring noise the swirl of conversation makes during the intermission. It adds to the roar of blood pounding in his ears. It is so very difficult to think.

—

Even before Simone comes back up to the box to tell her mistress that she has met the widow Kharlamov, Marguerite recognizes the woman beside Thomas.

It takes Madame Dufour a little longer, but when the same recognition comes, she places a hand on her cousin's shoulder. "I'm so sorry, Marguerite." There is a pause. Then, "though not surprised."

Marguerite flexes her shoulder to get her cousin's hand away from her. "We have to go," she says.

—

"What did he say?" Hélène asks Thomas. Since the incident at the Opéra three nights ago, Thomas is staying with her on the upper floor of the tailor shop. Hélène gives up possession of it in five days.

Thomas closes the door. He leans against it as a momentary support. Then he pushes off and brings himself to stand before Hélène. She is seated on the well-worn divan and is in the middle of darning socks.

"That he understands."

"That he understands?" She places the socks down beside her, and slides over to give Thomas room to sit. She peers into his unreadable face.

"No, he said a bit more than that. He says he's seen similar cases, more than I might think. In his opinion, when it's not the first time, but the second or third, there's not much point in even trying to patch things up with the wife."

"Well, I knew that. Isn't a magistrate judge supposed to be smarter than the rest of us?"

"He recommended I take a leave. Not quit, but an open-ended leave. That I go away from Paris for a year, maybe two. That I add more experience to my already illustrious career."

"Really?"

"Well, he didn't say illustrious. He didn't use any adjective at all." Thomas shrugs. Hélène flexes her eyebrows.

Thomas continues: "Later on, after Marguerite is out of the picture—"

Hélène snorts. "Poor woman. Everyone wants her dead."

"Later on, I can come back. He said he'd be pleased to have me work for him again. That he did say."

"Well, that's something. For later on. For you." Hélène holds out a hand. "How much did you tell him about it?"

"Enough, though I did not give your name. I told him Marguerite will not even let me in. Had a locksmith come to change the locks."

"That says it all." Hélène retrieves the wool socks and the darning needles.

"He gave me this." Thomas reaches inside a pocket of his coat. He pulls out a folded-over piece of paper. "A letter of recommendation. Let me read you the best part. Here it is. 'Thomas Pichon is as loyal, hard-working, careful and clever a scrivener and clerk as there could be.' I can't complain about that."

"I'd say not." Hélène gives him a suspicious look. "Did you write that yourself?"

Thomas pretends surprise, then allows a reluctant smile. He nods. "He asked me to draft the letter. He signed it without reading a single word."

"But it's not sealed. Don't you need his official seal?"

"I'll add that tomorrow. It'll be my last day."

"So, the only thing left for you to decide is where you're going to pass your year or two away."

Hélène picks up the socks and needles from the divan and places them in the wicker basket at her feet. She pats her thighs, inviting Thomas to lay his head in her lap. He carefully lowers his refolded letter of recommendation to the floor and does as she asks.

"Did I ever tell you I like your eyes, Hélène?"

"You did, along with a few other parts."

"It's true."

"So, where will you go to advance your already illustrious career?" Hélène arches her eyebrows. "Lyons? You often say you've never been to the south."

"I'd rather not."

"You'd rather not? What does that mean?"

"I'd rather go to Londres."

"To London?" Hélène jostles her thighs, bouncing his head. She pulls him up into a sitting position. "Is that a jest?"

"It's not. I'm free, as free as I've been in a long while, so why not do as I please? I'd rather go with you."

Hélène's face goes as serious and rigid as she can make it. She will not grant this man a glimmer that so much as hints at whether she is either pleased or saddened by what he's said.

"Would it be all right," he asks, "to come along? To England with you?"

Hélène looks down at her hands. They're cupped in her lap, her thumbs twirling round. Only when the thumbs stop does she look up into Thomas's eyes.

"Why? Why would you do that?"

"Because I like you. I'd like to see if we could live together, openly for once." He leans over and kisses her lightly on the lips.

She kisses him back, just as lightly. "All right, but it's going to be a new start."

"Which means what?"

Hélène hunches her shoulders. "Just what it says. I'm free too. I have my money left me by Pierre and from the sale of this place. You have whatever you have. We are two, not one. It's a new start, for both of us."

Thomas seems to study her face like he's never really seen it before. "Do you not trust me, Hélène?"

That brings what she knows is a slow, wide smile. "Oh, please." Hélène gets to her feet. She holds out her hands for Thomas to take hold. When he does, she pulls him to his feet. "Let's go somewhere nearby. Let's get something to eat." She crooks her elbow with his.

"Then come back here and...." Thomas gives her a knowing look.

"We'll see. We have a lot of things to do to get ready, don't we now?"

"We do."

V

Across

En route
November 1731

"Sixteen seventy-four," Thomas mumbles to himself as he catches a first glimpse out the window of the approaching Porte Saint-Martin. "I think that's what it is."

He glances at Hélène to see if it's worth his while to make her pay attention to him and to the gate that's coming up ahead. They've been bouncing and swaying in the diligence since they and a half dozen other passengers climbed aboard a quarter hour earlier in front of Paris's Hôtel de Ville. Thomas and Hélène each have a satchel up top on the coach's roof, as well as a trunk that contains possessions belonging to them both. Clothes and shoes, hats, canes, parasols and wigs, and, heaviest of all, a good portion of Thomas's library and archives. He pleaded through the door at Marguerite's for these last two. He asked that they be put out on the landing. Marguerite must have had her servants do the work. When he came back the next morning everything was there in wooden boxes beside the locked door. He couldn't take it all, but he made his picks. He imagines Marguerite burned or gave away what he left.

Neither Thomas nor Hélène would get into the diligence until they'd made sure that their two satchels and the single trunk were well tied down with a rope. They represent all they own in this world. Well, that's not quite true. They each have certain other valued items with them where they sit. He understands that Hélène has a good quantity of coins in a poche hidden away under her dark-blue linen travelling dress, but of what total value he does not know. Nor does he know the amount of the letter of exchange she has hidden in the lining of the dress. But he knows it must be a goodly sum. It would be for the bulk of what she received from her late husband's estate and the sale of his shop. She will take the hidden promissory note to a banking house when she arrives in London.

"You are not my husband," she said when he asked how much the note was for.

What could he say? He will not ask again, but if she would ever like to confide, he will not object.

They are a couple in certain regards, but not in other ways. How much money each has in this world is at the top of both their lists of what they keep to themselves. The world is filled with risk, countless menaces and threats. They both understand the need to look out first and foremost for their own interests.

Like Hélène, Thomas has a pouch of coins, and a few particularly high value coins where his socked feet rest in his shoes. It's an old trick that once served him well as a boy coming away from Vire. He has not one but two documents sewn into the inside of his dark brown justaucorps. One is a letter of exchange for seven hundred livres, which he will convert to British currency when he gets to London. The other is the signed and sealed letter of recommendation given to him by the magistrate judge. Thomas doubts it will be useful in London. The English would only raise their eyebrows, or maybe even mock him, if he brought forward a letter from a French judge for a position having to do with the law in their land. Nonetheless, he has to safeguard it for when he makes an eventual return to France. Doors to good positions do not open by themselves. That letter will be a knock too loud to be ignored.

Thomas turns back to the window on his side of the diligence. The Porte Saint-Martin looms much larger than it did before. "Sixteen seventy-four," he says aloud. He reaches out to touch

Hélène's wrist. With the other hand he is pointing through the window.

"What is it?" Hélène asks. She has been following the stream of bodies, faces and clothes out the window on her side ever since the coach started rolling.

"Up ahead, the city's northern gate, the Saint-Martin. Erected in 1674."

Hélène puts a finger to his lips. "Don't say everything that comes into your head."

Thomas pouts. He looks away from her, back to the window where he can take in the gate, now looming larger. It's a threshold that marks their official departure from Paris after more than a decade and a half.

"Turning point," he says quietly to himself.

He turns to see if Hélène has second thoughts about listening to what he has to say. No, it seems not. She's back looking out the window on her side.

"Ludovico Magno," Thomas intones loudly and deeply like a priest.

That draws several turned heads from the other seats in the diligence. Hélène flushes with colour. "What are you doing?" she whispers.

"Have a look." Thomas points at the Latin inscription in giant letters on the topmost part of the gate. He has forgotten she barely reads, and what she is able to recognize does not include chiselled letters in Latin in stone.

Hélène leans his way, low enough so she can fleetingly look out. "Oh, a gate," she says in mock surprise, then returns to looking out the window on her side.

The diligence rolls under and through the immense gate. The bright morning sunlight is blocked for a moment, making the interior of the coach as dark as twilight. Then it rolls back out into the sun again.

"Au revoir, Paris," Thomas hears Hélène say.

"Goodbye, Pair-esss," Thomas ventures in English, emphasizing the *s*.

Hélène sends him a happy smile. Her eyes are bright. They've been practising their English on each other over the past few days, but this is the first time either has ventured anything with others around. It sounds fine to Thomas's ears. How hard can that foreign language be? Gallatin mastered it. Surely he and Hélène can do the same.

—

"Well, when then?" Thomas is shouting in French at a burly, hairy man. The man seems to be ignoring him on the leeward side of the wharf.

The wind is gusting strong and steady. It makes it difficult to hear and be heard. Yet the man is wearing only breeches and a chemise, as if it were summer weather. It is anything but. Thomas and everyone else on the waterfront of Calais are bundled up with greatcoats as tight as they can be. Thomas removed his wig before going out on to the wharf, just in case it sailed off into the sea. Now he has his tricorne in hand, clasped to his waist. Though the wind is blasting cold, the hairy man doesn't seem to mind at all. He's taking his time coiling up rope that is as thick as his arms.

"What's that?" the man shouts back at last.

It dawns on Thomas that this man, were he not wearing clothes, might be mistaken for a bear. He looks to have hair everywhere. On his head the dark brown tangle is long and wild. It blows wherever the wind decides. The man clearly hasn't shaved in weeks or maybe months. He has a beard climbing up onto his cheeks. It has spread nearly a foot down from his chin. And from what Thomas can see of the man's chest and arms, his whole body is covered with a thick mat of even darker brown.

"When can we go?" Thomas yells. "In your boat. Set sail."

"The wind," says the man. He shakes his head at Thomas like he shouldn't have to say any more than that. The man stoops to pick up the rope he's just coiled. It's a giant circle made of hemp. He hoists it upon his shoulder and back.

Thomas glances at Hélène. She's still standing guard, so to speak, forty feet away beside their single trunk, their two satchels at her feet. She's down where the wharf joins with the Calais quay. She raises her arms to ask him yet again: when the hell can we board that boat? Thomas spins to catch up to the bear. The man is moving quickly away, farther out toward the end of the wharf. The coil of rope he's carrying is nearly the size of a child.

"Is the wind too strong then?"

"Is that," the bear allows, and scratches the top of his head through his wool cap. "The tide's wrong as well. Tomorrow maybe. Or maybe not. That's the sea." He bats a hand at Calais harbour. "Not like a road on land."

The man walks away from Thomas. He carries the rope over his shoulder like it's nothing at all. Thomas sees his conversation with the man is done. He trudges back to the quayside end of the wharf.

"Won't be today," he says to Hélène. "He says the wind's too strong, too risky. And the tide's not right. I guess he wants it fuller than it is. So the earliest he'll consider heading out into the Manche will be tomorrow."

"Does he promise? Does he say for sure?"

Thomas shakes his head. "He can't. And that makes sense. No one controls the sea and the wind. We could be stuck here for days unless there's a change. I noticed an inn over that way." He points toward a stone warehouse.

Hélène's hands go to her hips. "Well, did he at least promise he'd save a spot for us? I want to get going. We're this close."

"Have you ever been in a boat? Out to sea, I mean? Men lose their lives all the time."

"I've crossed a few rivers. I know danger. My parents, you'll remember, they were drowned."

"Your real parents? Or the other ones? The noble ones you invented for Marguerite?"

Hélène wants to look angry at Thomas but she cannot. She has to smile. "Both."

Thomas reaches out and taps her shoulder. "Wait here. I'll ask him not to take us across to Dover but all the way. Right into Londres direct."

"London. Yes, do that."

Thomas hurries the length of the wharf. "Hey," he yells to the bear.

The man is down in his boat, checking the ropes and lines to make sure everything is fastened down. When he finally looks up, there's a scowl on his lips. Clearly, he doesn't like to be disturbed. Or maybe it's that Thomas is shouting at him without using his name.

"Don't know how to address you. What's your name?"

"There are them who call me La Barbe," says the captain. He strokes his beard, evidently pleased with its feel.

Thomas nods. He might have guessed.

"Well, La Barbe, the lady and I are wondering: can we hire you— can we arrange to go farther than Dover? Up the river that flows to Londres? How much farther would that be? I mean how much extra would you charge? What do you say?"

"I say no and yes. I can't take the boat that far. The English don't permit it. But there's a port in the estuary of their river that's fine. Gravesend, they call it. As far as I can go. Done that a few times."

Thomas makes a face. Is Gravesend not English for death? A burial in the ground? "Graves end, that's what it's called?"

"That's it. High ground with marshes on either side. There's a ferry, a long ferry. It takes people the rest of the way."

"To London?"

La Barbe raises his hands to the air.

"I'm sorry. How much?"

La Barbe tilts his head and glances toward the open sea. He gazes beyond Fort Rouge and the Calais harbour mouth. "Could be hours or could be days. It depends on...." La Barbe tosses a thumb over his shoulder. "Any time away from here and the regular Dover run means money lost to me. You understand?"

"I do."

"Well, it's a longer run. So, five times what I told you before. Best I can do. Five times."

"We can't afford that, the lady and me. How about two times?"

"Three and we're set."

"We're set," Thomas repeats.

La Barbe clenches his fist and brings it to his chest. He taps it where the heart lies. Thomas's eyebrows go up. He's been working for years in a world where every agreement goes on paper. He hopes this agreement with the sailor will be as good. Thomas makes the same gesture as the bear, a fist tapped to his chest.

"One-third now," says La Barbe. "Another on departure. The last when we reach Gravesend. You hear that?"

"Yes. I'll have to get the first third. It's not on me, it's— I'll be back. Where might the lady and I find a room?"

"Cheval Blanc."

"Cheval Blanc?"

"Over there." La Barbe points. "Behind the warehouse. There's a sign. If you're there, I'll know where to find you when I'm ready to sail."

"All right." Thomas turns to go.

"Hey. No agreement till I get my first third."

"I know. I'll be back."

———

A loud thumping on the door startles Thomas and Hélène from deep sleeps. They're in an upstairs room at Au Cheval Blanc. The pounding tests the hinges.

"Thomas!" Hélène embeds her fingers into his arm.

"Who? Who's there?" Thomas calls out. He unclasps Hélène's grip. He puts his bare feet to the cold wooden floor. He's wearing a chemise, the same shirt he wore yesterday. And the day before.

The pounding has become heavy thuds.

"Who is it?" Thomas asks, face pressed against the door.

The pounding stops. "Open up. Time to go."

Thomas squints at the window, the only source of light in the room. It's still near full dark, only lightening a bit. Full dawn is yet a ways off. Thomas slides the bolt. He opens the door. The bear of a man is there, his face and full beard dimly visible in the faint light. La Barbe is shaking his head. "Time to go. First light."

"La Barbe," is all Thomas can say. He glances over at the bed, where Hélène is holding the cover up to her neck. "It's time to go," he says to her.

"Come if you're coming." La Barbe holds up both hands. "Wind's down and tide's about to turn. But I need my next third."

Thomas rubs a hand across his face. "All right."

Hélène jumps out of the bed. La Barbe looks away. She has on only a chemise. It comes barely to her knees.

"We'll need help with the trunk." Thomas points to where it lies. "To get it down the stairs and over to the boat. If you can—"

"Cart's below. Will lend a hand. Hurry, we take to the sea when the sea decides." La Barbe turns and thumps down the stairs.

Thomas closes the door and goes to his hat atop the small table. Yes, inside the crown of the hat he finds the coins he and Hélène put there last night. That next payment is already counted out. Nothing was taken from them in the night.

"Remember, it'll be cold on the water." Thomas is pulling on the warmest wool veston, justaucorps, breeches and socks he owns. He'll not be wearing any wig, not in an open boat out on the sea.

"I know, I know."

—

Hélène recalls sourly that she had wanted to make a good first impression when she arrived in London. She wanted to wear the finest dress she owns. Yet last night Thomas shook his head and said it's November and the sea air will be a lot colder than the air on land. Hélène decided he knew more about this than her. So she's putting on the drab green dress, the one she hates. Its one and only virtue is its warmth. Once they've set foot in England, however, in the place called Gravesend, she'll change into the new burgundy dress she bought the day before they left Paris. She will not take her first steps in London in any drab green dress.

Thomas helps Hélène finish off her dressing. He ties the strings, wraps the cloak round her shoulders and tells her how very pretty she looks.

"A lie, but thanks." She gives him a quick kiss.

"Ready?" he asks.

"I guess."

Thomas opens the door and shouts, "La Barbe, La Barbe."

No answer comes from below, but Hélène is relieved to hear the sound of heavy boots climbing the stairs.

"You are ready, you?" Hélène uses the formal 'vous' with Thomas for the first time in their years of knowing each other. She does so by design.

"That I am, Madame." Thomas adjusts his shoulders so he is standing more erect.

As the boot steps grow louder, the couple stands an extra few inches apart. Each finds a pose and an aloof expression that they hope says they're not lovers, just travelling companions. Yes, La Barbe has seen that they slept in the same room, even the same bed, but he doesn't know any more than that. Besides, he's not going to be telling tales to anyone in England, is he now? He'll be returning to France after he has taken them to Gravesend – so it doesn't matter what he's seen.

From this morning onward Thomas and Hélène are cousins, nothing more than that. It helps that some of what they are going to tell people they meet is true, or nearly so. The story henceforth is that each is recently widowed, she from a Russian tailor and he from a lovely lady. They're travelling together to offer each other the support and assistance of a friend. They'll worry about making adjustments to those stories after they've been in London for a while.

La Barbe fills the doorframe. "That it?"

He's pointing at the trunk. Thomas nods.

"Well, take your end. I'm not carrying it by myself."

Hélène picks up the two satchels while Thomas goes to the far end of the trunk. She can see that her new cousin does his best to carry his end of the weight as high up as La Barbe, but cannot. It's all he can do to stagger to the door and to the top of the stairs.

"Minute please." The strain is evident in Thomas's voice.

"The blankets, buckets and some food and drink," announces La Barbe. "Already in the boat."

Thomas and Hélène exchange a glance. They appear to have signed on with the right man.

—

"How long do you think this will take?"

Thomas waits for La Barbe's reply. The man has just cast off the last line and jumped down into his boat. It's a chaloupe, an open boat with no decking and only a single mast. The large sail is brown-stained. La Barbe swore with an upraised hand as Thomas and Hélène got into the boat that he has already made the crossing to England at least a hundred times. Only half a dozen of those trips, however, have been to Gravesend. Nonetheless, he knows the route.

"What'd you ask?" La Barbe says at last to Thomas.

"How long to Gravesend?"

"As long as it takes." He squints at Thomas then adds, "As long as that."

Thomas checks the horizon. It's barely the peep of day. He doesn't understand why the man he and Hélène have entrusted their fate to is so reluctant to just say how long the crossing will take. He turns back to the bear.

"But you must know from experience. On average, how long would you say?"

"Oh, on average." La Barbe grins like Thomas has made a joke. "Well, on average it gets a lot rougher once we've cleared this port. And once we're out there it's hard to say what on average means."

Thomas looks to the large irregular form covered by a canvas tarp that sits in the middle of the boat. Under there are their satchels as well as their trunk. Everything of value they possess is in that trunk, including what is sewn into the lining of their finer clothes. Thomas cannot help but wonder now if that was a mistake. What happens if the boat overturns? The trunk will go straight down. Thomas takes a breath. Too late now.

"Still," Thomas persists, turning back to La Barbe, "would you say a couple of hours? Maybe three?"

"We'll find out, won't we now? But I can tell you this. Dover's three hours at best and sometimes twelve. And we're not going to Dover but farther still. Even with the archangel Saint-Michel in charge of the wind, we'd never get to where we're going in as short as two or three."

Thomas studies how La Barbe is handling the rudder, then looks away. He notices Fort Rouge is now off to the starboard, no longer off the bow. He knows he should let the subject drop, yet he cannot. "Six or seven then?"

"From where do you hail, my friend?" La Barbe has a laughing look on his face.

"I— I'm from Paris, but I grew up in Normandy."

"Not along the coast it's plain."

Thomas's head ticks back. All right then, he'll keep his questions to himself. He turns toward Hélène, curious as to what she thinks of La Barbe's rudeness.

What is Hélène doing? When they first descended into the boat she had colour in her cheeks and a determined set to her mouth. Now, a little more than a quarter hour later, barely having exited Calais harbour, she has shrunk inside her clothes. Her face is pale and her lips are a shade of blue and trembling.

"What's wrong?"

Hélène holds up a wobbly hand. "The boat— the motion—"

Thomas grimaces. This is not good. The boat is just now going out where the swells are running higher and she's already feeling the roll of the sea. He kneels on the bottom of the boat and goes to her.

"You're getting seasick. Don't look down. Find something on land and stare at that. That's what I've heard."

"Leave me be."

Thomas moves on his knees back to where La Barbe is keeping one hand on the tiller and the other on the line tied to the boom.

"My cousin, she's getting sick. Is there anything you can do?"

Thomas thinks he can see grinning teeth through the sailor's beard.

"Do?" La Barbe shakes his head. "Quiet now." He's not looking at Thomas but a little farther out to sea. There's another boat, a schooner much larger than his chaloupe, approaching the entrance to the port of Calais. La Barbe's eyes switch back and forth between the fast oncoming schooner and the now flapping sail of his own boat. He's making adjustments as he steers.

At last, the wind fills La Barbe's sail and the chaloupe lurches ahead. The two boats pass safely, but with only twenty feet to spare.

Thomas clenches his lips as he waits. With the schooner now behind them, he speaks to La Barbe again. "I'm sorry, but you will have seen this before. A passenger who is seasick. What can she do?"

La Barbe swivels to meet Thomas's eyes. The grin is gone.

"Look, that's the way it is. Go back where you were and tell her she'll be all right."

"But—"

La Barbe offers a conciliatory shrug. "You never know who it'll be. Today it's her. Maybe the quickest I've seen. But you, you could be next. Understand? It's going to get a lot rougher soon. I say you go back to her."

La Barbe adjusts the tiller and the boat makes a quick correction. The bear of a man pulls out a flask and takes a nip. He offers it to Thomas, but Thomas shakes his head. Alcohol would only make him sick without delay. He crawls back toward Hélène.

"Hey," calls out La Barbe.

Thomas looks back.

"I'm aiming to get us there before dark. But dark comes early this time of year, so I don't know."

Thomas's head sinks down. The day has barely begun and La Barbe is saying they won't get there until near dark. Thomas looks up. "Thank you."

"There are two buckets. Over there." La Barbe gestures with his chin to indicate where the buckets are. "One's for the necessities. The other, well, I'd like it better if she'd retch overboard. Give it to the sea. It's hard to clean up the boat when someone spills their stomach in here. But that second bucket is there just in case she can't make it over the rail."

Thomas holds La Barbe in his gaze for a long moment. He watches him take yet another nip of whatever it is in his flask. He and Hélène are completely helpless in this small boat, open to whatever elements fate chooses to send. There have to be larger boats that make the crossing to England, ones that have decks and even quarters for their passengers. Yet he didn't see any like that along the wharves of Calais. So it's either they continue on with La Barbe in this boat and hope for the best, or they make him turn round right now and go back to Calais. Thomas clambers over to Hélène. He picks up an extra blanket and wraps it around her.

"Can you hear me?" he says in a soft voice near her ear.

She opens her eyes and blinks. "What?"

"Do you want him to turn round? Go back to Calais? He says it's going to take all day. We could forget Londres. We could move to Caen or Rennes instead."

Hélène shakes her head. Then a startled look takes over her face. Her frame trembles and shakes.

"I'm going to—"

She says no more. She grabs hold of the boat's rail and retches over the side, her entire body jerking as she does. Thomas holds on to her by the shoulders then rubs her back. When she finishes vomiting, he pulls her back and wraps her up in two blankets. He covers her from her neck to her feet. Thomas glances back at La Barbe. He gives Thomas a nod.

"She did well," the seaman shouts. "Not a drop in the boat."

Thomas rubs his eyes with his hand. Oh my God, and they've only just left the soil of France.

"Thomas." Hélène's voice is weak. "You're going to have to look after me. I can't."

Thomas enrobes her quivering frame with his arms. "Shush, it's all right. Just close your eyes. I've got you. I have."

"Thomas?"

"Yes?"

"If the boat sinks, the trunk won't float. We'll have to...."

"Shush, Hélène. Just try to get some sleep."

Thomas closes his own eyes. If the boat sinks, he thinks, it's not the trunk that needs worrying about. He can't swim and he doubts she can either. And even if they could swim, the November water would do them in. All three of them, La Barbe as well, would follow the trunk to the bottom of the Manche. Thomas exhales. He blinks away any thought that the boat is about to capsize. He looks back toward Calais. It's now not much more than a cluster of tiny buildings along a thin strip of shore.

"Hélène," he whispers, "do you want me to take your mind off things?"

Hélène's eyes remain closed. She does not reply.

"All right," says Thomas. "Did you know that Calais was under English kings for a few hundred years? That it sent representatives—"

"Oh no." Hélène's eyes snap open. Instantly there are beads of sweat across her forehead. She tries to grab hold of the rail, but the retch comes before she can free herself from the blankets. The first half of the stream splatters inside the boat. The stinking yellowish liquid bounces off the inside of the boat and over her and Thomas. The rest, mercifully, she sends out into the sea. Her two hands are grasping the side of the boat, the knuckles white.

"Did her best," says La Barbe from the tiller in a loud voice. "You've likely got her too wrapped up. But have a look. There's rags in one of the buckets. Wet them in the sea and clean yourselves up."

Thomas goes to get the rags. He wets them over the side.

"She won't be doing that all day long," says La Barbe. "No one does. A few more times, then she'll pass out for an hour or two."

Thomas does his best to clean the mess off the blankets and off his and Hélène's clothes.

With Hélène quiet and back inside the blanket wrap again, he shifts his gaze to the sea. From the wharf in Calais, the Manche looked so smooth in the distance. Out here, on its swells and valleys, the ocean is something else. Its waves roll up, then crest and spill, then re-form to do it again. And again. It's a giant sheet of liquid grey undulating of its own accord. The individual waves are of no import, none at all. What matters is the whole, which is beyond anyone's control.

Thomas puts both hands to his brow. He doesn't feel well himself. If only the sea would flatten out. He closes his eyes and takes a shallow breath. Then he takes as many breaths as rapidly as he can. He opens his eyes to look down at poor Hélène. She's cradled in his arms. Her pale face is peeking out from the blanket he wrapped around her head, her skin a greenish hue. Her hair is matted from the bouts of sweats. He cannot see how she is going to make it through as many as a dozen more hours of this. And what if—

"Bread and cheese in the hamper there."

Thomas turns La Barbe's way. The man is still nipping at his flask.

"Sausages and a couple of bottles of wine as well. If you get hungry, that is."

"No," Thomas replies, burying his face in his hands. The last thing he wants is to eat and drink. Especially not sausages.

"Your woman won't want a thing. But you'll need to get her to sip some of the small beer later on. Can't let her get too dried out."

Thomas raises his gaze to the thick November clouds swirling high overhead. He tries to recall better days. Nothing comes. He can't think of anything but the rolling sea. There's something wrong with his balance and his stomach is starting to feel warm while the rest of his body is growing numb. He grabs the third blanket and wraps it around himself. It doesn't do a thing. Shivers and trembles begin.

He can no longer smell the salt of the surrounding sea. What fills his nostrils is the stench of the vomit that remains on his and Hélène's clothes and on the bottom of the boat. It catches in the back of the throat. He closes his eyes and locks them shut. He decides not to look again at what Hélène spilled. He curls in as close as he can to her quivering, blanketed form. He does not care how pathetic he looks to the bear steering the boat.

Thomas swallows back the convulsions, gulping for air. The bile is souring his mouth. He swallows down a heave, but the next is too much. He gets up and leans over the rail. He splashes a yellow mess into the sea. He hangs out as far as he can, sucking in the cold air. But then his body is chilled, soaked from the sweats. He pulls himself back to the bottom of the boat to curl beside Hélène.

"You all right?" she asks.

Thomas shakes his head. She nods that she understands, and closes her eyes. He does the same. Maybe it would be best if the boat did go down after all. Wouldn't a minute of numbness in the cold water of the Manche be better than the world of agony he and Hélène are trapped within?

VI
Arrival

Gravesend & the Thames
November 1731

B ut for the slender swaths of purple and yellow along the bottom of the sky, it is nearly full-on night.

Thomas squints to watch La Barbe fasten the boat to the wharf.
He hears waves sloshing against the side of the boat. He hasn't
vomited in a few hours, but it takes all his energy to just keep
his eyes open. He looks down at Hélène, wrapped in her blanket
with her head on his lap. Eyes closed, breathing peacefully.

Thomas turns back to La Barbe. He's speaking with a skinny little man wearing baggy clothes and a simpleton's grin. The
skinny man quickly drops his grin. He points with repeated jerks
of his hand at a cluster of buildings not far from the quay. Oh,
how Thomas hopes the talk is about somewhere to stay. An inn
with a roaring fire, then a room with a bed. Even a paillasse in a
storage room would be good enough. He casts his eyes upward to
implore the darkness overhead to make it come true.

"We there?" It's Hélène. She stirs and sits up.

"We are."

She shimmies her shoulders to get free of the blankets. Her
clothes are a mess, stained in various places. Her hair and her face
look like she's been through a terrible ordeal.

Thomas unwraps his own blanket and confirms that he's in
about the same state. It'll be no easy chore to get the stains off

his clothes. He is the first to get to his feet. His knees and legs are wobbly for not having been stood upon in hours. And then there's the motion of the boat, even though it's tied to the wharf. He decides to sit on the rail before he extends his arms to help Hélène stand. She leans on him. He grabs her around the waist to make sure she doesn't fall.

"We made it." Hélène gives Thomas a hug. "Thanks."

Thomas helps her step from the rail of the boat onto the wharf. Then he does the same. He stomps on the wharf boards. How good it is to be back on something solid.

Hélène smiles at his stomping. "Who knew how good this would be. Dear Seigneur," she crosses herself, "please don't let me ever again be in any boat."

"Well, Hélène," says Thomas, speaking in English, and loud enough for anyone on the shore to hear how well he speaks this second tongue, "we need of a room."

"Good night," says Hélène, smiling. "Hello."

"Par ici," comes a shout in French from down the wharf.

It's La Barbe. The expression on his large hairy face is that of someone who will be glad to see the end of a long day.

"That little Englishman," says La Barbe in French, pointing at the skinny man in baggy clothes, "he says there's a coaching inn. Over there." La Barbe points at the cluster of wooden buildings alongside the road that leads up from the wharf. "But first, we have to go to their customs. Sign their papers. It must be done. It's the same on our side of the Manche."

Thomas nods.

"Et Londres? How to go there?" asks Hélène, wanting to try out her English.

La Barbe looks at her like she might be thick. He makes no effort to use the language of England. "Like I said in the boat. Coaches leave from the inn or there's the long ferry. Either way, nothing until tomorrow."

"The coach it is," says Hélène, sticking with English.

"No more boats," Thomas adds.

La Barbe shrugs. "Highwaymen," is all he says.

Thomas switches back to French. "We do not want to get sick in any more boats."

La Barbe laughs. "You might. But the long ferry is much bigger than my boat. It carries fifty or more. Besides, from here it's a river, not the sea."

Thomas sees Hélène's shoulders sag. They are both resigned to their fate and too tired to decide what happens next. They just want a bed and sleep.

"Here, La Barbe." Thomas puts his hand in the right pocket of his greatcoat and comes up with a handful of coins. He holds them out. "The final third. Thank you."

"Yes, thank you," Hélène says, though she looks like she might cry.

La Barbe takes the coins from Thomas. He doesn't count them or even give them a glance. He stuffs them in his pocket. "Any time you need to make that crossing, I'm your boat. Now, let's get to the inn."

"Mais...." Hélène is pointing at the large rectangular shape, covered with a canvas tarp, in the middle of the boat below where they stand on the wharf.

La Barbe claps his hands and laughs. "Oui, oui." He looks at Thomas and gestures for the two of them to get back down in the boat.

Thomas tenders a slight bow to Hélène. In French he says, "The day ends as it began, Cousin, with La Barbe and I carrying the trunk. A symmetry, I suppose. You'll carry our two satchels?"

Hélène curtseys back. "Toss them up. I'm not getting back in that boat."

La Barbe looks back and forth at the two of them. He shrugs, and steps down into the boat. Thomas does not delay.

—

Thomas knocks on Hélène's door as lightly as he can. He's not sure who else might be up at such an early hour. He can hear the seabirds shrieking as they whirl above the port, but that's it. He taps her door once more. This time he hears footfalls within.

The door opens a crack. A narrow slice of Hélène's face. She opens the door only a little more, just enough for him to slide in, then she closes it right away.

"What is it?" Hélène cocks her head. Like Thomas, she is wearing only a chemise.

"I just thought maybe...." Thomas reaches to pull her close. He presses his stiffness against her thighs. "I woke up thinking of you."

Hélène grabs his forearms and pushes him back. She's shaking her head. "That thing doesn't think. It just is. Especially at this time of day. Away with you."

Thomas is not deterred. He pulls her in. "We don't have to make any noise. No one will know what kind of cousins we are or are not."

She jerks a thumb to the left. "La Barbe's room is next door. I doubt he thinks we're cousins at all."

"He's heading back to France. Come on, you enjoy it once we start."

"No. Take your kindling and go."

"It's a log."

"Go." She steers Thomas to the door. "We have to be at our best."

Hélène opens the door and pushes Thomas out. He can hear people stirring down the stairs. There's a hum of distant conversations. "Half of an hour then?" he asks her in English. "We will go down?"

Hélène gives her agreement with a nod.

He reaches out with both hands to fondle the tips of her breasts through her chemise. With a sigh Hélène allows a bit of that. "Suffit," she says. She pushes Thomas away and closes the door.

Thomas turns round. There at the top of the narrow wooden stairs is La Barbe. The seaman holds Thomas in his gaze.

"Je— nous—" mumbles Thomas.

La Barbe says not a word. He takes the handle of the door to his room then halts. He turns to face Thomas, and says in French,

"Careful. This is not France. Things are different here. The English have some strange ways. Half price is all I would charge to take you back to Calais."

Thomas hopes his face does not betray too much of what he feels. But is this man crazy? Would he and Hélène get right back into that boat after what happened yesterday? "I think not," he says in French. "But a safe return to you, La Barbe. And thanks again for yesterday. We were in good hands with you."

"All right. But mark my words: the English are foreigners, they are."

Thomas cannot hide his laugh. But he makes a point of smiling kindly at the man's well-intentioned words. "Of course they are. They're not us, us the French." Thomas winks at La Barbe.

La Barbe shrugs and goes into his room.

Within his own room, Thomas's thoughts turn to his friend Gallatin. He has not seen him in five years. Will Gallatin not be surprised to have Thomas arrive in London unannounced? He knows the bookseller will do everything he can to ease the transition into his new London life. And Hélène's as well, of course. He's a good friend. Is there anything rarer or more valuable in this world than a friend? Thomas thinks not. And he has two, Gallatin and Hélène. He could not be luckier. Well, he supposes he could. He could find in this new English setting a position like the one he gave up with the magistrate judge. It is not at all clear to him how in London he'll be able to find something that suits his talents and ambitions. He'd like to think his past experience will count for something. But then, as La Barbe said a moment ago, England is not France. What if being French should turn out to be a liability instead of an asset?

Thomas leans against the bed. Relax, he tells himself. This isn't Persia or China, with a sultan or an emperor and customs strange to behold. The English have a king – a German king at that – and they have a Parliament to keep their monarch at bay. Thomas likes the idea of that. Gallatin has been trumpeting the English way in politics for a very long time. The bookseller voted with his feet to come live in this land.

"So then, friend," Thomas says aloud in English to the empty room. He has to smile at how much better he feels today compared to yesterday. He goes over to the trunk containing his and Hélène's things, except for what she took out last evening. Thomas makes the day's first decision. He'll wear the same suit of clothes he wore leaving Paris a few days ago. What could be more appropriate, more symmetrical, than to arrive in the new city dressed as he was when left the old one behind? Yes, London, a world of new opportunity, is but a short distance away.

—

Thomas smells oranges as Hélène leads the way down the narrow stairwell, one creaking step at a time. She must have dabbed on an especially heavy amount of the orange-scented water before leaving her room. Clearly, she wants to start off her life in England in a strong, feminine way. It reminds him to apply some rose water on his own chemise before they leave the inn. His scent is likely sour after all the travel, especially after the bouts of sickness yesterday.

As they turn the corner at the bottom of the stairs Thomas loses Hélène's orange scent. The new smell is smoke. There's a haze in the room. Thomas looks first at the fire blazing in the rough stone hearth on the far wall. But the wispy haze is not from there, it's from the dozen or so men smoking clay pipes. Mariners and merchants is Thomas's guess, judging by their faces and clothes.

Every head turns their way, though not to Thomas but to Hélène. Aside from the wide-hipped serving woman bringing food to the tables, Hélène is the only woman in sight. And she is certainly not dressed like any servant. In her luxuriant blue dress, Hélène could be a lady entering a salon. Thomas smiles to see her stride just a half step ahead, not so much as glancing around.

"Over there, milady and gentleman." The large-hipped woman points across the room. "The painters' table. All there is I'm afraid."

Hélène looks quizzically at Thomas. He's sure his face shows the same doubt. A table for painters?

140

"Go on, go on," insists the serving woman. "They won't mind. Cheery types, in fact. The rest of them must still be sleeping it off upstairs. There's two open chairs."

Thomas inclines his head at the woman. Though he has not understood every word, he grasps where she wants him and Hélène to sit.

"French I'll bet," Thomas hears a gruff voice say as he and Hélène walk by a noisy table.

Thomas takes it as a compliment and makes sure his shoulders are back. He and Hélène thread their way toward two men wearing what Thomas recognizes as floppy painters' caps. Beyond their table is a window that looks out to the port. Thomas can see gulls wheeling in the air, but he cannot hear the cries over the roar of conversation in the inn.

"Hello. Good morning. Good day." He's not sure which greeting is used in the morning so he's saying all the ones he knows.

The pudgy painter stands up. He looks to be about Thomas's age. He nods at Thomas, and to Hélène he offers a slight bow.

"Bonjour yourself." He smiles as if there is a private joke. "I take it you are French. Your accent."

"You have guessed." Thomas controls his smile. Learning to speak English may not take too long at all. "You call me Tyrell. Thomas Tyrell."

He sees Hélène's eyes go wide. He has not told her he's decided to go by Tyrell in England. It will protect his real name for when he returns to France. There is no advantage in giving away anything about oneself.

"I am here to master your langage," Thomas continues.

He sees the painters share a look, then a grin. The standing man turns to Thomas. "Well done so far, Tyrell. I am Hogarth. William Hogarth."

The painter extends his hand, which Thomas grasps. The two men heartily try to shake the living daylights out of each other's hand.

"It makes me a pleasure. Thank you." Thomas withdraws his hand and gestures at Hélène. "Voici ma cousine. She calls herself Hélène. Elle est une veuve. Me, I am veuf. Man with dead wife."

Hogarth's expression shifts from amusement to concern as he follows Thomas's words. "Ah, a widow and a widower. Heavens. So sorry. And both so young."

He pauses to make a gesture toward his seated friend, the other painter. "May I present my colleague, Samuel Scott."

Samuel Scott puts down the half slab of bread in his hand and wipes his lips with a handkerchief from his lap. He climbs slowly to his feet. It takes a moment for him to produce something like a smile.

"Of course and by all means. Why don't you join us, our new French friends?" Scott waves at the empty chairs. "We are travelling with three others, but last night's excesses are keeping them in their beds."

Hélène curtseys twice, once to Scott and once to Hogarth.

Hogarth pulls out the empty chair beside his own. He offers it to Hélène. As she sits, Hogarth slides her chair in. "Je vous en prie, Madame." Hogarth offers a courtier's bow.

"Un très gentil gentleman," says Hélène, fluttering her lashes.

Thomas tries not to roll his eyes. He takes his seat between Hélène and the painter called Scott. "You appreciate our need. Thank you."

But once more he spies the two English painters exchanging a look. Again they wear tiny grins.

"I say mistakes?" Thomas holds out a hand.

"No, no." William Hogarth's face is now one of regret. "Your English is far better than our French would ever be. Is that not so, Samuel?"

Samuel Scott is back in his chair, applying with a spoon an orange coloured paste to a slab of bread. "Mais oui," Scott says.

"My friend is a man of few words at this time of day."

"Hogarth," Thomas says softly to himself. "William Hogarth," he repeats, loud enough for all at the table to hear.

"Oui, Monsieur," says Hogarth, leaning in, "à votre service."
"I know your name." Thomas looks at Hélène to confirm. She
hunches her shoulders in return.

"An engraver and a painter of note." Hogarth winks at Samuel
Scott. "Known across the water in France, it seems. That's something, Samuel, is it not?"

"It is indeed." Samuel Scott's brow wrinkles, then he adjusts
his floppy hat. "If it's true, then my name should be known as
well. My specialty, sir, Monsieur Tyrell, is maritime scenes. Ships
in calm seas, for storms have been overdone. Perhaps you've heard
of me?"

"Peut-être," Thomas says to Scott, but he turns at once to William Hogarth. "But it is your name a friend of mine wrote in his
letter. Do you know a Frenchman in London?"

"Many dozen," Hogarth laughs. "Maybe more. London is
filled with the French. More than any other stranger group. They
say there are forty or fifty thousand. Your friend is one of the
Huguenots?"

"Jean Gallatin, un Huguenot? Un croyant et un hérétique?
Non."

"Huguenots are not heretics in this land." Hogarth stiffens.

"Bien sûr, I am wrong. This is England." Thomas waves a hand
in front of his face. "But you know him? Jean Gallatin? I am confident he write of you."

"Gallatin? Oh, John Gallatin. A bookshop near St. Paul's. Of
course, I know him. I did a trade card for him not that long ago.
Fielding introduced the two of us. Earnest John we call him."

"Earnest?" Thomas asks.

"A nickname. It means serious, sincere."

"Ah, sincère. That is him, toujours sincère. He had a store of
books back in Paris. Before he London came. To come. Went."
Thomas shakes his head.

Hogarth's eyebrows go up and down as he tries to follow
Thomas's words. "In any case, yes, I know the fellow. He's thinking of buying a press to print pamphlets and engravings. To go

along with the book selling. Doing all right, he is. But how about that? We've just met, Tyrell, and already we have a friend in common."

"Petit monde, we say in French," Hélène says to Hogarth. "Small world maybe you say in English?"

"That we do, Madame, we most certainly do." Hogarth raises his eyebrows at Hélène. Not once but twice. "You came over from Calais?"

Hélène's expression says it takes her an instant to grasp what the painter has asked. Then she nods. "Yes, it was Calais." She makes an undulating motion with one hand and with the other pats her belly, while her face presents a grim look.

Hogarth laughs before he offers a sympathetic face. "All depends on the weather, does it not? My wife Jane made that crossing and has sworn ever since she'll never do it again."

Thomas sees Hélène's shoulders slump and her lips go flat at Hogarth's mention of a wife.

"I think I did not give cousin her entire name." Thomas speaks first to Scott then looks at Hogarth. "Hélène's marriage was to dead man Kharlamov. He was Russia."

Scott blinks at Thomas's tidbit of news. Hogarth covers his mouth to hide what Thomas thinks is another grin.

"It is true." Hélène offers a small shrug. "A tailor. Pierre."

"Well, Madame the widow Kharlamov," says Hogarth as he glances at Samuel Scott. He then returns his focus to Hélène. "As a beautiful French woman with a Russian name, you could not choose a better place to come than here. I assume you are London-bound?"

Hélène nods. Thomas does the same.

"Well, our little London is the gateway to the world."

"Not so little." Thomas is eager to share what he has heard and read. "What I hear is six thousand. No, I must mean six hundred thousand. Bigger than Paris."

"I cannot confirm any number, for how could I?"

144

Hogarth's eyes glow as he speaks to the subject. "No one could ever count all the people in the alleys and closes. Any number must be wrong."

Thomas nods at the painter as decisively as he can. Has he not said the very same thing himself about Paris and its population counts?

"But I tell you this, my French friends." Hogarth leans back in his seat. "London may have crowds and dirt, squalor and thieves, gin and whores – excuse me, Madame Kharlamov – but it's more alive than any other place. It bursts with freedom and ideas. It is the drama of life itself."

"But Paris." Thomas holds open a single hand.

"Paris?" Hogarth makes an incredulous face. "If it offers so much, why then are you here at Gravesend and not still in France?"

"Because," says Hélène, as if that is explanation enough.

"Yes, because," Thomas adds. "Because we choose."

Hogarth looks down at the table for a moment. When he again makes eye contact, first with Hélène then Thomas, he says, "Forgive me. I was rude. I said too much."

"Our Willy sometimes sounds like he wants to be Lord Mayor." Samuel Scott gives his friend an indulgent smile. "He'd be a good one, I have no doubt, but he'd have no time to paint. That would be a loss."

"I write," comes out of Thomas's mouth. It surprises him.

"But in French, I suppose?" Samuel Scott asks.

Before Thomas can reply, Hogarth calls out, "Here she is!"

Thomas sees the serving woman approaching with a tray.

"Sally, our new French friends here were saying terrible things about you. They said you'd forgotten all about our food."

"That right, sir?" Sally winks at Thomas. "Doubts it very much. This is a true gentleman, here. But you painters, on the other hand? You're a different story."

She lowers the tray onto a corner of the table and slides it in to fill half the tabletop.

"Here's a start, milady and gentleman. Take your share before these other two dig in. Back with the rest as soon as I can."

Hélène and Thomas stare at the tray. There's a stack of four small plates, a large omelette, half a roasted chicken, two kinds of cooked whole fish, a dozen sausages, a pile of smoked herrings and a full loaf of uncut dark bread.

"There is mistake?" Hélène asks Thomas. "Mistake?" she asks again of William Hogarth and Samuel Scott.

"Yes, it is," Thomas says.

Hogarth and Scott swap self-congratulatory smiles.

"We English," offers Scott, "we are a robust race. We take breakfast seriously. Best meal of the day."

"True enough." Hogarth takes the carving knife in hand and slices off a thick slice of the chicken's white breast. "This is our fifth day here at Gravesend and each starts off more or less like this. When Sally comes back, I expect she'll be bringing our bowls of oatmeal. This inn has the most delicious sweet cream."

"And," adds Samuel Scott, "a pitcher of small ale and tea."

"Mais comment?" says Hélène.

Thomas cannot take his eyes off the spread of food. "But it is petit dejeuner, not the evening meal."

"Welcome to England." Hogarth opens his hands like he's the host.

"Hear, hear." Samuel Scott is handpicking the sausages he wants.

Hélène shakes her head. Thomas shrugs.

"Il faut s'adapter," he says. "We join our new friends, Hélène. Bon appétit."

———

"Yes, it'll be a little crowded," says Hogarth as he reaches up to take hold of Hélène's hand. With his help she steps on the rail then down into the boat. "But it won't be too bad. There is room for your things. We left London in a hurry and did not come away with much." In a whisper close to Hélène's ear, he confides, "We took this boat for our outing, but we're going to put it back."

"Vraiment?" Hélène looks at the painter with new eyes. Could he not be hanged for such a thing?

"In any case," says Hogarth, returning to a normal voice, "our boat will be better for you and Tyrell than the long ferry. Not only will we not charge you a penny, but we're good company to boot."

Hogarth glances round. None of the others in his party seems to be listening to a word he says.

"You are kind," says Hélène.

"Ah well, Madame Kharlamov, you'll not be disappointed with our wit, nor with the basket Sally has packed for us. We'll not go hungry on this trip."

Hélène looks round to see where Thomas is. She finds him up near the bow. He's in conversation with Samuel Scott and one of the other painters in this group of Englishmen. The other two men, whose names she's been told but immediately forgot, are using a rope and a couple of oars to put up a sheet of canvas around a bucket in the middle of the boat.

"Hogarth, why they put more sail like that?"

Hogarth looks embarrassed. "Ah, that's for you. For when and if...." He hunches his shoulders. "You understand."

"Oh. Thank you." Hélène hopes her face is not as flushed as it feels. "Excuse me."

Arms outstretched for balance, Hélène wends her way slowly toward the middle of the boat. She wants to speak with Thomas, who has just taken a seat atop a canvas bale.

"Thomas, have you all the names?" she whispers, staying with the English she wants to learn.

"Un deuxième William, un John et un qui porte un nom drôle. C'est Eb ... en ... ezer."

"Painters all?"

Thomas shrugs.

"Ah bon." Hélène stands as best she can in the gently swaying boat. It's still tied to the wharf. "Thomas and me, we thank you kind English. You are gentlemen. Merci William, William, John, Eb ... en ... ezer et Samuel. Un grand merci de nous, Thomas et moi." Hélène curtseys to the bow of the boat and to the stern where Hogarth is making sure his easel and paints are safely stowed.

As Hélène retakes her seat beside Thomas, it's Hogarth who replies on behalf of all five men.

"Gracious Madame, and pleasant Tyrell, we ask only one thing of you both as we sail up the Thames."

"What's that?" shouts out Sam Scott.

"That they listen to our lies and laugh at our jokes."

Scott bats the air. Hélène and Thomas laugh, a little after the others.

"As French," Thomas rises to say, "we too know lies."

"That's for sure," shouts one of the three English whose name is either William, John or Ebenezer.

"But," Thomas continues, "we do not lie about this. Your hospitalité is loved by us. By Hélène et moi. Merci."

"You're welcome, but that's enough." Hogarth loosens the last line keeping the boat tied to the wharf. "Casting off."

—

As the boat makes its way up the Thames, rolling with the incoming tide and pushed by a wind that billows its one large sail, Thomas is content for a time to simply sit where he is and study the distant sights on the opposing shores. At this great distance he could not tell England from France.

It pleases him to see Hélène smiling and chatting with the Englishmen. After yesterday's nightmare coming out of Calais, he was worried she'd be sick again. Yet right from setting off, she seems fine. The river's rolling swells are having no effect on either of them.

Hélène has the gift of appearing like she's listening to every word the English are telling her. He wishes she would pretend to listen to him like that. He supposes that she does not because she knows him so well. Whereas these strangers might offer her a path toward something better in her new life, which at the moment Thomas cannot.

"You see at this point how the Thames begins to twist and turn," says Samuel Scott in a loud voice. He's looking directly at Thomas. "Like a snake."

"I do see," Thomas says.

"Altogether, it's a little over twenty miles." It's the other William telling Thomas this. "From where we started this morning to where we dock. At Billingsgate."

"Bills Gate is London?" Thomas asks.

"That's right."

Thomas sees Hogarth shaking his head. "I think all our guests want to know is that we'll be in London before dark. Am I right, Tyrell?"

Thomas looks at Hélène. She gives a subtle nod. "Yes, Hogarth. But nous— we appreciate hearing talk. Interesting, we think."

Hogarth does not hide his broad smile this time. "Well, we'll let you be for a while. Hear that, chaps?"

There are mumbles from several mouths.

Thomas breathes in the rich salt smell from the river and the wind. He turns to watch the seabirds, some shrieking, others silent as they circle and swoop. A few come down to bob upon the waves. Large and small, some black, most white, but some with many shades of grey, they're on a constant quest for what keeps them alive. No different than for those inside this boat, except ambition is as important as food.

"Look!" shouts the one called John. "Dolphins."

First Hogarth, then everyone else aboard spots the creatures out in the middle of the river. Arms stretch and point. No one says a word. Half a dozen pewter-coloured arcs glide up and down and in and out of the water.

"Thomas," asks Hélène, "why is the dauphin the title of the premier fils du roi?"

Thomas shakes his head. "I do not know."

"Always wondered that myself," Hogarth offers. "But then, one doesn't expect things to make sense in France." The artist arches his eyebrows at Thomas.

"You make joke?"

"Yes, but it isn't much of a joke if you have to ask."

"Monsieur Hogarth?" Hélène taps the painter lightly on the arm.

"Yes, Madame."

"Your England, it was ruled once a time by the queen?" Hélène's eyes look very bright as she waits to hear Hogarth's reply.

"Oh, at least twice. Most recently by the late Queen Anne."

Hélène looks at Thomas as if to say, "See."

"The most famous," Hogarth continues, "was Elizabeth, our great Virgin Queen."

"A vierge?"

"So she said." Hogarth hunches his shoulders.

Hélène looks at Thomas meaningfully, but what the glance means is lost on him.

"A fine stretch of the river is it not?" Samuel Scott has moved down to join the conversation. "Perhaps not so much at this season, but from spring to autumn it is a veritable delight."

Scott's remark triggers something in Hogarth. A pensive look spreads across his face. He stands up in the gently moving boat. With one arm outstretched for balance he places the other upon his chest, above his heart.

"Above all rivers thy river hath renown

Whose boreal streams, pleasant and preclare—"

"Ah, Dunbar," Scott interrupts. "But what does 'preclare' mean, pray tell?"

"It means, or rather, two hundred years ago it meant clear, very clear," says Hogarth. "Excuse the ill-bred Scott, will you please, Monsieur et Madame?"

Thomas is delighted to hear some verse and to see the sport between the painters. It reminds him of his own circle of writer friends and Gallatin. Thomas glances at Hélène. She too is much amused. And it is Hélène who with a gentle wave of the hand urges Hogarth to continue on with his verse.

"Merci, Madame, but I think it best to jump closer to the end. I doubt our unrefined companions will allow me to recite the whole.

"Where many a swan doth swim with wings fair,
Where many a barge doth sail and row with oar,
Where many a ship doth rest with top-royal.
O town of towns, patron and not compare,
London, thou art the flower of Cities all."
Hogarth bows with an outstretched arm extended toward the
Thames flowing by.

"Bravo," says Thomas. "Poésie. I did not expect. Well done,
Hogarth."

"Oui, yes," adds Hélène. "London comme une fleur. Pretty."

"Willy has found an appreciative audience at last," says Sam
Scott. "And they've not even seen your real work."

"The very first stop." Hogarth winks at Scott. "I'll make them
admire my canvases one by one before taking them to their lodgings."

"Ah, perhaps not this day," says Thomas, brow wrinkled.
"I— we wish to go chez Gallatin. Maybe another day to see your
paintings, Monsieur Hogarth."

Hogarth shows an enormous grin. "Another joke, Tyrell. Of
course we'll get you to John Gallatin. Does he live near his shop,
close to St. Paul's?"

"He writes Church Street."

"Oh my."

"You do not know a Church Street?"

"London must have three dozen Church Streets." Hogarth
looks to his English friends. Each confirms with a nod that it is
so. "Almost as many as there are Cock Streets, Alleys and Lanes."

"In one letter he say silk weavers from France live all around."

"Aha, the Spittle Fields, or maybe the aromatic Sewerditch."
Hogarth's expression is that of someone much pleased with
himself. "I'm pretty sure there is a Church Street right beside
Hawksmoor's new church. I've sold engravings at the market
nearby. That was before my work became well known in France."
Hogarth looks at Thomas with an expectant face.

Thomas gives the painter the smile he wants.

—

"We're not too far now," says Hogarth as he sits down alongside Thomas. They each have a mug of small beer in their hands.

"Joy! Two days long." Thomas sees the painter chuckle. He knows it's the way his words come out. He must practise and practise until the English cannot tell he's not one of them.

"As long as you promise not to tell your King Louis," says Hogarth before he takes a sip, "I'll tell you what's round the bend." The artist points toward the front of the boat.

"But I am obliged to write the king every week." Thomas's face is deadly serious.

Hogarth leans back.

"A joke, Hogarth."

"So you do have humour in France. Excellent!" Hogarth takes another sip.

"We have everything."

"Yet you're here, you and the beautiful widow with the Russian name."

Hélène turns round at that. She smiles at Hogarth and winks at Thomas.

Thomas takes a good drink and sits back. It is only the first day in England – an ascent up a wide, fast-flowing river – but he likes what the day has brought him so far. The company is most pleasant, and all is well with Hélène.

"As I was saying," Hogarth says, addressing himself alternately to Thomas and Hélène, "if you look on the south side over there, you can make out different clusters of masts. Some with booms and rigging, some without."

"I do," says Hélène.

"Yes, me as well."

Hogarth assumes a serious face. "We're going by two, no, I must correct myself, *three* reasons for England's might."

"What is might?" Hélène asks.

"Pouvoir," says Thomas. He looks to Hogarth for confirmation.

"Yes, pouvoir. We are the mightiest naval power of all." Hogarth pushes his shoulders back. His eyes take on a challenging look.

"Is right," comes from Sam Scott. He's sliding past, sniffing the sausage in his hand.

"When you say *we*," Thomas queries Hogarth, "you mean England?"

"Great Britain."

"Ah, oui. C'est plus que l'Angleterre."

"That it is. Scotland and Wales as well. And for our naval might, we have three major bases right along this stretch of the Thames." Hogarth points up ahead.

"That's Greenwich. It rises from the shoreline up to the top of its green hill. That's a naval hospital at the water's edge, designed by none other than Wren. You know the name of Wren?"

Thomas and Hélène shake their heads.

"Well, you'll know it soon enough. Sir Christopher Wren, God rest his soul, was the greatest English architect there's been. Died and went to his reward seven, maybe eight years ago. His London churches – there must be fifty of them – are the finest buildings in the land."

"Catholique et Romaine?" asks Hélène.

Hogarth tilts his head and blinks at the widow with the Russian name. He laughs. "Very droll, Madame."

"And over there and there," Hogarth makes sure he has their attention as he swings his pointing finger. "Those are the dockyards of Deptford and Woolwich. But two of the dockyards where we Britons build and repair our ships."

"And does King Louis know about these places your George has?" Thomas offers the painter a grinning face. Though he's joking, he wonders if Brest, Rochefort or Toulon match up with the English yards Hogarth has just described.

Hogarth purses his lips and nods. "Oh, you can bet he does. There are no secrets about our naval strength. We also have dockyards at Gillingham and Portsmouth."

"So we, les Français, we should cede to you, les Anglais?"

"Why, yes, that's it in a crux, my friend. Well done." Hogarth taps Thomas on the back. "And you too, Madame widow, you too should switch sides. That is my advice."

Hélène smiles, as placidly as Thomas has seen her smile in days. For his part, Thomas hunches his shoulders. He makes his face as obliging as he can and tenders an outstretched hand. "Are we not here, in this your land?"

"That you are. Just make sure you don't slip back to the other side."

"Monsieur Hogarth, what is that?"

Thomas hears genuine wonder in Hélène's voice. He looks to where she points. It's farther upriver than the Greenwich shore they are now gliding by. She is pointing almost straight ahead, just slightly off to the right of the bow. There is what even at this distance appears to be a giant dome. Dozens of slender spires prick the air on either side. Thomas could easily guess, but he looks to Hogarth for the obvious answer to Hélène's question.

An intake of air swells William Hogarth's chest. "That, Madame, is your new home. The dome is Wren's great masterpiece, St. Paul's. All around is but a hint of our fair London town."

VII
Welcome

London
November 1731

The man holding the tiller, the one named William who is not Hogarth, ignores the shouts of abuse that rain down upon him. The anger is coming from the three men aboard the fishing vessel alongside. They have been outmanoeuvred by the painter. Hélène and Thomas each check the faces of their fellow travellers in the boat to see what one does in London when others with red faces shake their arms and curse. Apparently, you pretend you're deaf. Their boat glides into a spot beside a set of stone steps.

As soon as contact is made with the stone, the five Englishmen dash about like their boat is on fire. Two jump to the quayside, where they secure the ropes to the closest bollards. The other three remain aboard, but each is hurriedly packing up his things. Hélène recalls that Hogarth had whispered to her hours earlier that the boat was liberated for an adventure without permission.

"Oh, mon Seigneur." Hélène pinches her nose. Thomas covers his face with his arm. The stink from the river where they are now docked is horrendous. They look down at the choppy water and see a thick slurry of God knows what. Sewage from some of London's six hundred thousand asses and offal from one or more slaughterhouses is Hélène's guess. And this is November. She cannot imagine how bad the stench must be in a summer's heat.

Hélène swallows back a lurch. She sees Thomas does the same. She turns to focus on the reactions of the Englishmen aboard. Not one is letting on that their noses are picking up any hint of the stink. Are they simply used to it? Or are English noses like their ears? They select what they allow to get in.

Hélène looks skyward at the seabirds wheeling and diving overhead. Their cries are making it hard to think. She looks at Thomas and pretends, for an instant, to cover her ears. But then she realizes that it's not the birds but the shouting men in other boats or those toiling on the docks who are making it so deafening. She sees dozens of carters rolling their iron-capped carts and wheeled barrows up and down the docks. Hélène cannot make out what is being yelled, yet she hears enough to know that the words are sharp and fierce. They are curses of some sort. Will everyone in London be as angry as this?

—

Thomas feels his chest go tight. He covers his nose so as to not take in the foul air. He hopes he will not lose his hearing amidst all the calls and shouts. He cannot help but think this journey to England may be a mistake. He could have found some level of comfort in a small city in France that was better than this. The English capital is a jumble of confused, rude sounds. And it stinks.

But wait, thinks Thomas. This is but the main landing point for London when coming upriver from the sea. The rest of the city will not, could not, be like this. Their king, their government, their notables all live here. What was the line of verse Hogarth sang out? "London thou art the flower of Cities all." Thomas will hold his judgement until he has seen, heard and smelled more than this dock. Paris has its abattoirs and shitty sewers running through the streets. Those are simple necessaries, like this Bills Gate. The wailing labourers are but playing their noisy parts, just as lawyers stride into rooms as if high born. Here at the docks everyone yells at the top of his voice. And her voice as well, for Thomas discerns there are more than a few women onshore. Their faces are just as red and angry as those of the men.

Thomas snorts out the stink. Yet his nostrils fill again. It will clearly take a while before he gets used to it the way Hogarth, Sam Scott and the others are.

Thomas swivels to study farther upriver, toward the city that stretches out on both sides of the Thames beyond where the boat is tied up. Great warehouses of brick and stone line the water's edge. There are spires of what he assumes are churches nearly everywhere. A high column stands out. It has a golden shape at the top. That must be the memorial Hogarth mentioned, the one that pays homage to the Great Fire of 1666. Two hundred and five feet high and standing two hundred and five feet from where the fire started in a bakery in Pudding Lane.

Yet even that column is dominated – the very word for it, thinks Thomas – by the immense dome of St. Paul's. It looms high above and over every single thing. It is odd to think that not one of the church steeples he sees is of the Roman Catholic faith. Though there must be secret Catholics about – because there have to be – most of the English belong to what the Protestants claim is one or another of the many Reformation cults. Their beliefs are heretical to what he was taught in France, yet here they are ortho-dox. What sense does that make? You get in a boat and sail across the Manche and all at once the world of religion is upside down. Gallatin is surely right when he says that all religious beliefs serve those who have something to safeguard. Thomas wonders if his friend still detests all religion, or might he have mellowed and gone over to the Protestant side now that he has been in London for five years?

Thomas brings his gaze back to the water level to his immedi-ate left. Not far away – maybe a hundred feet – is what he's been told is London's one and only bridge. Imagine, a river city with only a single bridge! Yet, as he has seen, the Thames River is much wider and its tide more of a force than the Seine. The Thames can rise and fall, according to these Englishmen, some twenty feet twice a day. Its breadth of churning waters makes it an understandable challenge for engineers and builders. The one bridge he does spy is a most top-heavy affair. Above its low stone arches is a wobbly looking wooden structure several storeys in height with individual buildings overhanging the edge. They must be houses or shops. How they bulge and sag. Hard to believe the bridge is safe. Why do the English not build something like the Pont Neuf?

Samuel Scott says there's talk of raising another bridge farther upriver, at or near Westminster where the houses of government sit. The watermen who run the ferries on the strength of their arms and oars are much against it, the painter explains. Scott also says the arches of London Bridge are so narrow and low they do not permit vessels of much size from passing under. Only shallow craft without masts – the rowboats, wherries and barges – are able to run the gauntlet of the rapid water that flows beneath the arches. The painter says each year a dozen watermen lose their lives taking that risk.

Thomas feels Hélène tugging at his sleeve.

"What are we going to do?" She is speaking in French and pointing at the trunk.

"C'est vrai." Thomas switches to English. "Monsieur Hogarth, can you bring us assistance for this?"

"Ah yes, your trunk." Hogarth puts down his own belongings beside a bollard. "Keep an eye on these," he asks of the man called John. John grimaces but nods agreement.

Hogarth is biting his lower lip as he slips back down into the boat. "Hadn't forgotten you. Worry pas. It's just that we as a group—" he wiggles his fingers at the four other Englishmen, all of whom are standing dockside and looking down into the boat, "Well, we've had a rather good frolic and are now eager for its end. Yet we did invite you to come along. So we must see this through. Tyrell, you take that end and I'll take this.

"Madame Kharlamov," Hogarth gestures with a nod, "would you mind stepping out of the boat? It would give us more room to hoist."

With her own satchel and Thomas's clutched to her chest, Hélène steps up on the rail of the boat and then onto the quayside, beneath the wooden gable roof overhead.

"Now?" asks Thomas. He is stooped over and has his knees bent. He has both hands beneath the trunk.

"On the count of three. Once we get it up onto the dock I'll see if I can get you a hell-cart."

"A Hell cart? L'enfer?"

"The same. It's a fitting nickname for the wretched things. You'll see. One, two, three. Lift."

—

With the trunk tied down with crisscross ropes atop the luggage wagon being towed behind the hackney coach Hogarth calls a hell-cart, Hélène and Thomas climb inside the passenger compartment.

"No windows?" whispers Hélène. She wants to practise her English even though only Thomas can hear her.

Thomas reaches out to touch the surface where in France a window of glass or translucent paper would be. He taps it hard. It gives a metallic sound.

"Only little holes. Does it go down, Thomas?"

Thomas finds a handle, and yes it does. The late afternoon daylight floods in. An instant later, Hogarth's round and smiling face is looking in. He must be standing on an outside rung.

"It's like being trapped inside a bucket, is it not? The tin blinds are to keep the weather out," the painter explains. "And dust and soot and smoke. It depends on the day and where in the city you are. Less expensive than glass."

Hogarth jumps down to the ground, but shouts so Thomas and Hélène inside the coach can hear.

"I'm going to come along. I want to make sure you end up where you should. My brother-in-law John will look after my things. Be right there."

Though they cannot see him in action, Hélène and Thomas listen intently as Hogarth yells at the driver of the coach.

"Mary Hill to Little East Cheap then left until Grace Church Street and turn right. Climb Grace Church till you're well up on Bishopsgate. No other route than that, good fellow, no deviations. Understand? Won't stand it, we won't. Then head for the new church near the market at Spitalfields. We're looking for a Church Street thereabouts."

With that, Hogarth is up and in. There's a crack of the whip and the coach jerks away. The conveyance has barely gone ten feet and already all three passengers are bouncing sharply up and down.

"Mais pourquoi?" Hélène reaches out to steady herself as best she can.

"What is it wrong?" Thomas's imploring hand goes out to Hogarth.

"As I said, hell-carts. No springs, just leather straps. This awful bouncing is the result."

"Less expensive?" Thomas does not hide the pucker on his lips.

Hogarth smiles as he reaches out to steady himself. "You're beginning to grasp this city, my dear Tyrell. Business first and business last is London's creed. All the rest, mere trappings that come and go."

Hélène looks at Thomas then back to Hogarth. "So, to succeed here, Thomas and me need business place?"

"Either that or marry up. If not, you'll be heading back to poxy France." Hogarth winks at her. "Our London's a great city, but it's not for the idle or faint of heart."

—

The advance of the hell-cart is slow. It's more stop than go. Keeping his gaze out through the lowered window space as much as he can, Thomas sees London's streets are crowded with an endless flow of people with barrows and carts. Many coaches and many people simply walking about. The stink and the yells of the docks and fish market are soon but memories. The outside sounds are the more familiar calls of sellers on streets, and the creak and grate of their carts. Except for the fact that the words are English, not French, it's like travelling up a Paris street.

There are women, men and children of all levels and stations. As in Paris, Thomas notices, those walking keep to the sides. The middle is for carts and coaches. He sees several dark servants, or maybe they're slaves, from Africa or the sugar islands. They appear to be more numerous here than in Paris. He knows there is great wealth generated by the labour of slaves for the wealthy in both England and France. The overseas colonies are more and more important with each passing decade.

It surprises him to hear snatches of shouts and conversations in not only English, but also German, Portuguese and French.

"People are from everywhere, il semble," Hélène says. Judging by the expression on her face, she is pleased by what she sees and hears.

"That they are. The entire world." Hogarth speaks as if London might be his first-born son.

"From China? Indians from the Americas?" Thomas leans back. He knows he is offering a smug look. He believes Hogarth will take such teasing well.

Hogarth smiles and reluctantly shakes his head. "Not so many perhaps. But our London does have coffee shops where all you'll hear are strangers speaking their own tongues. French. Spanish. German too. My father once opened a coffee shop for Latin-speakers."

Thomas cannot keep a bemused expression off his face.

"You are right," says Hogarth, "it did not do well. But to change the subject, London has twelve papers. By that I mean newspapers."

Thomas nods approvingly.

"And countless pamphleteers, book publishers and that most high craft, engravers like me. London is the greatest friend the printing press has ever had."

"So my friend, so *our* friend Gallatin writes." Thomas pretends to keep listening to Hogarth as he goes on, but his thoughts are his own. He has always wanted to try to write for a living. Could he do that in England when he could not in France? But can he write in English? He's far from sure.

"What's that I taste?" Hélène asks.

Hogarth looks out the window for an instant. "Ah, you were more likely used to wood smoke. We English burn more coal than wood. It gives a hint of sulphur, I suppose. You soon won't notice it at all."

Thomas runs his tongue along his teeth. There is a grit, and it has a bitter taste.

"From time to time," says Hogarth, continuing on, "our Thames freezes over."

Thomas looks to Hélène; they share doubting looks.

"It takes a prolonged cold snap, of course," Hogarth continues, waving their doubt away. "The small arches of London Bridge keep the ice from shifting downstream with the tides. So the ice builds up. It's not happened in a few years, but when it does, we have a Frost Fair. The entire city, it moves onto the Thames. Entertainment, food, we artists, even the whores, excuse me Madame, but everyone sets up shops and booths on the ice."

Thomas thinks he hears Hélène sigh. Or is it he himself? He glances at her face. There is fatigue showing around her eyes. And, he notices now, she is wringing her hands. Well, no surprise. They have put in two long, long days.

"Oh," gasps Hélène as the hackney coach dips in and out of a sudden large rut. Thomas grabs for the side of the coach.

"An adventure, is it not?" Hogarth says. He's beaming like he's having the time of his life.

"Hogarth," ventures Thomas, "I see no lamps?"

"Of course we have lamps."

"No, in Paris we have lamps that hang on ropes with large candles in glass boxes across many streets. It makes our darkness safe. Well, safer than no lamps."

"And who pays for that?"

"I do not know. The city. Those who govern." Thomas holds up his hands.

"What I thought. No, that is not London's way. We have lamps here and there, especially in front of the great houses. But one can go anywhere, as long as one hires a boy."

"A boy? Un garçon?"

"Yes, lads. Link-boys, we call them. They have torches made of pitch and tallow. You pay a farthing and the boy lights the flame and accompanies you to where you have to go. Then they extinguish them and wait for the next gentleman to come by. It works better than what you describe. The cost is borne only by the man who is out and about, no one else."

Thomas blinks and sits back in his seat. He does not know what to say.

"Tell me, Tyrell, your Paris has a police force as well as lamps, does it not?" Hogarth narrows his eyes.

"Of course it does. For the threat, especially of the night. Me, I was once chased by a gang of thieves. I—"

Hogarth waves his hand to interrupt. "There, you see. Your lamps and your police did not prevent a thing. We've all been chased, and sometimes caught. It's just how it is. But we draw the line on police. We value our liberty too much. Your most famous writer agrees. He wrote we were a 'paradise of tolerance'."

"My most famous writer. Who is that?" Thomas leans back firmly in his seat.

"Voltaire. He lived here for a few years a while back. Must have drunk fifty cups of coffee a day. Which kept him in a spin. Still, a pleasant enough chap. Though I can't say I much like the perpetual grin he keeps on his face."

Thomas and Hélène share a look. When she declines to comment, Thomas decides he should say what's on his mind. "Voltaire has a fine plume, Hogarth, I agree. Fine words, cependant, are not always true."

"Could not agree more, Tyrell. But your Voltaire is right about London being a paradise."

"All is perfect then?" Thomas says deadpan.

"Good God, we've a hundred wrongs, but the point is, fewer than anywhere else."

"Ainsi soit-il," Thomas mutters.

Hélène turns quickly away. Thomas can see her gently shaking her head.

"And this," Hogarth goes on, raising his voice to get his should-be listeners' attention back, "here more or less begins the Spittle Fields. Some spell it S-P-I-T-A-L fields these days. Comes from an old hospital that once stood somewhere up here."

Thomas and Hélène stare at Hogarth.

"Spitalfields," repeats Hogarth more slowly. "Huguenots and silk."

Thomas and Hélène each shrug. Hogarth purses his lips.

"Where your friend John Gallatin lives? On a Church Street among the Huguenots?"

Thomas puts his hand to his forehead. "Oui, of course."

"Well," Hogarth points out the window at an extremely tall and slender spire. "That is the new Christ Church. And beside it, if I'm not mistaken, is the street you seek."

Thomas's eyes jump wide. "Excusez-moi." He leans out the open window of the coach as far as he can.

He can taste the grit in the smoky air, even more than when he was inside the coach. Nonetheless, he stays where he is. He studies each group and each individual as the hell-cart bounces by.

There's a herd of boys at the entrance to an alley. Thomas surmises they are bent over doing something they should not. He hears their snickers and guffaws. It brings to him a smile. Though his youth was in France, he supposes it was similar to theirs. He notes that an aged mother and what looks to be her daughter, both in middling finery, have to step around the scruffy boys to get by. They move out into the street and nearly pay the price. A man with a patch on one eye comes barrelling at them with a barrow filled with bricks and sand.

Farther along, in the centre of the street, Thomas sees the porters of a sedan chair huffing and puffing along. Their footfalls fairly pound the cobbles. Their wide-eyed expressions say, "Look out, we're not yielding to anyone."

On the right, two carpenters atop scaffolding are speaking what to Thomas's ears is an unknown tongue. It has a lovely, lilting cadence. He wonders if that's what Irish sounds like.

"If you look out the window," Thomas hears Hogarth say to Hélène, "way up to the top of the houses, do you see the large panes of glass?"

Thomas listens in. He does as Hogarth suggests, only on his side of the coach. He looks up to the tops of the buildings as the hell-cart bounces by.

"I do. Big windows," says Hélène.

"All that glazing," Hogarth goes on, "is to bring in light. That's where the Huguenots put the looms, up in the attic space. They sell the finished silk products in shops at ground level. Living quarters are in between. Clever and efficient, is it not?"

Thomas does not catch Hélène's reply, but he agrees it is clever.

Back to scanning the ground level, Thomas focuses on a tall, thin man with a long-out-of-date wig. He's bouncing along faster than anyone should ever walk. He passes an apothecary's shop then an upholsterer's before he ducks into a lane and out of sight. The fleeting sight of him makes Thomas laugh.

Way up ahead on the right, just passing beneath the wooden sign showing riding boots, a solitary figure catches Thomas's eye. A wigless man dressed in greys. He's strolling in a familiar way and reading a folded-over newspaper as he goes along. His head inclines slightly from side to side as he walks and reads. Thomas expects the fellow to bump into the abandoned cart in his path, but at the last instant he looks up and carefully steps around, then goes right back to reading the paper in his hands.

Now the man comes to a halt. He's standing in front of a colonnaded portico of a church, looking around. The hell-cart is catching up.

"And that," Thomas hears Hogarth explain to Hélène, "is the new Christ Church. Nicolas Hawksmoor is the architect. Splendid, is it not? The street you seek is there, right beside the church."

The man in greys is staring at something Thomas cannot quite see. Something on the other side of the stone wall in front of the church.

The cart rolls another few yards and Thomas sees what it is. Two men, one short and wide and the other tall and lean, are taking turns pushing each other in the chest. There's anger on their faces and they're only moments away from throwing fists. The hell-cart rolls past the scene.

"Can we stop and regard some silk?" Hélène asks.

And that's when the man with the newspaper turns to look inquiringly at their hell-cart as it bounces by.

"C'est lui!" Thomas shouts. "C'est lui."

He brings his upper body back into the coach and puts a hand on Hogarth's knee. "Stop. Make stop. Gallatin. He is right here." Thomas is pointing out the window opening of the coach.

Hogarth thumps his fist on the underside of the coach's roof. "Coachman. Coachman. We stop here."

—

Hélène watches their embrace. Thomas is obviously relieved and pleased. The face of the oft-talked-about Jean Gallatin moves from being astonished to delighted to see his long lost friend. Their chests press together, the arms of the one enthusiastically hugging and slapping the other's back.

Standing apart, hands still clasping the other's sleeves, for a moment neither has anything to say. Hélène is satisfied to be a bystander to the show. By the tiny grin she sees on Hogarth's face, so is the English artist. It is Jean Gallatin who speaks first.

"Whatever are you doing here, Thomas? How good it is."

Hélène is not surprised that Gallatin makes his greeting in English, but it looks to her as though Thomas is. He's blinking at his old friend. He's lost for words.

Jean Gallatin shuffles his feet at Thomas's silence. He pulls back, letting go of Thomas's sleeves. He bows ever so slightly to Hélène and Hogarth. "Master Hogarth. Greetings to you. Is it you who found this fellow and brought him here? Well done."

The painter seems much amused but says not a thing. He merely makes a fraction of a bow and a courtly gesture with one arm.

"You sound like a true Englishman," Thomas says. "Accent and the rest. Five years, I guess."

Hélène makes her own appraisal. She has not laid eyes on this bookseller before, and she often wondered if he could live up to what Thomas has said: sharp of mind, opinionated, strong-willed and earnest to a fault. Well, she sees none of that. The man has kind eyes and a slender form. He's a little taller than Thomas, and handsome in his own lean way. She likes the way he is so fond of Thomas and not afraid to show it to anyone passing on the street. Hélène slowly unfolds the pale-blue fan she's been holding in her hand. She lifts it to her chin, then higher still to cover her mouth.

In the momentary lull, two beats of a human heart, Jean Gallatin bows toward Hélène a second time.

"Madame," he says.

"Ah oui," says Thomas, "je m'excuse." He glances at Hogarth and switches to English. "Jean, I must introduce her. It is Hélène."

"Hélène?" Gallatin twists his head. "But— your wife is Marguerite?"

Hélène turns to Thomas. She's curious to hear how he will explain the situation to his friend, and in front of Hogarth. Will he stick to the story they agreed to only a couple of days ago?

Thomas yields a nervous laugh. She can see that wheels are spinning in his head. Whatever he's written to Gallatin over the span of five years, as far as Hélène knows he's not written to him in the past few weeks.

"Oui, Jean, yes. I understand the confusion of your face. My wife Marguerite, she had to die."

Gallatin's face registers shock at the news. Hélène suspects that Thomas's English wording was not the best, because Hogarth gasps.

"Thomas, I am so sorry." Gallatin clasps his friend with both hands. "I did not know. You should have written. I would have come to Paris to share your grief."

"Very kind, but it was sudden. It was that. Alors, ma cousine ... I introduce you to Madame Kharlamov. That is her widow's name. Hélène is prénom. She demand I travel with her on this journey to London. Me voici. And so here we are."

Gallatin bows yet again at Hélène, only this time stiffly and with a grave expression. A moment of instant mourning has apparently descended.

Hélène cannot entirely hold back a smile. She steps forward half a stride and curtseys to Gallatin, lower than she usually does. On the way up, to amuse Thomas's friend, she whispers a little joke to Gallatin that occurs to her.

The few words bring surprise to Gallatin's face, then a laugh. Good, Hélène thinks. After all, with Marguerite still living, as far as anyone knows, mourning for her pretend passing should be short.

—

Thomas sees Hélène's lips move as she puts on her show of courtly deference to his friend. He cannot hear what she says to Gallatin, but he sees Gallatin's embarrassed look before he laughs. Thomas shakes his head. Hélène can be playful when she wants. He'll ask later what she said.

"Chère cousine." Thomas reaches out to draw Hélène closer to his side. He wants her to understand that she has to be careful how she acts and what she says.

The bell in the slender steeple of Christ Church, towering overhead, begins to chime.

"So," Hogarth shouts above the resonant gongs, "I don't think they've asked you yet, Earnest John. They're wondering if they can stay with you. You French may beat around the bush, but I do not. On their behalf of course."

"Mais oui." Thomas puts a hand to his chin then to the tricorne atop his head. "C'est vrai. Ma cousine et moi, could we find a bed with you? Two beds, I mean. Under your roof?"

The church bells stop, having rung five times. The vibration of the last ring is still in the air.

"Bien sûr. Of course." Gallatin's smile stretches across his face. "I'm in an entire house and there's only me. My housemate, Johnson, who rents it with me, is off to see Europe on his grand tour. He writes he'll likely be another six months. I have a servant, Polly, who comes in during the day, but she keeps herself busy in the basement kitchen and on the ground floor doing a bit of sweep and clean. Doesn't stay the night. So yes, by all means. Please, please come along. It's not half a block from here. We'll figure out the sleeping arrangements when we're there. Hogarth, I assume the trunk on the wagon behind the hackney comes with these two, is that right?"

"That it does. I'll give you a hand before I head off. I have a wife and children chez moi."

"You are very kind," Hélène says to the two men hoisting up the trunk. She hands the two satchels to Thomas.

"What did you say back there to Gallatin?" Thomas whispers in French to Hélène.

She smiles and shakes her head. She displays the barest hint of arched eyebrows. Thomas has to let it go.

They enter Gallatin's place and undertake a rapid tour of the first two floors. He explains that Polly has left for the day, but she has kept the house warm and reasonably clean. Everything smells of smoke and burning candle wax. Hogarth nods at what he sees in each and every room. Here and there he offers a compliment to Gallatin: the fragments of Roman sculptures and pediments on display in one room and the blue and white Delft tiles fronting a fireplace in another.

After offering his kind words, Hogarth is quick to say his goodbyes. He speaks first to Hélène, who tells him that she is pleased to meet him and hopes their paths cross again. Then, after descending the stone steps on the front of the house, standing on the cobbles of Church Street, Hogarth says to Gallatin, "John, you're part of a group of writers and booksellers that meets once a week, is that not so?"

"I am. Wednesday nights. Would you like to come along?"

"I think I would. I'd like to hear what's being said. Keep in the know."

"We'd love to have you, William. We meet at the Friend at Hand. It's in a close off Threadneedle Street, near the Royal Exchange. Sign on the wall indicates the way. A painter such as yourself would be most welcome. Raise the tone." Gallatin winks at Hogarth.

"I doubt that, but who knows. And you," says Hogarth turning to Thomas, "I expect our paths will cross again. London's too small for anything else. Perhaps at the Friend at Hand with John and his friends. Unless of course you scamper back to that other land across the way. Au revoir, Tyrell." Hogarth extends a hand to Thomas. The two men shake like tradesmen parting company after completing a job.

"Tyrell?" queries Gallatin after Hogarth has headed off up the street into the fading light of day. "Thomas, you've given yourself a new name?"

Thomas makes a face, eyebrows arching up. Instead of speaking of this out in the street, he puts an arm around Gallatin as they mount the steps and go into the house.

"Lost your tongue? What was the name? Was it not Tyrell?"

Thomas glances into the parlour to the right. "Une belle salle, Jean."

"I see. Another of your little secrets?" Gallatin halts their progress down the hall. He offers a disapproving face. "You've not changed. Secrets to you are like bread to the rest of us."

Thomas laughs. "La maison est très agréable."

"Merci, mon ami. Johnson and I are both bachelors yet, but we like it here. Let's go upstairs and see if your cousin needs help settling in."

Thomas reaches out to stay Gallatin's climb up the stairs. "You insist on speaking English. Tiens, so will I. The name Tyrell is just a little insurance. Not other than that. A disguise while out of France."

"A nom de plume?"

"Only without the book. I reason if ever France, after my return, asks where I was for this time of my life, I will say I was a commis with the French army in the Pays Bas et les états allemands."

"You already have a story?"

Thomas shrugs. "There will be no record of Thomas Pichon. Not in England. Only Thomas Tyrell."

Jean Gallatin looks at Thomas long and hard. Then he shakes his head. "Such camouflage is foreign to my nature, my friend. For better or worse, I feel obliged to give my true thoughts on anything and everything. Even if I wanted to hold back, I doubt I could."

"Who is to say which is the better path through life? We are each who we are."

"So it seems," says Gallatin with a sigh. He begins again to climb the stairs. "Look, I'm sorry to put you in the attic, Thomas, but I think I must. I'll give your cousin the better room on the first floor, as long as Johnson's on his grand tour."

"Of course. That is right."

"All right then. I have a couple bottles of wine in the cellar. From Italy. Maybe over a glass or two you'll tell me about what has been going on in your life. At least the quarter or half you think I can be trusted with." Gallatin halts at the top of the stairs and pokes Thomas in the ribs.

"For you, vieux ami, I risk telling the complete half."

Gallatin laughs. "Perhaps the virgin widow will have a glass with us?"

Thomas tilts his head. "Virgin widow? Veuve vierge?"

"Her term, not mine."

"I do not—"

"Your cousin, Madame Kharlamov."

"Is that what she said in your ear?"

"It is. It took me by surprise."

Thomas draws a deep breath. "Hélène is not like any woman I've ever known, Jean. A maker of mischief, she is."

"I believe it."

Thomas glances at his friend. Can he really see his lover's mischievous side as quickly as that? No matter. Thomas must quickly decide just how much of his story he will share with Jean Gallatin. Should he confess that Marguerite is not really dead? No, maybe not. Because that will raise the question as to why Thomas fled Paris and the life he had there, choosing instead uncertainty in England. Gallatin will not believe it was just to come see him. Sooner or later, any explanation Thomas comes up with will have to include Hélène, because here they are, arriving together at Gallatin's house. The one thing Thomas knows is that it is always better to say less than more.

Besides, keeping the truth from Gallatin is probably not such a bad thing. It'll only be for a few weeks. At most, a few months. However long it takes for him and Hélène to get on their feet in their new lives. Once they have come to know London, and have positions suitable to their talents, they'll move into their own place. Then Thomas will tell Gallatin the truth – well, more of it, in any case – and tell him of his real relationship with Hélène.

VIII
Seasoning

London
Spring 1732

She removes the layers one by one, never taking her eyes off Thomas. He is sitting on the straight-backed wooden chair ten feet across the room. He is at the table where he has had to put down his quill. It goes into the waiting slot of the blue and white faience inkwell. Thomas is wearing only his chemise. He has pushed aside the manuscript he was working on, its ink now dry, the latest page atop the thin stack of others. He wants no distractions as he watches her unfasten and peel off her clothes.

The attic room is tight and airless. The solitary candle on the table is the only light there is. It flickers and gives off a wisp of smoke.

As she unlaces and undoes her strings and ties, the garments come slowly off. The entire procedure is going to take a while, but that is precisely the point. We are not animals compelled by nature's shift of seasons to quickly rut. No, this is pleasure as pleasure should be.

It comes at last down to only her chemise and the little cloth cap. The usually hidden contours of her curving body are visible beneath the linen. In the candlelight the linen seems to glow golden as Thomas looks on from his chair.

For the final touch she pivots, turning to highlight her back. Slowly, as slowly as she can, she slides her bare feet backward across the chill wooden floor. Coming to him where he waits. As she advances backward she raises the chemise inch by inch, higher and higher still – slender calves, then the backs of her knees. The thighs rise to her rounded bottom. Honestly, Thomas thinks, is there anything on earth more appealing than a woman's bum? The two crescent outside curves, the crack and best of all the hint of the flat area which underneath in shadow waits. Thomas smiles.

She lifts the chemise a little higher still. The tapered top of the bum merges with the small of the back. Then all at once she bares her entire back. There's a mole upon the shoulder blade Thomas had not noticed before. He watches her flex her shoulders, rolling them like they might be on wheels. She's completely naked from her heels to her neck, where the fabric of her chemise is all bunched up.

Less than an arm's length away, she turns round. Her smile is broad and it's clear that she loves her naked body every bit as much as Thomas does. She inclines her head slightly to the left. She removes her small white cloth cap and tosses it to the floor. With both hands now she takes hold of the rolled-up chemise and pulls it up over her head. She sends it sailing across the room. She pretends to quiver like she's cold though it's just for fun. The movement wobbles her breasts and releases her long brown hair to make it dance where it falls down her back and onto her chest.

"Oh my God," Thomas mutters.

Why has he allowed this dark hour's fantasy to go on so very long? You'd think he was still fifteen and back in his attic room in Vire. He adjusts his breeches and pushes his chair away from the table. The candle gutters with the jarring, but the flame re-finds its wick. The empty room shimmers in an incriminating light, nowhere near as golden as in his imagination. Thomas stands up abruptly, angry at himself. As he springs up the wooden chair he was seated on topples to the floor.

"Thomas!" It's Gallatin calling up from his bedroom on the floor below.

"Thomas, are you all right?" Hélène's worried voice comes through the floorboards from her room, also on the floor below.

"The chair. Just the chair," Thomas yells. "It— it fell over."

"Oh, all right," says Hélène. Thomas hears the worry fading from her voice, replaced by bewilderment. "Well, good night then."

"I'm here if you need help," says Gallatin.

Thomas rolls his eyes at the idea that he might need help to right a chair. He will not reply.

He picks up the chair and sets it down softly, then sits at the table that serves as his desk. He closes his eyes hard and tight. He needs to send away completely the reverie of the woman undressing and making herself available in his room. Where did that figment come from? He was working on an essay, one comparing London to Paris, when suddenly there she was. Thomas shakes his head.

His thoughts turn to monks and priests living in their lonely rooms. Whatever do they do with their own unruly rising cocks? Is the roughness of their homespun habits enough to keep things down? If not, do they have trusty pieces of silk? Or do they find willing fellow monks or obliging parishioners to satisfy their urges? Some do, of course. Thomas saw the looks and heard the whispers when he was a boy in Vire. And Gallatin, of course, always makes it a point to spread calumnies about every errant priest and brother he hears about, with no worry if true or not.

Thomas is no monk, though this attic room is definitely a cell of sorts. It could not be much barer. Not that much different from the room he had as a child at the top of another chilled house. The major difference, because it's Gallatin's place and not his parents', is that there are no religious images, nor any rosaries or bénétiers anywhere in sight.

Thomas squints to make sense of why his mind – or rather his autonomous loins – would summon a naked woman to his room.

"Oh," he says softly to himself. "That."

—

The dessert is very good. A flaky pastry, a rissole, with a delightful pistachio-flavoured cream. Hélène licks her lips after each tiny spoonful goes into her mouth.

"Thomas, I know you sometimes tire of hearing my enthusiasm for Rome and Romans," says Gallatin, after he has dabbed his lips with his napkin, "but I believe there has never been any sculptor to match what was produced in antiquity. I thought of this today as I went by the rather drab stone statue they have put up to Charles II in Soho Square."

Hélène sees Thomas bristle. She's not sure whether it's due to the taste of pistachios in the rissole or the topic Gallatin has just raised.

"Really, Jean." Thomas holds out an impatient hand. "The Greeks, for instance."

"Of course, they were masters, without a doubt. Before the Romans. But since Roman times, we have not seen the like." Gallatin prepares to dip his spoon again.

"Ridiculous," Thomas mutters. He puts down his spoon.

"Now, now," says Hélène. "Thomas, I think you will admit that Jean has studied Roman art and history more than you."

Thomas stares wide-eyed at Hélène. Slowly, he shifts his gaze to Gallatin. "I am no expert, I admit." He taps his chest to underline that point. "But, in truth, neither are you."

Now Hélène sees Gallatin's eyes go wide. She imagines her own do the same.

"Have you seen what Bernini and Michel-Ange produced?" asks Thomas, his gaze almost fierce. "The recent Italians, why today's Italians, they're as good or better than any Roman sculptor you could name."

"They can't be named, Thomas."

"No? Well, if they could, they would be journeymen to Bernini and the rest."

"You can't be serious." Gallatin is folding his napkin. It looks to Hélène like he will not be finishing his dessert.

"Of course I'm serious." Thomas's voice is raised.

"Whoa, wait." Hélène makes eye contact with each man in turn. "You two are arguing about sculptures, nothing more than that. Who cares?"

Thomas shakes his head. He takes a breath. Then there comes an impish smile. It reminds Hélène of Voltaire.

"I think you're forgetting Paris, Jean. Do you not recall how many delightful bare female buttocks there are in the city parks? Marble bums, I mean."

"I suppose I do."

"Well, let's just leave it at that." Thomas stands up and pushes the dish containing the rest of his rissole aside. He tosses his napkin onto his seat. "Oh, maybe this. What would you prefer, Jean, an ass made of marble or one made of a woman's warm flesh?"

Hélène feels her head jerk back. Gallatin's expression says he's appalled.

"I have some work to do upstairs," says Thomas over his shoulder as he leaves the room.

—

Thomas shudders as he recalls the discussion. He saw the disapproving look on Hélène's face as the argument went on. Too late he sees he should have let the subject drop long before he did. Poor Gallatin, poor Hélène. After all, the bookseller is still their host, however unsatisfying these lodgings. Jean has become Hélène's employer as well, ever since Thomas suggested he give her a position in his shop, and to Thomas's surprise, he did. Even though she cannot really read or write. It was either that or—well, who knows what?

He and Hélène have been living under the man's roof for four long months. Have they overstayed their time? Indeed, they have. Yes, they contribute to the rent and pay their share of the food and coal. But it's becoming clearer with each passing week and month that it's time for the two of them to move out, regardless of whether or not Gallatin's Scottish roommate is ever coming back. There is a natural course to all things, and lodging with a friend is no exception. It's time to find new quarters.

—

One of the few consolations Thomas has in his London life derives from what he can accomplish through his quill. It has not yet been possible to find any kind of position comparable to the one he left behind in Paris. So far he has two jobs to keep him busy during the days. Uninspired though they are, they keep him from spending the sum he brought with him as a letter of exchange from France. Admittedly, he does not buy a thing, other than food and drink. His fine clothes brought from Paris are beginning to show wear and tear from their constant use.

Three mornings a week he goes to a great house near Soho Square as a French tutor of an aristocrat's two ungrateful sons. Then five afternoons Thomas toils in a cloth shop on Thrift Street. Would not his father and mother – if they are still alive – would they not be surprised to learn their son is back to sorting and selling bolts of wool, flannel and cotton, linen, muslin and silk? Maybe "surprised" is not the word. "Delighted" might be closer to the mark. He suspects they yet harbour a grudge and would like to see him down the ladder to stand on the same rung as them. It's been twelve years since he saw them in Rouen, seventeen since he lived with them in Vire. One of them at least, his father is his choice, is likely dead. He begins to make the sign of the cross but then puts his hand back down. Reason, not religion, he says to himself.

Thomas turns to his manuscript, which he thinks is coming along well enough. It's a two-city travel memoir, an extended comparison of London and Paris. To challenge himself, he's writing it in English. He finds it a wonderful way to master what he hears at work and in the streets during the days.

Of course, he still has much more to see of the City of London and of adjacent Westminster. For instance, he has not yet crossed the river to the south side. Nor gone into all the nooks and crannies, as he used to in Paris when he was first there. Some of the seamier corners, for instance, like the Seven Dials, call out for inspection. A comparison of two great cities must include all angles and aspects.

He rereads what at the moment he sees as the opening to his book. He knows that a month from now it will have changed, but one has to start somewhere. Thomas frowns to admit it, but he has to give silent thanks to Gallatin, to whom he has shown the pages twice now. Though a bookseller, not a writer, Jean made the English grammar and vocabulary far better than Thomas was able to on his own in his first draft.

Our focus in these pages is on two river cities, each ultimately connected to the same sea. Yet it is London's ocean link that is by far the stronger of the two. Ocean-going ships of all sizes and shapes can come right up to London's docks, at least up to the sea side of the rickety London Bridge. A good wind could blow that structure down. The Thames is a true watery highway out to the sea. The Seine is as well, but Paris lies far inland. Before the great French river arrives at the coast, it meanders quietly along. In contrast, the English river connects London directly to all the ports of that country's vast empire of commerce and trade. Paris would resemble London only if it was lifted up and placed closer to the coast. Perhaps if it were merged with Nantes or Le Havre.

Thomas nods at what he has so far. It reads fairly well. Better still, it's true. It will only improve as he revisits it in the nights ahead. And when he shows it or reads it to his English writer friends. Fielding, for one, has said he would be glad to have a look and offer comments.

Thomas shuffles the pages and comes to something he jotted down about public celebrations.

On Lord Mayor's Day each October, the Thames becomes a spectacle of movement and pageantry. All the livery companies of the city make an effort to be afloat. So too everyone else who has the means to get into a boat. Hundreds of barges and boats make a great procession on the river. It is

Thomas frowns. He cannot yet write much more than that, for he's not yet seen the watery procession with his own eyes. He's simply condensing what Hogarth has told him and put it into his own words. He and Hélène arrived a few weeks after last year's event. He'll see the procession for himself October next.

Thomas shuffles the pages again and settles on rereading what he has so far about the different nature of Paris and London streets.

The shop signs in the English capital are larger than those in the great French city. Most are ringed in iron and extremely thick. Some shops have no signs at all. Rather, they are models pertaining to the business or trade and are fabricated in wrought iron or carved in wood. A tailor, for instance, might have a pair of giant scissors. Everything hangs far out on iron brackets. The weight is great. From time to time, the brackets give way and the signs or models come crashing down. People, so the author has been told by those who know, are sometimes killed. In this regard, Paris offers safer streets.

Turning to the threats that exist in all cities at night, that dark period that is the mother of all surprises, Paris has a police force as well as lamps. London does not. In the city on the Thames, people of quality have to hire link-boys – urchins who carry lighted torches – to get them about in the dark. And as for police, the English absolutely refuse to arm anyone. They say they value their liberty too much. As a Frenchman, this author does not understand why they prefer risks over the possibility of having a force that might assist them in a time of need. But that is the English way.

Yet, one must not fault the English for their love of sweet liberty. Though their fear of police may be at odds with Reason, it is a land that has broken with the yoke of Rome. They do have an established church, and that church has the ruling monarch at its peak. And that same approach to religion is one that allows thousands of dissenters to have their own meeting houses. London has many churches of these splinter faiths. Why, even the Jews now have their synagogues while the Quakers own the brewing houses.

Going over that last paragraph again, Thomas shakes his head. What a tangent! He'll copy over his words about religion and use them somewhere else. Such observations do not belong in a section about streets.

Thomas looks at the candle flickering away, then over to the room's lone window. A flutter of snowflakes is trying to brighten the dark. As it was in Paris, so it is here. March is a month that doesn't know whether it's still winter or time for spring.

He looks again at what he has on streets and religion. He has to laugh. He has missed the most obvious of the obvious. He has not said a word anywhere about churches. How well he came to know those houses of worship during his Paris years, though not once for the purpose for which they were built. Wonderful places for rendezvous is what they were. And nothing is more prominent on the London skyline than the countless spires of its churches and the one great dome. It's a rare street that does not offer a peek at some slender steeple or other. And to think that they were built by people of differing religious beliefs. It makes for an interesting contrast with Paris, where all its churches are of the one faith.

Thomas smiles. He had nearly thought, the one true faith. What is inculcated when one is young gets embedded, does it not?

He might as well begin his tour of London churches from where he lives. If he were to stand and go to the window, he could make out the tall, slender spire of Spitalfields' own Christ Church. It's the design of Nicolas Hawksmoor, as Gallatin and Hogarth seem to enjoy pointing out nearly every time he walks by the front portico with them. Apparently, there are five other Hawksmoor churches in London town, or near enough. Thomas cannot see why he should not visit them all and take notes. Hogarth says Hawksmoor is still alive, in his seventies. Why not track him down and get a quote or two? Then after checking Hawksmoor's churches off the list, Thomas can turn to the even greater Wren. No interviews with him, alas.

Thomas stands up and tucks the pages he has written inside the old book cover he has had since he was a boy. While it used to be home to his youthful verse, the leather cover is now where he keeps whatever essay is his current project. He opens the table drawer and places his work-in-progress inside.

If he can keep writing at this pace, and if Gallatin will continue to contribute improving touches, the book will write itself.

—

"You're sure?" Hélène hopes her face is not showing too much doubt. Thomas has been at her for weeks about tomorrow's outing. He swears she'll be safe.

Thomas sighs. "Yes, I'm sure. You'll not be the only woman there, I know that. They say it's the most popular sport in the land."

"Sadly, he's right." Gallatin dips his spoon into the two-fish soup. "Mmm, smells good. Polly has outdone herself."

"Should we ask Jean to come along?" Hélène's spoon comes up with a good-sized chunk of cod. She looks at it while she waits for Thomas's reply.

"But of course. Gallatin, will you join us in our exploration?" Thomas cracks off a chunk of baguette. His expression suggests he'd be just as happy if his friend said no.

"Merci, mais non merci," says Gallatin. "I went once, not to Clerkenwell, but over to one on the south side. But it's the same. It is safe, Hélène, have no fear. Everyone goes, women and children along with all the men. So you two go and see what you think. We can talk about it at tomorrow's dinner."

"There, it's settled." Thomas puts down his bread and picks up his spoon.

Hélène wonders if Thomas's smile could be called a smirk. Not quite, but halfway there. "Yes, settled it is." Though Hockley-in-the-Hole still doesn't sound safe to her. English names are so strange.

—

Thomas sees that for the outing Hélène has decided to wear the one new dress she's purchased since arriving in London four months ago. Well, new to her. It's a violet-coloured linen one she purchased at a second-hand shop last week. This will be the first time she's worn it outside her room.

"It's very pretty," says Thomas when he sees her in the downstairs hall. "Almost as pretty as you."

He leans close to kiss her neck. But Hélène raises a hand and turns him back. Oh right, Gallatin is in the parlour. It's possible he would see any such kiss or clinch.

"You're looking very gallant, Monsieur Tyrell," says Hélène.

"Thank you," Thomas replies, and wonders what her words and that elusive smile upon her lips might mean today.

—

Hélène sees the shadow of confusion cross Thomas's face as they stand near each other outside the parlour. Her words and smile are to let him know that though they're continuing to live this fiction of being cousins, and to sleep in separate rooms on separate floors, she wouldn't mind having him make love to her once in a while. Of course, only when Gallatin is not around, and she's not in her fertile time. She's finding she's missing the intimacy they used to share.

—

The first sight of what might be as many as three hundred men gathered in a circle, with their shouts and raucous laughter filling the air, makes both Hélène and Thomas slow their pace.

"Where are the women?" she asks.

"There are a few. Et des gosses aussi. Come on." He reaches out and takes her by the hand.

As they weave through those on the outer layer of the crowd, Hélène is reassured. There are indeed quite a few women here, and lots of children. Boys and girls are pushing past people's knees to try to get as close as they can to the wooden rail. Nearly everyone looks to be in a joyous mood, though there are fierce expressions on the faces of a few. Those will be the ones who have wagered large bets is Hélène's guess.

"Par ici." Thomas is tugging her hand, pulling her out of the crowd.

"You don't want to see it after all?" she asks.

"Over there." Thomas gestures at an empty cart. She nods. He's right.

Once they are atop the cart, Hélène and Thomas can see exactly what is going on inside the circle here at Hockley-in-the-Hole.

An enormous black bull is tied to an iron stake. It's held by a thick rope about fifteen feet long. The bull is snorting the air and pawing the ground.

A man dressed in shabby clothes, a handler of some sort, approaches the beast from behind, a small can in his hand. The onlookers seem to hold their breath. The man reaches up and out and turns the can upside down. He's sprinkling something close to the bull's nose. The huge beast shakes its head with loud snorts, its horns rending the air and breaking the dirt. An enormous cheer rises from the crowd.

"What was that?" Hélène asks.

Thomas shrugs his shoulders. "Pepper?"

Almost at once, a tiny round dog, yapping fierceness, runs into the ring. He goes underneath the bull's belly. The bull's legs kick out at the dog, his hooves raising dust. The dog darts in and out, again and again. Hélène watches in horror. It looks like the little round terror is trying to sink his teeth into the bull's most vulnerable place.

"Mon Seigneur," she hears Thomas say.

The bull catches the dog with its horns. He does not pierce its body but catches it between its legs and raises the little thing up in the air. With a strong flick of its head, the bull sends the dog flying through the air.

"Look at that," Thomas cries out.

Someone in the crowd has caught the dog. Why, he's putting him down to get back into the fight. The dog must be wounded or dizzy, because he does not dart like he did before. This time, when he scampers underneath the bull's belly, teeth bared, the bull is able to strike him with a hoof. The bull crushes the dog's back. The high-pitched cry from the dying dog silences the crowd.

"Oh, Thomas," Hélène says.

An instant later, a second dog is let loose. A different colour than the first, but everything else is the same.

"Let's get away from here," Thomas says.

Hand in hand, they get down off the cart and hurry away.

"What's the sport in that?" she hears Thomas ask. "A staked animal cannot win."

Hélène looks down at her clothes. She got dressed up for this?

—

Thomas follows Gallatin through the entrance door. They slide past a crowd of men standing in the larger of the two rooms on the ground floor. The voices in the room are loud, bouncing off the dark beams overhead. Each speaker is straining to be heard above the rest. Gallatin and Thomas do not even pause to look around. They know their friends will not be up here. They will be one or two floors below, where conversations can be carried on without shouts.

Gallatin and Thomas take hold of the rope at the top of the stairs that lead to the below-ground rooms. The rope at the Friend at Hand is thick, the kind used aboard ships. Here it serves as a railing heading down the steep and uneven stairs. The descent is narrow, reminding Thomas of a crypt. Here, however, no one is buried, at least not as far as he knows. Parts of the building are said to date back to the time of Henry VIII. Its half-timber framing and hand-hewn beams are visible everywhere. The structure stands just outside the zone where the Great Fire levelled so much of London. Thomas does not doubt that portions of the place, especially beneath the ground, could date back to Tudor times, for in the months he's been coming here he's noticed in several spots tiny rose designs embedded in glass or plaster. They are not decorations for decoration's sake but long ago declarations of support for the Tudor claim.

The first floor below the ground level has half a dozen tables, a couple of booths and a counter behind which labours a serving wench. Two smouldering lanterns and a few candles give off a burnt orange glow. The air is thick. Half the tables are filled with men smoking clay pipes and nursing cups of coffee. There's a thin bewigged man, a customer, standing at the counter. He's handling one of the pewter measuring vessels that belong to the establishment while leering at the serving wench. It is her lot in life to have enormous, swelling breasts and it is these that are the objects of the man's gaze. Thomas can see that the poor server is doing her best to ignore the man. She holds her chin up high and is keeping her eyes on the other patrons in the room.

Gallatin pauses and looks around. He takes the few extra steps required to leave the stairwell so he can peer into a booth. Sometimes this is where their group is forced to meet, should one of the rooms on the floor below be taken. Gallatin's inquiring squint is greeted by a dismissive wave of the hand.

"Must be below," he calls over to Thomas on the stairs. Then he goes and gets two cups of coffee from the server at the counter. He makes a point to turn his back toward the leering man as he pays the girl and gives her a tip. Thomas shows his approval with a forward tilt of his head.

Coffees in hand, Thomas and Gallatin continue their descent down the next set of stairs. The smell of freshly chinked mortar competes with the rich aroma rising from their steaming cups. In the week since Thomas and Gallatin were last here the owner must have had some work done on the wall. Thomas traces two fingers along the fresh white grooves between the stones. He likes the smooth cool crack of a mortared wall.

"There they are. The Frenchies! Just in time."

Thomas and Gallatin squint through the dim light to see who it is calling out. It's Hogarth, and he's on his feet. With a broad smile he's beckoning them to hurry on, to join him, Sam Scott, Henry Fielding and another at their long table. There is room on the benches for the newcomers. Two tall candles stand in the middle of the table. Each of the four men already has a cup in his hands – talking juice as Fielding calls it. Coffee certainly is that. In the centre of the table, between the candlesticks, Thomas makes out the usual two stacks. The higher of the two, as always, is a pile of newspapers. The other consists of pamphlets. Members of the group bring along whatever pieces of writing they want the others to discuss and debate. Everyone gets his turn to show how smart or polished or contrary he can be.

There is only one face at the table Thomas has not seen before. He's easily the oldest in the group. He looks to be at least fifty. He has a rounded, jowly sort of face with a soft floppy nightcap upon his head. Thomas hopes his face does not betray any of his disapproval. Nightcaps, he believes, should be worn only inside one's home, not out on the town.

"Neither of you has a stake in this question," Hogarth announces in a loud voice, gesturing at Thomas and Gallatin to take the empty places. "Two strangers to our land. So we should have their impartial continental judgement on the matter, I think."

"What weighty matter is that?" Gallatin winks at Thomas as he sits down beside Hogarth.

"I am sorry," Thomas says, hand outstretched to the man he does not know. "I don't think we've met."

"I'm sorry, Thomas," says Gallatin.

"As am I," adds Hogarth. "I thought everyone knew everyone. My apologies."

The older man rises from his seat and takes Thomas's hand. He has a smile affixed to his face.

"Edward Cave," he says, then immediately, as if it were a part of his name, he adds, "*Gentleman's Magazine*. Always looking for new writers, you know. We're in our second year."

Thomas knows the publication well. It is the brightest and most talked about of London's magazines – that word borrowed from the French and made to mean in English a storehouse of stories and ideas.

"You have your office in Clerkenwell, do you not?" Thomas seeks out Cave's hand to shake it a second time, this time out of desire, not protocol. Cave is slightly surprised at this gesture.

"Yes, we're at St. John's Gate. Are you a writer or a bookseller? Or an aspiring printer like Earnest John?" Cave extricates his hand from Thomas's grip.

Thomas finds himself lowering his voice. "Oui, I am a writer, I am."

"I did not catch the name."

"Thomas Pi— Tyrell."

"Well, Thomas P. Tyrell, bring us something to consider. Always interested in a foreigner's view of London, as long as it's filled with praise, that is." Cave makes his eyebrows dance.

"That is what I have." Thomas's chest inflates. He speaks loud and fast. "I compare Paris to London. Streets, buildings, customs, religion too. Many differences but not so many after all."

"I see. I'm not sure. Is it a pamphlet or a book?"

"It's not complete."

"Ah, well." Edward Cave reclaims his seat. "You'll have to finish it before— before someone else gets me their work first."

"Yes, of course." Thomas takes the chair beside Cave. He will not speak any more about this project until it's done. He does not want to be yet another name on the long list of writers who talk about books and articles they could write but never do.

—

The biggest problem in London is unquestionably the excessive consumption of gin. That particular alcoholic drink is everywhere, and easily obtained. It is so inexpensive, even the poor can afford it easily. It is the source of ills too many to name.

Thomas lifts his quill. Should he name those ills or leave it to the readers of his eventual book to deduce? Surely they understand what excessive alcohol consumption does to a land. Thefts, violence, prostitution, burglary, sickness, filth. He'll ask Gallatin if he needs to spell all that out. In addition to improving Thomas's English, Jean is wise about these things. No, what is Thomas thinking? He can decide that by himself. It's his book, not Gallatin's. Thomas puts down that page and picks up a clean sheet. He begins to set down his thoughts on a different topic.

Although Londoners, and the English or Britons in general, like to think themselves a people completely apart from the French, it is amusing for a visiting Frenchman to see how closely they follow all the news from Paris and Versailles. This is especially so when it comes to fashion. For where do the fashionable people of London look for the latest cuts and fabrics, periwigs and all the rest? They gaze longingly across the Manche, to that great capital on the Seine.

Thomas blows out a jet of air. No, he'd better change that. He must remember that to the English, it's the Channel, not the Manche. And he has to be recognisant that the readers of the *Gentleman's Magazine* are not going to want to see themselves depicted in a dependent light, especially where that dependency is on the French. Perhaps he will not include anything on fashion at all. It is one area of life where the English are weak.

Still, he cannot avoid the truth. And one truth is that there are in London very mixed emotions about the French. He refreshes his quill in the inkwell.

There are a great many French in London, with the Huguenots making up the largest number. They are concentrated in the eastern part of the city, in areas known as Spitalfields and Shoreditch. There are hundreds of Huguenot master weavers in this general area, with perhaps ten thousand looms. That makes them an important part of the English economy. Because of religious prejudices then, what France lost by persecuting the Huguenots turned out to be England's gain.

Thomas looks up from the page. He must be careful about that as well. He expects to go back to the other kingdom one day and to work for its officials and all the surrounding attitudes, policies and protocols. It's never wise to burn any bridge. Then again, this book will not be traced to anyone named Pichon. It will be the work of one Thomas Tyrell.

The Huguenots have their own churches in London and since 1718 a major hospital in Rochester. Many of that belief system are also said to reside in the county of Kent. They're supposed to be especially thick in Canterbury.

Thick doesn't sound good. He'll have to find a different word than that. He'll ask Gallatin.

Thomas looks at the small clock on the table beside his bed. It's getting late. But he does want to jot down something about the Great Fire before he snuffs the candle out. Though Paris has had many fires, it has not had anything as widespread as the famous London blaze.

In 1666, four-fifths of London burned. Though that was nearly seventy years ago, the recollection of the conflagration is still in every Londoner's thoughts. It began near Billingsgate, where the travellers coming up the Thames go ashore. A man confessed to starting the fire, a Frenchman he was. They hanged him for what he'd done, though now there's talk that the man who took the blame was not well. His claim was false.

Christopher Wren, the greatest of English architects, proposed that the City of London take advantage of the opportunity that the fire presented. He laid out a plan for a new city that would be laid out on a more geometrical grid, rather than the ancient twisting streets, some of which date likely back to Roman times. However, in the haste to rebuild, Wren's design was not used. The new construction was carried out upon the old, often narrow and non-aligned streets.

In the rebuilding of London there was a great use of bricks, unlike in Paris where the structures are mostly of quarried stone. The brick buildings of London are mostly black or red, or painted so if their clay was not that hue.

Thomas sits up straight, re-reading what he just wrote. He shakes his head. No one is going to want to read this. He's simply wasting his time. He puts down his quill, tidies up his pages and goes to relieve himself in the chamber pot.

In bed, with the only light coming from an unseen milky moon, Thomas cannot still his mind or slow his breathing. He decides that he needs to remember that what he has written so far is only a start. He'll improve it as he goes along. Adding and taking away. He has some good bits and some chaff. He just needs to figure out which are which and what goes in front of which. And it needs to move along. There's no need to despair, not yet. He has to continue on. Whether or not his inky pages will be of interest to Edward Cave is not something he can control.

—

Seated in the parlour, sipping her bittersweet evening drink, Hélène enjoys hearing Thomas and Gallatin clown about in the hall. It's not always this way. After months of living together, tensions sometimes arise. When they do, each usually tries to get her on his side. In those instances, it's not easy for her. She wants to remain friend and confidante with both. So when arguments begin, Hélène tries to hold back, remain aloof. She's known Thomas for years. They have much in common and have been lovers in many different rooms. Yet Gallatin is her employer now, as well as the person who owns the house where she lives. He is thoughtful and open about what he feels and thinks. In any case, there is no friction between the two men at this moment. It's a Wednesday evening and they are in high spirits as they set off to gather with other men at the Friend at Hand. Hélène would be interested to see and hear how they talk and behave when they are out, but she does not ask to go along, and of course it does not occur to them to invite her. So she sits in the parlour waiting for them to leave, sipping her chocolate.

"We won't be late, Cousin," says Thomas from the hall. There's an odd look of mischief in his eyes, one that Hélène cannot place.

"Don't believe him." Gallatin's smile is broad. "Late is obligatory on these nights."

Hélène sips her chocolate. "Tomorrow then." She tenders a vague wave.

With the closing of the door, she gets up with the intention of washing the dishes the three of them ate from a short while ago. The baked eel was all right, she thinks, though not exactly to her taste. A little too oily. But she loved the oyster casserole with the Parmesan crust. She would not mind having that again. As she waits for the water to heat in the kettle she has put on the fire, she hears hurrying footsteps out on Church Street. Then comes the sound of a key in the front door. Hélène picks up the poker from the fire.

The door swings open. It's Thomas. He's grinning like he might have just stolen the crown jewels.

"Quick," he whispers. "Quick, upstairs."

Hélène lowers the poker to her side. "What?"

"I told Jean that I'd forgotten my sample pages. What I am to read to the group tonight. So we've got a bit of time before I hurry on. Come on."

"You lied to Jean? Why?"

"Why do you think? Come on. We can have a quick one." Thomas arches his eyebrows.

Hélène looks down to the floor, then over to the kettle hanging from the metal arm close to the flames. Returning her gaze to Thomas, she shakes her head. "No."

"No?" Thomas comes over to her. He puts his hand on either side of her waist. He pulls her close.

Again Hélène shakes her head. "I'm not giving you a tumble just because you've lied to your friend and found a quarter hour." She removes his hands from her waist. "Why don't you go to London Bridge? Or the ones in St. James's Park? They'll give you what you want."

Thomas makes his puppy eyes. "No, I want you. And I apologize for the rush. I'm not taking you for granted."

"That's exactly what this is."

"I'm sorry."

He kisses her lightly on the lips. Then buries his warm face on her throat and neck. She feels something stir. It's true, it has been a while. Far too long. Yet why does it always have to be so fast and furtive, as this is going to be?

"All right," she whispers near his ear. Fast and furtive is better than not at all.

———

When they are done, they lie side by side, faces flushed and bodies wet with sweat. Thomas finds his hand going back to his favourite place.

Hélène gives him a tolerant look. "Delve and span," she says.

Thomas stops. He props himself up on his elbow. "What's that?"

"That's what Jean said the other day. It's a little verse the English have. Do you know it?"

Thomas shakes his head. "Maybe. What is it?"

"When Adam delved and Eve span, who was then the gentleman?" Hélène gives him a little smile.

Thomas frowns. "I don't think Gallatin should be talking to you about something like that."

Hélène grins. "It's not about the act of fucking. It's about that in the beginning there were no kings and queens and lords and ladies. It's about— what did Jean say ... it's a verse that speaks to a time when there were no classes or inequality at all."

Thomas leans back. He feels a tightness in his chest. "Say it again."

"When Adam delved and Eve span, who was then the gentleman?" Hélène gestures with her hands. "Tu comprends?" She twists to sit up on the bed, and picks up her chemise from the floor and pulls it on.

Thomas does the same, rolling off the bed on his side. "Yes, I think maybe I have heard that before."

He sees Hélène set her lips as tightly as she can. Apparently she does not want to say another word.

They dress quickly and in silence. Since she is not putting on a fine dress, but only her stockings, chemise and skirt, Hélène has no need of any help.

"Sorry if my little verse annoyed you," she says as she wanders over to the table where Thomas writes.

"It didn't." Yet Thomas has to admit that there's an annoyed strain in his voice.

He watches her pick up the sample pages he is going to take with him in a moment when he hurries off to the Friend at Hand. They are the bits and pieces he has selected to read aloud to Hogarth, Sam Scott, Henry Fielding and whoever else might be there this evening. Gallatin has already heard and read them all, and improved a good many. Thomas is hoping Edward Cave is not among the crowd tonight. He'd prefer to get suggestions from the others before he submits anything to the *Gentleman's Magazine*.

"What are you doing?" Thomas asks.

Hélène swivels to meet his inquiring gaze. "I'm reading what you've written. It's about London."

"*You* ... are reading?"

"Not every word, but most. What is this?"

Thomas looks at where her finger points. "*Ultimately.* How did you learn, Hélène?"

"Jean instructs me at the shop when there are no customers around."

Thomas's gaze is locked. He cannot think of a thing to say.

—

"Should we not hire a link-boy?" There's a waver in Thomas's voice.

"Nah," replies Hogarth. "The dark makes the heart beat faster, does it not?"

"Ah ... is that what we want?"

Thomas is keeping up with the fast-walking artist, but only just. His companion promised to take him somewhere he would find interesting for the London parts of his book. "You need more grit," is what Hogarth pronounced after Thomas had read a few pages last Wednesday evening. "Some seasoning to your stew."

Thomas asked what he would suggest. Hogarth shrugged, then replied, "Come with me on Saturday night. I'll show you what I mean. We'll get you some seasoning, we will." And so here they are, following a route William Hogarth clearly knows, even if Thomas does not.

They go through narrow, stinking alleys, where abandoned crates and broken barrels have been cast aside. The smell reminds Thomas of meat or fish that has been too long in the sun. The sound of scurrying rats makes his heart race. Hogarth brings out a perfumed mouchoir to block out the stink. Thomas has only a regular, unscented handkerchief. It's not much help. Beyond the nasty smells, there's more than the usual sulphurous grit in the air. It bites his nose and throat.

"Scratch an itch, fellows?"

It's a woman's voice coming out of the dark. Thomas nearly jumps, which makes Hogarth laugh. The woman is leaning against a wall at the entrance to a close. There's a smell of rotting fish coming from a barrel of something godforsaken not far away. The woman, who looks to be not much more than twenty, hikes her skirt up well above her knees. "A guinea for you both. What say you to that? No better price."

"No thanks, dear," says Hogarth, not even breaking stride. "We're going to a different church."

"Anything you want," the woman calls after. "Make it quick, I can."

"We're going to a church?" Thomas puts a hand on Hogarth's sleeve.

"Honestly, Tyrell, you really are something sweet. No, we are not going to a church. But listen, my friend, under no circumstances do you ever go into an alley with one of them. Understood?"

"I was not tempted," Thomas explains as they hurry on.

"Good thing. Did you notice the black patches on her cheeks?"

"I did."

"They hide sores, I'm willing to bet. And if the diseases don't get you, her billy-boy, who was likely hiding somewhere nearby, will."

The dark thins as the two men turn a corner. All at once there is open sky overhead. A little more than half a moon gives the cobbled ground and surrounding buildings a milk-white glow. There are lamps in front of several buildings.

"Ah," says Thomas, recognizing where they are. "Covent Garden."

"The one and only. So you've been here before?"

"Of course, for the market."

"At night?" Hogarth scrutinizes Thomas's face.

"I have not. Is this where my seasoning starts?"

"It is indeed." Hogarth waves vaguely at the northeast corner of the piazza. "Around here, if I may change the metaphor, is the church I spoke of before."

In the dark Thomas can just make out a small crowd of men standing in front of a couple of establishments on the north side. There are several coaches, with horses pawing the ground, and three sedan chairs. So, quality are at whatever place that is. "Theatregoers?" Thomas asks.

"Of a sort. Only the plays they're in have no scripts. It's life itself."

Thomas laughs. "Where are we headed?"

"Across the piazza to a place called The Rose. It's my inspiration for a series of paintings I'm working on. I thought it might do something for you as well."

"Lead on, my friend."

—

"You mentioned this place inspired a painting of yours," Thomas says as he and Hogarth give way to two men who exit through the front door of The Rose.

"A series of eight I'm going to call 'The Rake's Progress'."

"What is a rake?"

"Ah, an example to avoid. It's a gentleman who follows his immoral whims and inclinations, and pays the price." Hogarth points a thumb at the tavern they're about to enter. "This particular place is where I have placed the third scene. It accelerates the rake's decline."

"The Rose, then, it is not safe?"

Hogarth's face crinkles in amusement. "Safe? In what regard?"

"For our purses?"

Hogarth laughs. "Once inside, most men gladly give their money away. So don't worry about theft."

Thomas furrows his brow at the reply. The entrance to the tavern is now clear. Coming from within he can hear oohs and ahs, followed by silence. He glances at Hogarth. The painter nods.

"Just wait," Hogarth says.

There comes a loud roar.

Hogarth gives Thomas a knowing look. "Cardamom and ginger, I think."

"What?"

"The seasoning you're about to experience. Lead on, Tyrell."

Within The Rose Thomas finds a room packed with a crowd of standing men. On each man's face is an expression Thomas has seen before. Excited and slightly glazed. They seem to be holding their breath and the shortest are up on tiptoes. All eyes are trained the same way. Something is going on in the centre of the large ground-floor room. Whatever it is, Thomas can see that it must not be a fight. No, this must involve a woman.

"Though I've not been robbed on any visit here," Hogarth explains, "it's always sage to be on your guard. It's not always the poor who steal," he whispers, waving at a couple of tables of well-dressed high-born types. "That's how many of the rich got their start."

Thomas smiles and nods that he agrees with this assessment.

"Here, let me go first," says Hogarth. "We want a table up front. Otherwise, there's not much point in being here at all."

Thomas follows Hogarth as he clears a path. "Excuse me. Make way. Coming through," he hears the artist utter as he pushes his way through the crowd. What amazes Thomas is that some of the men actually stand aside. It must have something to do with the tone of voice. Thomas can learn from that. As he follows in Hogarth's wake, Thomas mutters, "Thank you, thank you." It doesn't seem that anyone hears or cares.

The advance halts abruptly when Thomas bumps into Hogarth. "Easy there, Tyrell."

They have come to a table that has six men seated at it, each looking immensely pleased. Thomas follows where their attention is directed. He spies a completely naked woman walking away, heading toward a darkened doorway. She swings her hips side to side like no one would ever do walking down a street. Every voice in the room gives vent to a roar. She pauses at the doorway, sticks out her ass, then disappears from sight. Thomas swings his attention back to the men at the table before him and Hogarth. Their eyes are slightly dazed. Their grins are wide.

"Gentlemen," Hogarth says.

All six faces, plus a few from nearby tables, squint the painter's way. Hogarth holds up a fist. Suddenly he's a magician performing a trick. All eyes go to the upraised hand. The conjurer opens the fingers of that fist and reveals two bright coins.

"A reward for a consideration." The painter's gaze does the circuit of the table. "Two seats, no more than that. A coin for each."

Four men are up and off their seats.

"Two, I said, only two."

The first two men to get to Hogarth – both costermongers is Thomas's guess based on their frayed clothes – take what's in the hand.

"Well done," Hogarth says. "Kindness is alive and well in London town." He grips the back of one of the two emptied chairs and gestures for Thomas to do the same.

"Are you richer than I thought?" Thomas asks close to Hogarth's ear.

The artist smiles. He leans to his side so only Thomas can hear. "The pretence of wealth is great fun."

"Who are you?" asks the chap seated directly across from Hogarth. He's an aging fellow sporting a long wig filled with curls that is at least a decade out of style. The man is reaching underneath the wig to scratch his head. The smudges of ink on his fingers tell Thomas he's a printer by trade.

Hogarth stands and bows. "I am from the Duchy of Utope, and this...." He turns a deadpan face Thomas's way. He flicks out a hand. "And this is my plenipotentiary to France, Tommy Jene Saisquoi."

The long-wigged questioner and his tablemates cast dubious looks at the answer. "Utope? Where is that?"

"In the north." Hogarth scans the table, looking closely at each of the four faces. "Our Utope is what stands between dear England and that barbarous land above." Hogarth pretends to look around the room as if he is in some conspiratorial game. He lowers his voice. "No Scots, I say, no Scots."

"That's it," beams the bewigged man with ink-stained hands. He looks to his tablemates and each one nods in turn. "We're with you, sir. That's what we say as well."

"No Scots! No Scots!" rises from the table like a chant. Thomas hears a faint echo of it here and there around the room.

"All right then," says Hogarth when the chant is finished. "Where are we with the night's entertainment?"

"The next moll will be along," the long-wigged tablemate says. "I think we're due for the candle."

"That we are," chimes in another.

"What luck. That's why we're here." Hogarth gives Thomas a knowing look.

Thomas maintains a non-committal face but beckons Hogarth lean his way for a quiet word. "Why does he talk of a candle? Une chandelle?"

"The same. They call them posture girls. Ah, here she comes."

Thomas, and every other man in the room, turns toward the doorway through which a naked woman departed a few minutes before. Now there's a woman with long brown hair wearing a skimpy gown, a long linen chemise. It goes down to her ankles.

She's standing in the doorway looking around the room. She seems to be looking for someone or something. Thomas hears a few shouts from around him.

"The candle!"

The woman raises a single finger as if she's just recalled what it is she is looking for. She pivots and goes back into the dark, out of sight. The whistles and boos are loud.

Out she comes again, this time with a metal tray. She parades in a circle twice around the small stage. She holds the tray up at the height of her eyes.

"Candle, candle," is shouted from here and there in the room.

The woman nods and smiles. She brings down the pewter tray low enough for all to see. There is indeed a candle there.

"Here we go," says the bewigged printer across the way.

"What I thought you should see, Tyrell," whispers Hogarth into Thomas's ear. "First, she does the sculpture garden, then— then you'll see."

The woman peels off as slowly as she can the almost see-through linen shirt. Completely naked at last, she starts to pose. She becomes a statue in a park or on the grounds of some great estate. It's quite a sight. She crosses her ankles and makes like she is flying a kite. Then her legs go wide apart and she is using a bow. Or she's seated on an invisible bench reading a book. Each pose brings a cheer. Then she covers her charms with her hands and puts on a shocked face. It brings a roaring laugh.

"Come on, you know what we want," cries out a voice far off to the right.

The woman speaks. "And can you not wait?"

"No!"

"'Tis a problem with you men, isn't it?"

There is much laughter and a few shouts of "Shame!" and "Not me!"

Now the woman holds up her shiny pewter plate. It brings a cheer. At once she fixes her gaze above the heads of the onlookers and seems to go into a trance. She starts to use the tray as a mirror, standing, squatting and lying on her back reflecting her curves and crannies to a wide-eyed, breathless room. Then comes the final act, the one everyone has been waiting for. She takes the candle and makes it disappear. There isn't a sound in the room.

—

"See what I mean?" Hogarth is looking at Thomas like he has just imparted a valuable lesson in life.

"How could I not?" Thomas takes a deep breath.

"Anything like that in Paris?"

"Not that I ever saw. How can such a thing be allowed?"

"Allowed?" Hogarth blinks. "This is England. We don't put up with French regulations or police."

"So I'm often reminded." Thomas's eyes narrow in thought.

"We had good seats." Hogarth is making conversation, apparently trying to determine Thomas's mood.

"Any closer and we'd have been up her ass."

"Tut, tut, no need for that."

"No?"

Hogarth chooses not to keep the exchange alive. The silence allows Thomas to reflect on the so-called posture girl. Of course, he was aroused. His loins decide that all by themselves. But his cock is not his brain, thank God. It saddens him to see a woman having to splay and spread-eagle like that. He loves women and the delightful mysteries of their bodies as much as anyone. Yet this kind of public display of their private parts is wrong. Such secrets and pleasures should not be on display in some leering room. It reminds him of the poor bull tied to the stake. Only here the men are the dogs. A posture girl is not about sex at all. It's about the power of being an observer who gets to watch someone doing something they'd never do themselves.

"The show didn't please?" Chin resting on his fist, Hogarth is staring intently at Thomas.

"No, it did not." Thomas exhales loudly. "C'est mauvais."

"What did you say?" A frowning William Hogarth meets Thomas squarely in the eyes. "Mauvais? As in bad?"

"I did."

Hogarth leans back with a satisfied expression. Thomas nods at his friend. Does the painter also disapprove of what just went on, he asks with his eyes? Hogarth nods back. Aha, so that means this nighttime visit to The Rose was simply to give Thomas a peek into a part of London's nasty underworld. Thomas's chest relaxes at that thought.

Thomas notices that the four other faces at the table are either squinting at him or fixing him with a sour look. Oh-oh, he is showing dislike for a show they like very much. Thomas climbs to his feet. He makes four half bows, one to each of the strangers with whom he shares the table.

"Duty calls in distant Utope. My lord," he says, turning to Hogarth. "This plenipotentiary is off. Adieu."

Hogarth is startled by Thomas's sudden act, but he himself quickly stands. "My good man—" He reaches out to grab hold of Thomas's upper arm. "I must away as well, alas." The painter turns to the table, zeroing in on the fellow with ink-stained hands. "Enjoy the rest of your evening, gentlemen."

"But Rhymin' Rosie's next," calls out the printer.

"Our loss, I'm afraid," says Hogarth over his shoulder as he strides off with Thomas.

—

As the two men hastily leave The Rose, Thomas nearly bumps into an aged knife-sharpener wearily pushing his tarp-covered cart up the street. "Veuillez m'excuser," he says.

"Fuck yourself," the old man replies.

"Eye-opening, was it not?" Hogarth asks as they hurry across the Covent Garden piazza.

"Depressing is more like." Thomas slaps his arms and shoulders to warm up. Coming out of the packed tavern into a cool spring night is only momentarily refreshing. He begins to feel a chill. "If it was meant to inflame our passions, I'm afraid it did the opposite for me." Thomas looks at Hogarth hoping he will agree.

"Oh, I concur. But do you not think you should write it up? Include it in your book? That's why I brought you here."

"I'm not sure how, but, yes, I think I must."

"That's what I thought. London may be the greatest megalopolis there is, but we have our nasty parts. As I'm sure your Paris does as well."

"Megalopolis?" Thomas gives Hogarth a dubious look. "Yes, Paris does. I knew those areas once."

"You sound wistful."

"No, not really. Well, maybe for the youth I once had and spent." Thomas sniffs the air. They must be passing through a downdraft of coal smoke. "So, Hogarth, heading home or going down some other dark path? If the latter, I leave you here."

Hogarth laughs. "I may paint a rake on his descent, but I am most assuredly not one of them. I'm off home to my sweet Jane."

Thomas shrugs. "Ah, right. A married man. What we all aspire to. Remind me, you have children or not?"

"Yes, foundlings we've taken in. None yet of our own, though we still have hopes. But you tell me, Tyrell, speaking of wives, what about that cousin of yours, that pretty widow with the Russian name?"

"She is not my wife, Hogarth."

"Relax. Do you know how suspicious you look?" Hogarth lays a calming hand upon Thomas's shoulder as they stride along. "I'm not chasing her. All I mean is that she once was someone's wife. What is her Christian name?"

"Hélène."

"That's it. And now the widow Rusty Cough."

"Kharlamov."

Hogarth shrugs. "Close enough. I've not laid eyes on her since that trip up the river from Gravesend. Is she well?"

"She is." Thomas gives the painter another close look as they stride off the piazza on the far side. Are his questions as innocent as they seem?

"And she's still staying with you and Earnest John at that Church Street address?"

"Soon to be moving out. Look, why are you asking all this?"

"Just conversation, Tyrell. It's what people do as they walk side by side."

"Do they? Well, I'd prefer to leave my cousin out of it."

"Of course." Hogarth puts his hands up.

Thomas gives the painter a sour look. "Another topic, Hogarth."

"The recent closure of the convulsionist site in Paris? Reports of the grave-robbing vampires in Hungary?"

"The former, please. For I once knew that site well. The Church of Saint-Médard it's called."

"Really? I'm all ears."

IX
Education

London
Spring 1733

Thomas can feel his heart thumping in his chest. He wants it to slow down but he knows not how. Tonight is supposed to be the night, and that means he's thought of almost nothing else all day long. For several days, in fact. Edward Cave has had his manuscript for three weeks, maybe a month. Cave as much as said that he'll let Thomas know what he thinks of it the next time they get together at the Friend at Hand. He was not there last week, so surely he'll be there tonight.

Thomas supposes he'll be able to tell with just a glance. If Cave greets him with a smile and an embrace, then Thomas will know that he will have his work published soon enough, likely as installments, a chapter at a time. If the reception is good, someone may want to put it out as a book.

But what if Cave looks away, up to the ceiling or down to the floor? In that case, the man will not need to say a thing. The rejection will be written in his face.

"And if he doesn't come at all?" Thomas mumbles aloud.

"What's that?" Gallatin leans forward to get a better look at Thomas as the two of them walk along. "If who doesn't come?"

Thomas shakes his head. "Nothing. Nothing at all."

"Cave? Am I right?"

Thomas slows his pace. "How did you know?"

"Ever since you gave Cave your pages a month ago, you've not been yourself."

"I know. I'm sorry."

"Don't be sorry. He'll like them, I'm sure. You didn't share the final package with me, but I'm confident they're good. Very good.

You're a clever lad." Gallatin hesitates then adds, "And—" But then he says no more.

"And if they're not?" Thomas completes Jean Gallatin's thought. "What then, Jean? I still have my tutoring position and the job in the Thrift Street shop?"

"One step at a time, Thomas, all right? Wait until you hear what Cave has to say. Before— What I mean is there's no sense in souring your humour with worries about something that probably won't come to pass."

"I know, but just let me stew a little more nonetheless. Will you do that?"

"As you wish." Gallatin pretends to take a key to his lips.

In the silence of the next few minutes, as the two friends grow steadily nearer to the Friend at Hand, Thomas finds his thoughts no longer dwelling on the pages he gave to Edward Cave. Something Gallatin just said, about Thomas's humours being soured, has struck a chord. That is exactly what has happened to him. Not just since giving his manuscript to Cave, but since coming to London.

His once promising Paris career is gone. He makes his living doing what anyone could, anyone who speaks French and knows a bit about cloth. As for Hélène, the woman he left his previous life and position for, he hardly gets to be alone with her at all. For well over a year they have stayed in separate rooms. All because Thomas lied about the nature of their relationship at the start. A story once told is difficult to change. And it's only every month or two they even get to be alone. Lately it requires pleading or convincing on his part. The old Hélène has been replaced by someone else. The new one is satisfied with working at Gallatin's shop and reading novels when she's at home.

So, yes, Gallatin is right. Thomas's humours are out of sort. If Thomas still had as much of Hélène as he used to, he might not care what Edward Cave thinks of his pages. But since he does not, not until they move out, Cave's acceptance is all he has.

—

The instant they arrive in the bottom-most room of the Friend at Hand, Thomas hears Gallatin mutter beneath his breath, "Not him."

Thomas looks. There are half a dozen men at the usual table, but none is Edward Cave. So no answer tonight after all, unless Cave arrives later on. Thomas hears a loud exhale come out of his friend. "To whom do you refer?" he whispers to Gallatin.

"Cleland," the bookseller mutters. "He's beside Fielding, on the right. In green. I don't like or trust the man. Can't say why. I just don't."

"Good to know," Thomas replies. "And who are the other two? Between Hogarth and Sam Scott?"

"John Goodenough and Adam Whynott."

"Why not? Pourquoi pas?"

"Oui. Les Anglais, n'est-ce pas?" Gallatin shrugs. "Both aspiring writers like yourself. Pleasant enough chaps."

Thomas reappraises his friend. He does not like to be lumped in with two men of questionable talent he does not know.

"Gentlemen," exclaims Gallatin in a loud voice. "A good, good evening to you all."

Thomas's eyes go wide, then he remembers. As a bookseller and a printer Gallatin does business with these people. He has to pretend he is a good friend to one and all, even the one he doesn't like, called Cleland, seated beside Henry Fielding.

"Enough chit chat." Hogarth climbs to his feet. He taps the table to have all eyes directed his way. "You two, take your seats."

Gallatin does as he is told, choosing to sit beside John Goodenough. The only other open chair is next to the man that Gallatin does not like or trust. Thomas goes there.

"My good friend over there...." Hogarth gestures at Sam Scott. It sounds to Thomas's ears like the painter is about to make a speech to get elected to the English Parliament. "Yes, the celebrated Sam Scott. My colleague maintains that London was founded *not* by Romans, which is what we were all taught, but by Trojans. Yes, those lucky few who escaped from ancient Troy. Do I have that right, Sam?"

"It is written down." Sam Scott gives an embarrassed shrug. "That's all I ever said. It's in a book."

Thomas glances at Gallatin, the greatest admirer of the Romans he has ever met. His friend is giving Scott a steely gaze.

Hogarth makes as if he's astounded by what Scott has just said. "So, if it's written in a book, it must be true, is that it? Can the rest of you attest to that?"

There is silence at the table. No one wants to torment poor Scott any more than Hogarth already has.

"Fielding, you've written a few books. More than the rest of us combined. What say you? If something is in a book, does that make it true?"

Henry Fielding glances at Sam Scott with an apology in his eyes. "Depends on the book. Some are more reliable than the rest."

"Well said." Hogarth's face is triumphant. "And you, sir." The painter turns to Gallatin. "If you only sold books that contained the truth, how many books would you sell?"

"Impossible to say."

Thomas recognizes a smug smile forming on his friend's lips.

"How so?" Hogarth frowns.

Gallatin holds out a single outstretched hand and raises his pointer finger before he speaks. "First, one must define what is meant by the truth. It is not a synonym for facts."

"Bah." Hogarth swivels in his chair. "Let's not get into that. You, Tyrell, you have a quiet, learned air. What say you to Scott's belief that the Trojan horse was here?"

"Willy! Please." Sam Scott shakes his head. "I never said—"

"Shhh, I know. Disregard my joke about the horse. Tyrell, come on, the clock is ticking fast." Hogarth holds out his hand.

"But you've changed the question, Hogarth," Thomas ventures. "You started with the Trojans possibly coming to London and then switched it to books and the truth. Should we not discuss them one at a time, not in a blur?"

"Bravo," says Sam Scott to Thomas in a quiet voice. "Hear, hear," say some of the others.

Hogarth sits down, a deflated expression on his face. "All right. What a strange night is this. I seem to be in need of correction. Like a comet in the sky, it shall not be seen again."

"But— but comets do come again." Thomas glances around for support.

"Of course they do," says the man to Thomas's right, the one Gallatin does not trust. "That's what makes them comets and not something else."

"What a crowd." Hogarth shakes his head. "Let's move on. Enough about the Trojan wars." The artist gives an impish smile.

The table, especially Sam Scott, looks delighted to let the subject drop. Three separate conversations begin to fill the void. The man who backed up Thomas's remark about comets rises from his chair, hand outstretched.

"Cleland. John Cleland," he says.

"Tyrell. Thomas."

They regain their seats, but Thomas has taken closer notice of this Cleland's carefully coiffed wig and well-cut clothes. The dark-green coat looks to be of the finest wool, tailored carefully to the man's frame, not picked up at any auction sale. The coat and the matching breeches will have cost him a lot. Whoever he is, he seems to be a man of some means.

———

"Well, I ask you this," a suddenly impassioned Henry Fielding nearly shouts, "who here has seen a man kicking the air as he fights for his life?"

There are stunned looks on every face. This is not a usual subject for a Wednesday night. The latest pamphlet or book, yes; the supposed threat of the Jacobites; or whether or not religious writers absolutely need to be so tedious and dull. But the practice of hanging criminals? No, that's not a subject they discuss.

"Whatever do you mean, Henry?" inquires John Goodenough. There is a hint of trepidation in his voice.

"I was eighteen when I saw Jonathan Wild hang from Tyburn's tree." Fielding's voice is serious. "I sometimes see him still."

"I've not heard this before." Hogarth brings his hand up to scratch his chin. "You were really there that day?

"Along with everyone else. We were thousands, if not tens of thousands. There were tickets sold for the best viewing spots. The huzzas I'll never forget. You'd think it was a coronation."

"Who was this man Wild?" Thomas asks.

"An inspiration, it seems," offers Cleland.

All eyes turn Cleland's way, surprise on their faces. Thomas notices Gallatin is shaking his head, a disgusted expression nearly showing through.

"For writers, I mean," Cleland clarifies. "Defoe was quick off the mark. Then old John Gay. There'll be more to come, mark my words. The world loves a thief. Just as long as his hand is in someone else's purse and not their own."

"True enough, that," mutters Hogarth, and the entire table agrees. "You, Tyrell, and even you, John Gallatin, you're not that long from France. Are thieves there celebrated as well?"

Gallatin and Thomas exchange a look. The bookseller nods that Thomas should reply. "Not by those whose pockets or chests are robbed, but by the untouched, yes, they can be celebrated, I suppose. Just as Monsieur Cleland here said."

There's a momentary lull in the discussion. Thomas assumes it's because no one knows how to get the subject away from hanging thieves.

"Well," says Fielding, "I don't know if Defoe was at Tyburn that day or not, but his book sold well enough. And John Gay's *Beggar's Opera* had over sixty performances at the theatre at Lincoln's Inn Fields. I've never had anything do as well as that."

"No fault of yours, Henry." Sam Scott gives the writer an understanding look. "The public is an ass."

The silence that follows lasts but half a breath. Then everyone at the table, including Scott, guffaws and sputters.

"An ass, perhaps, but it farts out the money to pay our bills." Hogarth smiles warmly at Scott.

"Indeed it does." Scott sends an apologetic series of shrugs around the table. "Forget I said anything."

—

"So, what brings yet another Frenchman to our dear London town?" Cleland asks.

"This and that," Thomas replies.

"Ah, this and that. The French do that so well." Cleland makes his eyebrows dance.

Thomas cannot help but laugh. Though Gallatin has warned him about this man, Thomas has not seen or heard anything yet from him in the past hour's conversation he does not like. He is very well dressed and seems bright, even funny at times.

"Like the rest of us, except the artists, I assume you're here because you write?" Cleland asks.

Thomas inclines his head.

"Saving your best words for the page, I see. Very wise, Tyrell." Cleland takes a sip of the rum he switched to half an hour ago. "The trick," John Cleland takes a second sip, "is to find a niche. It's as simple as that."

Thomas is particularly struck by the man's way of speaking. It's as if each word or phrase is a cream-filled pastry in his mouth. It's how Thomas imagines a count or duke might speak, should he ever be in their circles.

"Easier said than done, I think," Thomas replies at last.

"True enough. Tell me, have I said enough?" Cleland leans toward Thomas and gives him a quizzical look. "Passed some quota you have for people you've just met?"

Thomas blinks. "Am I as rude as that?"

"Well, you were quiet to begin with, then you say less as the conversation goes on. Other than that, no, you're not especially rude. I find it's a natural French thing. Le style français, peut-être?"

Thomas glances at Gallatin, who is deep in a conversation with Sam Scott. Why does Jean not like this man? "You speak French?"

"No, but occasionally foreign words come out my mouth. A salon trick."

"A good one to have, I bet."

"You know, Tyrell, French is good for but two things."

"French the language or the French?" Thomas taps his own chest.

"I'm afraid I don't distinguish." Cleland waves to get the servant's attention. He indicates he wants a top up of his rum and some for Thomas as well.

"Thank you," says Thomas, "you're very kind to someone you've just met."

"It's easier to be kind to strangers, don't you find? We know our friends too well. After a while they don't deserve a thing. But tell me, sir, are you not curious about what I think of the French?" Cleland tilts his head.

Thomas sighs. "Not really. I'm sure I have heard every French joke there is since coming to London." He sips the rum that Cleland has paid for. It's good. He lets Cleland know with an appreciative nod. "All right, Monsieur, what two things are the French good for?"

Cleland smirks. "Lace and whores." He hunches his shoulders as if to say he's sorry, but it's the truth. "The one complements the other, don't you think?"

"Is that a joke?"

"I wonder, is it?"

But then Thomas sees the laughter in Cleland's blue eyes. So Thomas forces a reluctant laugh for his new friend, a man who bought him a drink. "Funny," Thomas adds.

"It seems not. Oh well. I tried."

Thomas's attention goes to Gallatin. Gallatin's eyes are burning into him and he's beckoning Thomas to come over to his side.

"Excuse me for a moment," says Thomas to John Cleland. "My friend wants a word."

"Of course he does. Tame old Earnest John. He wants to warn you away from me. That's my bet."

Thomas blinks at Cleland. "Why would he do that?"

"Any number of reasons, I suppose."

"Alors, what's your guess?"

"That I'm disreputable. That would be a word John Gallatin might choose."

"Tiens, I'll let you know." Thomas walks around the end of the table over to Gallatin.

Gallatin grasps Thomas by the elbow and angles the two of them so that they are both facing the wall, their backs to the table. "Watch out, Thomas. That man is nothing but a rake. I don't know who invited him here tonight. He spends all his time in bagnios and brothels, then writes it up."

"He writes about whores and sex?"

Gallatin nods sternly. "No one publishes him, but I hear that's what he does. Disreputable, he is."

Thomas laughs.

"You think that's funny?" Jean Gallatin squeezes his eyes half shut. He looks at Thomas like he thinks Thomas has lost his mind.

Thomas composes his expression, making it the sternest he can. "You warn me away from him, is that it?"

"I do. Don't get too close."

As he pads back around the table to his seat beside John Cleland, Thomas cannot rein in his broad smile.

"So," says Cleland, "your friend made you laugh? But the question is: was I right? Am I someone to be shunned?"

"It seems you are. And, yes, disreputable was the very word."

"There you have it." Cleland leans back with a smile. "It must be so. Earnest John is not likely to be wrong."

Thomas gives Cleland a long look. "Do you know that I have submitted pages to Edward Cave?"

"I do not. Well done."

"No, nothing is done, not yet. On those pages I compare London to Paris, both ways."

Cleland arches his eyebrows. "Which two ways are those?"

"One against the other, what else?"

Cleland drains the last bit of rum from his glass. "I don't know. Front and back, up and down. You know, like making love. Or coupling, as I think of it."

Thomas snorts a jet of air out his nose. He darts a glance at Gallatin, who happens to be looking back at him, shaking his head. Thomas nods at his friend and understands that the bookseller is now glancing at the stairs. Oh, he gets it. Gallatin is asking him if he's ready to leave. Indeed. Thomas supposes he is. He stands up.

"I'm off, Cleland, but something tells me you could show me a different side of London than I've yet seen."

"You've been to The Rose at Covent Garden?"

"Yes, Hogarth took me there. Did not like it much."

"Not for me either. Better to play than watch, I say. How about the Shakespeare's Head?"

Thomas shakes his head.

"Well, there you go. A quite different den of iniquity, that one is. The man in charge has quite a list. Perhaps you'd like an education there some evening soon?"

"An education?"

John Cleland makes a funny face, then alerts Thomas with his eyes that someone is approaching.

"Come on, let's go." It's Gallatin. He's come to collect Thomas from his conversation and get him up the stairs and out the door.

"Another time, Bookshop John," Cleland sings out. "Must have a chat, I think."

Thomas covers his mouth to hide his laugh as he grabs hold of the thick rope to mount the stairs.

—

"Don't be fooled," says Jean Gallatin the moment he and Thomas push out into the cool air coming out of the Friend at Hand. "That Cleland is no one you want to know."

Thomas keeps his lips sealed for a moment. It's unlike Gallatin to be so visibly upset. And over someone who is as clever and amusing as the fellow Thomas sat beside tonight. Something must have happened between the two of them. "Perhaps you worry too much. He seems harmless enough."

"He is not. Trust me on that."

"In any case, my path and Cleland's are unlikely to cross again."

"I hope that's true. He's a rogue and a rake."

Two for one, thinks Thomas, but keeps it to himself.

Gallatin picks up the pace. He appears not to want to say any more, which suits Thomas very well. He has lots to mull over and figure out. At the top, as usual, is Hélène. His relationship with her remains unfulfilling. In the literal sense. He really must bring things to a head. The choice of words makes him smile. He recalls some conversation long ago when one of the Paris writers made a joke to the effect that the big head cannot think straight if the little head is blocked. Well, that is certainly the case. Eros, his old ally, has practically deserted him. Thomas has bided his time for far too long, leading a monk's life up in the attic of Gallatin's house. He has to get them out of that place. The sand in the glass is running out.

—

The air is close, unseasonably warm and sticky for this early in the year. Of course Hélène knows it cannot last more than a day or two, but such knowledge is no relief. This day must be gone through to get to tomorrow. It's the kind of weather one expects to find in London occasionally in summer, not this early in spring.

Nearly every face shows the effect. If they are not slick with perspiration, they have bedraggled hair or wigs. People are fanning their well-oiled faces with either hats or hands. The only dry brows are those where a mouchoir has just rubbed the sweat away. Many people, especially the older ones, are searching for a clearing breath, for London is blanketed beneath a hot and gritty shroud.

Hélène feels Thomas's fingers tighten round her right hand. They are wending their way through the oncoming sea of unyielding shoulders and determined faces. He appears to find it reassuring to give her hand a tug and make her turn around. She thinks he must feel that he's giving her safety and security in this bustling place. She doesn't mind. She always gives him a tiny smile. Truth be told, she comes through the Covent Garden piazza twice most days, on her way to and from Gallatin's shop.

She doesn't really have anything in mind to buy. It's just that if she and Thomas are going to go somewhere for a walk, it might as well be somewhere she likes. The piazza is one such place. The Spitalfields market close to where they live has all the same fruits and vegetables as does this place, but not on the same scale, nor with so many people on display. She is not vain, but she likes to think that with her blue parasol and blue dress she is the match of anyone on the market square.

—

Thomas takes a shallow breath. The air is so heavy with humidity that it weighs upon the inside of his chest.

Why, for the love of humanity, does Hélène want to go through the piazza and not around? Because of the unprecedented heat, the place stinks like nowhere else. Not as bad as Billingsgate, but for an inland square, it's pretty bad today. And it's coming off the crowd of bodies that carry the hundreds of sweating faces.

Thomas closes his eyes for a moment as he lets Hélène lead them through the human sea. Snippets of passing conversations come and go. He cannot yet distinguish among the different accents the way the English can. They can tell in an instant where a person is from and the class or occupation to which he or she belongs. He supposes he could do the same for France and will eventually be attuned to England should he continue to live in this land.

Thomas hears a woman complaining about some mean thing her absent husband said before he stormed off; how some man's bowels are as loose as a cat's; how a cock-fight bet won five guineas last night; how a merchant woman lost a bundle when a crate of Chinese porcelain was dropped coming off the ship. Half the dishes were cracked.

"What are you doing?"

Thomas feels the edge in Hélène's voice and the squeeze of her hand. "Rien," he says, eyes opened wide. He switches to English. "A bit of fun."

"Well stop it, all right?"

Thomas makes his eyes go very wide, but Hélène does not laugh. She turns around and they continue their winding path across the crowded market space, no longer hand in hand.

It's funny. Thomas knows Hélène better than anyone else. Yet sometimes he wonders if he knows her at all. There's been a change in her since they arrived in London. What that change is precisely he's not sure, but he is certain it stems from the minimal amount of time the two of them spend together and alone. Gallatin has become an influence that is not always for the best, in Thomas's view. Lately he has noticed how Hélène raises her hand, pointer finger up, just like Gallatin, each time she wants to object to something Thomas says. What was humorous with his friend is less so when it's his lover. It's what comes from their working in the same shop.

"You're far away," Thomas hears Hélène say.

"Yes, I suppose." He shrugs. "Another time, another place."

"When are you not?" Hélène goes back to admiring the display of asparagus spears before her.

Thomas half expects her to buy a few and to ask him to put them in his pocket. But she does not. Instead, she goes on to the next stand and admires the carrots. Hélène seems able to appreciate the colours and the scents of nearly everything. This is how it continues as they slowly make their way across the market display. It makes him shake his head.

Since the outing to the bull-baiting at Hockley-in-the-Hole, Hélène generally says no to any suggestion Thomas makes when he proposes exploring unseen corners of the city. So he has given up suggesting any new adventure at all.

It was "no" to taking a long-nosed wherry over to the Southwark side of the Thames. "But why?" she asked. "Don't we have enough dangerous quarters and tenter grounds on this side?"

"She's right," Gallatin had chipped in.

It was even "no" to Westminster. Hire an oarsman to row them there, saving them half of that long walk. Thomas had wanted to stroll through the royal parks. So far he's seen only the tops of the trees in St. James's and Green and Hyde from afar. He studied the latest London map for the manuscript he gave to Edward Cave, but that's not the same as actually walking through the real places.

"Enough for you?" Hélène asks. "It's enough for me."

"You mean you're ready to go?"

"I've been told I need a better education on London town. I was hoping you might be my guide."

"Sérieusement? Who told you that?"

"Jean."

Thomas instantly regrets it but he cannot hold back. He rolls his eyes. He can see that he has displeased Hélène.

· "No? Not inclined?" she asks.

Thomas recomposes his face. He bows. "Well, yes, I am inclined. I will be your guide." He makes a gentlemanly gesture at the north side of the piazza, toward which they have been slowly, though unintentionally, making their way. Though it annoys him that it was Gallatin's suggestion that has done the trick, he has nonetheless been waiting for this for a long time.

"Thomas, I think I should apologize. You're always suggesting places to go and I'm always putting you off. But not today. You choose and I'll follow where you lead. Though some place with a little shade and some quiet might be a good idea."

That sounds better. "I know such places. More than one."

After they leave Covent Garden he'll show her Soho Square, where, if she agrees, they'll be moving soon. Thomas glances up to the clouds. There may not be anyone or anything up there, but he gives a smile of thanks just the same.

———

It pleases Hélène to see Thomas's reaction to her suggestion. One good mood breeds another, does it not? She hopes it lasts.

She and Thomas weave in and around a maze of market tables and stalls. Her only stop is before a wild-haired woman with a tray overflowing with a bountiful display of sticky buns. "Don't they look good?" she asks Thomas.

"Would you like one?" Thomas thrusts a hand into the pocket of his veston, searching for a coin.

"No, no," she says, "I'll be a mess. Maybe on our way back. We could take it to Church Street."

"I'll hold you to that. I want one too."

"Thomas...." says Hélène. But then she looks around. No, it's too crowded, too noisy where they are.

"Yes?" Thomas leans closer so she does not have to yell.

"Nothing. Why don't you take me to find a wild goose?"

"What is that, a wild goose?"

"Un oie sauvage, j'imagine. But I'm not really sure. Jean said it the other day in the shop. It's an exploration of some sort."

"I do not know such an expression. Curious. But let's pretend. Let's wild goose St. James's Square then Soho Square. I have been wanting to show them to you for quite a while."

"Lead on."

Hélène sees Thomas pick at his clothes as discreetly as he can. She can imagine that he's probably wet in the armpits and in the small of his back, as is she. But she knows enough not to let on to anyone who might see. She's surprised Thomas is not more careful about the image he presents.

"In my opinion," Thomas says as he takes her by the elbow and begins to pick up the pace, "Soho Square is for people like us. Our level. I want to show you St. James's Square first, though. It's an address of the topmost ranks. Seven dukes and seven earls is what I hear."

"At that one square?" Hélène cannot stop herself from leaning back.

"So I hear, seven of each, dukes and earls."

Hélène feels the smile upon her face.

"I thought that might pique your interest." Thomas is smirking as he stares at her. "Better than a Russian tailor, would it not?"

Hélène gives him a glare.

"I'm sorry," he says. "Pierre was my friend as well."

"I thought so. He was a good man and his memory deserves better than that."

"Of course." Thomas chooses to be silent for a while as they walk on.

—

"So here we are. Surprising is it not, how from the outside the houses are so alike? It must be on the inside where they excel, the earls and dukes. Which is as it should be, I think. An elevated position is something owners should enjoy privately. Not display to people like us walking by." Thomas makes sure his shoulders are erect and his head held high.

"Is that how you would be, should fortune come your way? You'd keep your wealth hidden away?"

"I'd like to think I would."

He watches Hélène shake her head.

"Well, you'd be a crowd of one. People wear their level for all to see. You know that as well as anyone. For a man it's the cost of the fabric and its cut, the buckles on his shoes. The type of coach. A pocket watch or fancy cane. For us it's the dresses we wear. The jewellery and shoes. Display is how we live."

Thomas glances around the crowded square. He doesn't like being challenged by Hélène, but he acknowledges that she is correct. He spies three young women with wide, straw bonnets strolling side by side. It's obvious they are not servants of any kind. Watching the young women pass are two men of obvious standing. They are wearing close-cropped periwigs, the tail ends tied and covered by black taffeta bags. Another man off to the left has a wig that rises up like an ocean wave. A fop, to be sure, but one with a stream of income that means he doesn't have to think about finding work. Farther on an even younger man who clearly wants to be noticed as he struts by. His wig is powdered a brilliant white. "You're right," Thomas says at last.

He and Hélène wait for a water-carrier, a broad-shouldered young man, to pass by. Thomas catches Hélène's whisper after the man has passed.

"It's only monks and nuns who want to hide away. Those with wealth and leisure want everyone to know what they've achieved."

"Or been born into," Thomas adds.

Hélène gives Thomas a warm smile. "Not our lot, alas."

Thomas returns her smile. They are silent for a while as they leave the square. They follow behind a man holding up half a dozen cages of wild birds. Thomas wonders if they are for amusement inside people's homes or whether they are to have their necks wrung for food. Back on a street with shops, he and Hélène go past cutlers and silversmiths, linen-drapers and haberdashers, clockmakers and tailors, pewterers and perruquiers, bookbinders and wine merchants, leather breech makers and undertakers. Paris has lots of shops, but nowhere near as many as Thomas sees in London. He must remember to make that point in his book. If only he would hear from Cave. Does the man not see the value and interest that Thomas's comparisons will generate? And that means sales, in other words.

Hélène comes to a stop in front of Thomas Berry's shop. The display in the window of fine leather pattens and clogs halts her in her tracks. To see her study the different styles makes Thomas smile. Women and their shoes. Right up there with jewellery. He bides his time as long as he can.

"We're almost there, you know," he says at last. He nudges her with his elbow. "Five minutes at most."

"Almost where?" There is surprise, not consternation, on her face.

"Soho Square. Where we're going to."

"No, I don't think." Hélène's face is flushed. The warmth of the day is taking its toll on her.

"But it's just up ahead. See that carriage? The one painted black with gold trim? With two horses? It's turning into the circle that runs around the square. That's it. That's Soho Square. We're almost there."

"No," says Hélène.

The cast of her eyes and the set of her chin tell Thomas there is no going farther on this day. The visit to Soho Square will have to wait. Which means the conversation they need to have about leaving Gallatin's address also goes on hold.

"I'm sorry, Thomas. I see you're disappointed. But my feet are sore. And it's too warm. We'll have to get a hell-cart back home."

—

Inside the hackney coach, Hélène slides off her shoes. One at a time she caresses the soles of her feet.

She notices Thomas has gone silent. It's how he gets when he's angry with her. Oh well, he'll cheer up. "What's this area called?" she asks, just to get him speaking again.

"Leicester Field."

"Anything special here?"

"Frederick, the Prince of Wales, lives in that house over there." Thomas points half-heartedly.

"Are you angry with me?"

"No. Why?" His eyes sweep fleetingly over her face.

"You're chewing your lower lip and hardly saying a thing. It gives you away."

Thomas grimaces. It takes a moment, but he brings his eyes to meet hers. "I think you're wrong," he says at last.

"About?"

"Anger."

Hélène leans all the way back in the seat on her side. "Am I now? What about the strain in your voice and on your face?"

Thomas takes a deep breath. Hélène sees that for a while at least, he'll be keeping to himself. He has turned to the world beyond the window on his side. Hélène swings to the window on her side. Outside she sees a chestnut tree, its white billowy blossoms unfolded to their full extent. A small brown bird, a sparrow, she thinks, lands on the nearest branch. In its beak it has a twig – no, maybe it's a length of ribbon or a brushed-out tangle from some child's hair. The little bird must be building a nest.

"Tell me, Thomas," Hélène says, speaking in a tone that she hopes will tell him she wants their spat over and done, "have you ever thought of having a child?"

Thomas turns to her. "A child? Un bébé?"

"That's how they come."

"I—" Thomas puts a hand up in the air. He squints at Hélène to see if he perhaps misunderstood.

"That's all right. I was simply curious." Hélène goes back to the window. The hell-cart they're in has moved on. She can no longer see the chestnut tree or little bird.

—

They descend from the hackney in front of Christ Church. Thomas looks up to admire its most slender spire. So elegant, it seems to rise up almost to the overhanging clouds. It's only a five-minute walk to where they live. Bah, where they live in another man's house. Gallatin's, not theirs. Thomas feels a weight in his chest magnify. He scuffs his shoes on the cobbles as they turn the corner onto Church Street. Why don't things work out?

He feels Hélène touch his elbow. He looks up. There's an expression he doesn't recognize on her face. Clearly there's something she wants to say. He recalls her question about having a child. Is that it? She wants him to father her a child? If so, Thomas will have to tell her he will go along only if they move into a place of their own.

"Thomas," Hélène says, soft as wool.

But then she can say no more. A dozen laughing silk weavers are sweeping up the street from Brick Lane. Their chatter is entirely in French. Thomas pretends he is examining the brickwork and shutters of all the buildings on the street, but he is really listening in. The talk is of some newcomer recently come from northern France. What a bumpkin he is.

"Thomas." Hélène is shaking her head.

"You know, I miss hearing and speaking French," he says. To which he sees her gently shake her head.

Thomas examines her eyes. She really doesn't care which language she hears or speaks. It's just a means to an end for her. Him, he misses the nuances of ideas and expressions that can only be made in French. Her, she—

"Thomas, I—"

"Minute," he says, pronouncing it in French. He suddenly thinks that maybe a child would not be so bad. He could be a father, a better father than the one he had. He wouldn't force any son of his into the Church. Of course, it could be a girl. In that case, Thomas would—

Hélène grabs his sleeve. "I have something to say."

Thomas leans back. Her tone is insisting he not talk.

"Et nous voici," he says, surprising himself. "Chez notre cher Gallatin."

They are standing directly in front of number five. Thomas scans the windows on every floor. There is no sign of Gallatin or the servant Polly peeking out. He returns his gaze to Hélène.

For an instant, she looks down at the cobbled street. Slowly she lifts her head. He can see that she's worried about something. It has to be the motherhood issue she brought up. Yes, Thomas could be the father if he must.

Hélène reaches out. She takes a strand of Thomas's wayward dark brown hair and tucks it behind his ear.

"Je t'attends, ma chère." Thomas gestures with his hands for her to hurry up.

"You recall that Jean has a roommate, do you not?"

"Beside us, you mean? Yes. The Scot. The one on the grand tour."

Hélène's face shows relief. It comes out as a little laugh. "Yes, Johnson. That's right."

"How could I not recall? Touring Italy. Seeing the ruins. Which to Gallatin is a dream come true."

Hélène grimaces. "Well, he's coming back, Johnson is. A letter arrived yesterday. From Genoa. Jean passed it to me at the shop. I read it myself."

A smile slowly comes to Thomas's lips. Oh, he sees where this is going. "And Gallatin no longer has room for us? The Scot will want his room back?" *Finally, a way out.*

"Why, yes. And you don't mind, Thomas? It seems not, by the look on your face."

"Mind? Oh, Hélène, this is good. I've been thinking for a long while about just this." He grabs hold of her shoulders and presses his lips to hers.

Hélène blinks. She moves him back. "Well, excellent. You still have a fortnight at least. So there really is no rush."

"The sooner the better."

Hélène's eyes go wide. "Vraiment? Well, if you want."

"I've been thinking Soho Square." Thomas's whole body feels like it has come alive. "That's why in fact I wanted to show it to you today on our walk. We'll find rooms, I promise, that are to your taste."

"*My* taste?" Hélène squints at Thomas. Slowly she starts to shake her head.

"Quoi?" Thomas's eyes and mouth start to mirror what he is seeing in her troubled look. He does not understand why she's not as pleased as he is. "Yes, I learned that lesson in Paris years ago. You recall? You have to like our rooms. So," he says, holding out a self-evident hand, "I will not choose them by myself."

"Oh, Thomas." Hélène's eyes go watery.

Both of Thomas's hands go up, each confused.

"I'm sorry. So sorry." She appears to be on the verge of tears.

Thomas comes close and kisses Hélène quickly on the cheek, then slowly on each eye. He whispers, "It'll be all right. You'll come to prefer our new place." He leans back. He takes in her bewildered face.

"Thomas, Thomas." Hélène rubs her eyes. She swells her chest with an intake of air. It comes back out as a rapid exhale of breath.

He summons a smile to reassure her that everything will work out.

"Thomas, it's not we who are moving out." She inclines her head and looks at him with sorrowful eyes. "It's you. Only you."

——

"I had no idea. You have to believe me." Jean Gallatin's earnest face and one outstretched hand implore his friend to understand that he means what he says. The two friends are striding along a rapidly darkening street.

"Of course you didn't." Thomas makes sure his expression is indifferent, no matter how he really feels. "Je te crois, Gallatin. I do."

Five days ago Hélène told Thomas that she is now with the bookseller and he, Thomas, has a fortnight to move out. Over the course of those angry and disappointed days and nights Thomas has rationalized that no one has really done anything wrong. No matter how alone and apart Hélène's betrayal makes him feel, stuck as he is in a foreign city working at a level far below where he should rightfully be, he cannot blame Jean Gallatin. Thomas never told him the truth about him and Hélène. So it's a rough justice of sorts, where you get hoisted on your own petard. Or in this case, his own canard.

As for Hélène, she did what she's always done. That is, she went after what's best for her. Thomas cannot fault her for that, even though he wants to. If only it had been for a duke or an earl instead of Gallatin. That would have been better than this. Gallatin may be a friend, but after all he's only a bookseller and a minor printer, someone no better than himself. If Thomas had only known how important it was to Hélène, he would have taught her to read himself.

"You're sure?" asks Gallatin.

"I said so. Don't ask again, all right?" Thomas pats the bookseller on the back.

It's simple, really: Thomas will have to find another way to get along. He had a life without Hélène, before and after they met. He can do so again. He has already found a small apartment to move into, one that will suit him well. It's away from Spitalfields and any chance encounters with Hélène. When he moves his things in a few days he'll be at the far end of elbow-shaped Falconbridge Court, off Sutton Street. It's only steps away from Soho Square, where once he thought he and—

Through curled lips Thomas blows out a jet of air.

As a cul-de-sac, Falconbridge Court should be quiet if nothing else. He'll have ample room for his books and manuscripts. It goes without saying it will be a better place to write. No chill attic, no ex-lover living with his friend on the floor below. Two improvements there, they surely are.

"I did not ask her to say any such thing," says Gallatin as they continue to hurry along. "You have to believe me, you must. If you want to stay on a while after Johnson returns, we'll find a way, we will."

"No, it's all right." Thomas tries a smile, but he doubts it looks right.

"I was intending to tell you about Johnson's return. I was waiting for the right time."

Thomas glances at his friend. He looks as worried as Thomas feels bitter. "Jean, you could not have known about the relationship we'd had."

Gallatin slows to a stop. "Who are you talking about? You and Hélène?"

Hélène has not told him everything, obviously. Maybe not even very much. Thomas purses his lips.

"The weather has certainly cooled down." He rolls up the collar of his greatcoat and tugs on his hat. He has to be careful with every word. "Yes, I'm talking about me and Hélène. We've been friends. We shared ... a bit of a history in France."

Gallatin's eyes take Thomas's measure. "A history? What does that mean? Was this while you and I were friends?"

"Let's get going. We don't want to be late. I'm hoping Cave will be there tonight. I'm still waiting to learn what he thinks."

"Of course. It is getting too chilly to stand."

They pick up the pace toward the Friend at Hand.

"But back to what you just said, about you and Hélène having a history. Right from that first evening you arrived in London I could see the two of you were, well, close. Closer than one normally finds cousins, which she now tells me in fact you're not."

"She told you that?"

"Yes, she did. The way you two stood together, it wasn't the way people stand who are not close. A glance between you two was sometimes communication enough."

"Maybe sometimes it was."

"No 'maybe' about it. It was. But look at you, trying to make your face a mask. You do that, Thomas, when you are unsettled and have something to hide. Do you know that about yourself, my friend?"

Thomas rolls his eyes. "S'il te plaît. I do not hide and I'm not unsettled." He feels a surge of anger well up from deep inside. "Look, it's good that I'm moving out. It's good for you to be with Hélène. And I am thankful you let me stay in your house as long as you did. Merci."

Gallatin reaches out to make contact with Thomas's sleeve. He brings the two of them to a halt beneath a wooden sign that has a painted image of a pair of men's riding boots. "You sound so fierce. We should talk about this."

"What *this*? There is no *this*."

Two women approach, each dressed in washed-out greyish fabric and each with a white cap on her head. There are no holes in their clothes, but their skirts and jackets are threadbare. Thomas concludes they are servants not whores. They'd be dolled up in one garish way or another if their affections and bodies were for sale. For amusement Thomas tips his tricorne at them as they go by. The younger servant, with as plain a face as a face can be, gives him back an embarrassed smile. The older woman tugs her by the hand and drags her on.

Gallatin waits until the women have passed. Then he turns to Thomas and grabs him by the shoulders. "Come clean. No subterfuge."

Thomas finds a smile coming to his face. "As you wish. I'll tell you all you want. But can we at least keep walking? Il se fait tard, mon ami."

"All right." Gallatin sets his chin as he begins to walk. "Go on."

"No, you tell me what Hélène told you. I'll add or take away as I must."

"Well, I learned she is no cousin of yours. It was a pretence to protect her honour as you travelled into this land."

"Correct."

"And she was orphaned as a young girl and grew up with her uncle and aunt in Évreux."

"So I understand."

"And you two met in Paris."

Thomas mumbles his accord, though with a tentative tilt of his head.

"She married a Russian tailor, who was your tailor as it happened. You were often in the shop. And when he died— what? Is there something wrong with that?"

Thomas has rolled and bitten his lips, no more than that. So, Hélène's given Gallatin a much abridged version of her life, leaving out all the bits with Thomas as her lover over the years. And no mention of her time as a prostitute then a servant-cum-pretend-aristocrat in the service of Marguerite. Well, Thomas cannot blame her for that. He'd do the same. A life story needs to be tailored to its audience. Gallatin has accepted the story for what it is. Thomas is not about to dash her tale. Nothing to be gained in that. Who knows, someday maybe she'll do the same for him.

"No, no, Jean. I was merely interested to hear a few details I did not know."

"But you made a face." Gallatin bites his lips, only much more exaggeratedly than Thomas had done.

"The sausages I had at noon, perhaps?"

"Well, Hélène says you came to the Russian's funeral and offered your condolences. Then a few weeks later you were back in the shop. That was when you suggested the two of you might travel together to London. For the added safety and convenience that would bring."

Thomas does admire Hélène's ability to shape a simple tale. She understands that the trick is less what you put in than what you leave out. Let the listener fill in the gaps. "There is a little something I could add. One day in the tailor shop – Hélène used to help out the Russian – she was looking especially triste. I asked her what was wrong. Everyone knew Pierre was ill by then. She didn't want to tell me at first, but I insisted. At last she said she was mulling over what she would do if her husband's illness took him away. I happened to mention that I had a friend, a bookseller, in London who wrote of his satisfaction with England. C'était toi, Gallatin."

Thomas sees that Jean Gallatin is delighted to have been part of Hélène's story so early on.

Thomas continues. "I was bold. I asked her if she had ever thought of changing lands. Like Pierre, her husband, had once done. And like my friend, the bookseller. She replied that she had, back before she was wed. She said she'd once met some English travellers in an inn. Those various influences gave her a notion that someday she too would like to cross the Manche. To see what the other side was like."

"She did not mention that."

"Non?" queries Thomas. He hunches his shoulders. It would have been something if Hélène had told Gallatin a story Thomas has just made up.

"But tell me one thing, Thomas. Were you not married at that time? To Marguerite Salles? How could you speak to Hélène about leaving France when you had a wife?"

Thomas feels his eyes flicker. His mouth loses its easy rest. "Ah oui. Marguerite. Oui, oui, Marguerite. Yes, she had just died. It was around the same time as Hélène's tailor husband's death. So I too was un veuf, a widower, by then. Hard to recall. But yes, I recall. I came to the tailor shop to pick up a new funeral coat and Hélène reminded me of our earlier conversation. Or maybe I reminded her. So long ago. It does not matter, I think. We were each widowed and eager to start over somewhere else. Oh, look, our coffee house is just ahead. Notre ami is at hand." Thomas arches his eyebrows at his little joke.

"Thank you. Merci, Thomas." Gallatin actually shakes Thomas's hand. "Hélène did not go into such details. It's good to hear."

It comes to Thomas, looking into Gallatin's delighted eyes, that he could have a bit of fun with the fellow. He comes to a halt. They are not twenty paces from the doorway to the Friend at Hand. "Écoutez. There is one thing. One thing about Hélène you may not know." His tone is deep and worried.

"What is that?" Jean Gallatin's eyes narrow. His jaw appears readied for the worst.

"She is a believer. Did you know that? She still follows the teachings of the Catholic faith and its pope."

"Oh that." Gallatin's relief shows itself as a noisy laugh. "Come on, let's go in."

"But you have always said religion is—"

"I know, I know. But she and I have spoken of this many times in the shop."

"Et alors?"

"We agree to meet halfway."

Thomas blinks. "What is halfway between a Catholic and an atheist?"

"The Quakers. At least that's what we've agreed."

"The Quakers." Thomas mulls whether the self-described Friends, with their deliberately drab clothing and long serious faces, might fall halfway between a lavish Roman religion and a denial that there is any god at all. Why yes, they just might.

"We're going to attend a meeting of the Friends in the weeks ahead. We'll see if it will be enough for her and at the same time acceptable to me. The Quakers do much good, I admit." All at once Gallatin claps Thomas on the shoulder. "After all, religions are just stories we tell ourselves so we won't worry about our deaths. Their Quaker story likely won't do any more harm than having no story at all."

"I cannot disagree. In fact, I'm impressed."

"In any case, no more hard feelings? About Johnson coming back and you giving up your room?"

"All behind me now." Thomas reasons that if he keeps telling himself that he does not care about losing Hélène, eventually he will not. "Here we are." Thomas points at the wooden sign above their heads, its painted image of a large white dog with liquid brown eyes.

"You ever have a dog, Thomas?" asks Gallatin.

"No, but it's an enticing idea, is it not? Something being unquestionably faithful, no matter what."

Gallatin's eyes pinch. But then he looks up and over Thomas's shoulder. "Aha, here comes the man you want."

Thomas swings round. So it is. Edward Cave. When he recognizes Thomas, a great grin comes to his face. Thomas sees that he has what looks like a sheaf of paper tucked underneath his arm.

"Looks like good news, Thomas. Congratulations. Listen, I'll leave you two alone. I'm going downstairs." Gallatin tenders a wave. "See you in a bit."

"Hello, Edward." Thomas holds out a cautious hand. He thinks Cave's smile of recognition a good sign, though he wishes it were not quite so fixed, so apparently immovable on the man's face. "It's been a while, I guess."

Cave takes the hand, but the contact is weak. "It has, Tyrell, and I apologize for that. You see, I've been swamped. Everyone is writing something, it seems. And yes, I'm well."

"Should we get a table where we can talk?" Thomas nods at the manuscript under Cave's arm. "Where we can go over it?" He is surprised, embarrassed maybe, by how fast his heart is starting to race. He knows better than to get his hopes raised, but his heart does not.

The smile that was frozen on Cave's face melts away. "A table? Oh you mean inside. No. No, I don't think." The publisher holds out the pages for Thomas to take.

Thomas feels trickles of warmth starting in his armpits. "But you— you had a chance to read through the book? The manuscript I mean." He accepts the proffered package, but he finds he cannot hold Cave's gaze. Instead, he finds himself staring at the sheaf of pages like they might speak or come to life.

"It's an intriguing read, Tyrell, it really is."

Thomas looks up. Cave's expression is that of someone who has just heard grave news. More than that, the publisher is inching away from him. When Cave sees that Thomas is watching his feet, he comes to a halt.

"It's fascinating, quite fascinating in places, Tyrell. You have definite powers of observation, you do."

Thomas's heart slows to a crawl. He tilts his head to try and grasp what Cave is telling him. He's sorry if he's nearly squinting at the man, but it's the only way he can hear what he's saying.

"But the thing is—"

Thomas looks away.

"The thing is, I'm afraid, well, it's not for us. The *Gentleman's Magazine.*"

Thomas comes back to look Cave in the eyes. "No? It's not?" He hears his voice as if it's coming from someone else.

"No, but it's good, very good. Please consider us again. Something a little lighter and more entertaining. That's what our readers want, you understand. Stories, words that leap off the page."

Thomas nods but he can no longer look Cave in the face. The man raised his hopes then dashed them like that. Thomas will give him no pleasantries at all. No word of thanks, no good riddance. No parting handshake between two gentlemen and no gesture for Cave to go fuck himself.

Thomas sees Cave's feet take a few steps. The man wheels and heads back to wherever in hell he came from.

Thomas looks up at the dog on the painted sign. The one and only thing he can do is exhale. He tries to blow out his lost hope and his swelling disappointment with one long, foul breath. His fondest hope is gone. Disappointment remains.

He looks down at what's in his hands. A worthless bundle of pages covered with his handwriting in ink. So much time and effort, and all for what? Thomas shakes his head. Should he throw it away? No, he could use it to light a fire in a grate.

"Good Lord, man, whatever it is, it can't be that bad."

Thomas turns round. It's John Cleland striding up. He comes to a stop an arm's length away. "Looks like you've lost your best friend."

Thomas snorts a laugh. "If you only knew, Cleland, if you only knew. It's not been a good few days."

"I saw Cave beating it away from here a moment ago. Does your mood have something to do with him? Ah, you're clutching a manuscript. Let me guess. He just gave it back."

Thomas nods.

"Great wind out Edward Cave's arse, Tyrell, this can't be the first time you've been turned down."

Thomas shrugs.

"Hang on to the blessed thing. You'll find a way to insert bits and pieces of it into something else. Trust me, that's what we do, writers like us. Not much goes to waste."

"Keep it up and you'll make me smile, Cleland."

"That's the spirit. Come on, let's go in and see what disappointments the others have had. We all get our share."

Thomas shakes his head. "Not me. I'll not trumpet my failings before them. I don't want any phony commiseration."

"All right then, my French friend, how about I take you somewhere?"

"Where's that?"

"Just a place to give you a lift." Cleland winks. "It'll further your education, as I think I once promised you I would."

"Lead on then. Allons-y, Alonzo."

"Alonzo? What's that?" asks Cleland as he turns and begins to walk away from the inn, Thomas following at his side.

"Nothing. It's an amusement in French."

"Really, you French. By the way, I've thought of a third."

Thomas looks at him quizzically. "A third? A third what?"

"A third thing the French have contributed to the world. My mother Lucy sports a French name, so I'm partial to your race. I'm still waiting for the Spaniards to contribute something."

Thomas hoots, and feels his mood shift. "If memory serves, it was only lace and whores. Is that right?"

"True enough. Until I came up with the third.

Thomas shakes his head in amused disbelief. He's finding it hard not to beam at his friend. "Let me guess: our French writers, painters, musicians, perchance?"

"Good God, no. Not worth a scrap. Give up?"

"I do."

"Cundums is what."

"Cundums? Oh, condoms. French safes, as you English say."

"Le gant anglais, n'est-ce pas?" John Cleland inclines his head and makes a sly grin, then he picks up the pace, which Thomas matches.

"You seem to know a lot of French, Cleland. Why don't you speak it with me?"

"Ah, I choose not to be mediocre is why. So my French is only pour faire l'amour with the best French tarts." Cleland gives Thomas a wink.

"All right. But how about you at least tell me where we're going?"

John Cleland slows the marching pace for a moment. He turns to his friend. "Is that not why you're coming along? Precisely because you know not where we're headed?"

Thomas is taken aback. Cleland is right. That is exactly why he's drawn to accompanying this slightly mad Englishman wherever he leads. For as long as they're moving, future unknown, the adventure holds the promise of something better than what Thomas has now. Which is nothing.

—

"There he is. Knew he'd be around." John Cleland is using his outstretched hand to direct Thomas's gaze.

Thomas sees a thin, almost gaunt-looking man coming down a set of stairs into the large central room on the ground floor. They are in what the sign outside says is the Shakespeare's Head.

In one hand this man Cleland has identified has a rolled-up funnel of folio sheets. With his other hand he's making caressing contact with the backs or shoulders of nearly every person he walks past. He appears to have a quiet word for all. All spoken to and tapped respond with smiles and winks. If this were a court, Thomas thinks, this little man would be king.

"Only the head waiter," whispers Cleland, "yet our Billy Bing runs the place."

"Is that right?" Thomas does notice that those working in the inn, at the counter where the drinks are dispensed or the ones carrying trays to or from the tables, straighten up and move a little faster after Mr. Bing comes down the stairs. The head waiter's eyes never rest. Everything in the room is under his shifting gaze.

"Just wait," Cleland says. "Wait until you see what he has on those rolled-up sheets."

"Is that why we're here?" Thomas holds up the manuscript pages that Edward Cave returned. "Because we're not short of paper."

John Cleland's eyebrows lift. "Billy's list is literature of a different sort. Wait here."

Cleland glides over to Bing and touches his elbow. At once the man leans Cleland's way. Thomas watches as the two lean close and trade words. Cleland points at Thomas and says something else. The head waiter gives Thomas several knowing nods, which makes Thomas tilt sharply back. He does not wish to be so singled out. His back brushes against the wooden rack of pewter measures, sending one into the air. He catches it and puts it back. When he turns back to the room, Cleland and the head waiter are less than an arm's length away.

"Billy Bing," the waiter introduces himself. He's holding out his right hand.

"So I hear," Thomas says. He gives the man's hand a quick shake. "My friend here," Thomas gestures at Cleland, "sings your praises."

Billy Bing shrugs. "Well, friend here has known me for a while. I do what I can. In the service of nature and mankind."

Thomas tries not to look startled at such a claim. "I see." He looks the man up and down. He is not a physician nor a judge nor an apothecary. "How as a head waiter can you—"

"Billy," Cleland interjects, "please call him Billy, will you Tyrell. Why he's a purveyor. A purveyor of untold pleasures of—"

Billy Bing reaches out and taps Cleland on the forearm. "Best if we go somewhere to sit. Away from too many ears."

Cleland blinks his agreement. Billy surveys the noisy, smoke-filled room. It seems to Thomas that he winces at one particular table. Four foppishly dressed aristocrats are taking turns singing at the top of their lungs. It's a stupid ditty that amuses no one but their drunken selves. With a decisive nod to Cleland and Thomas, Billy tells them to stay where they are. He walks over to a table in a far corner of the room where two bleary-eyed men are nursing mugs of something much stronger than coffee. The two men stare stupidly at Billy for an instant before jumping to their feet. They shuffle off, though not without looking back with sour faces at the man who has made them move.

"Here we go," Billy calls out, his voice loud. He beckons Thomas and Cleland. "This table just came up."

Evidently pleased by what he has just seen, Cleland mouths to Thomas on the way: "That's Billy Bing."

Thomas does not think he smiles in return. He's been in lots of noisy places crowded with late-night men over the years. He has learned that such places are not really for him. It would be better if he were back at Gallatin's making sure he has packed up all his books and manuscripts. And deciding what to do with the pages Cave has rejected. The relocation to Falconbridge Court comes in two days. Nonetheless, Thomas has come this far. He supposes Billy Bing deserves a chance to show what it is he does that Cleland so admires.

All three men take a seat. Thomas decides to place his rejected book under his ass rather than on the table. An instant later one of the servants with a tray deposits two steaming mugs in front of them. Billy Bing waves the servant away.

"For you, my friends, warming coffees," he says. "Our Shakespeare's Head is here to help our customers relax."

Thomas forces an appreciative smile. He reaches out to the mug. Yet instead of bringing it closer he edges it a fraction of an inch farther away. He doesn't like to be told what and when to drink. Cleland, however, is taking a savouring sip. He nods at Thomas as if the coffee is exactly what he needs.

—

Thomas glances round, beginning with the framed engravings on the walls. They are bedroom scenes with women in various states of undress. So that must be it. This Billy across the table is a purveyor of flesh. Not much of a surprise there. Thomas wonders how long he'll have to sit in this place. Once again there's a lesson in this outing. Don't be seduced by any alluring talk of mystery. The sad truth is that having just passed his thirty-third birthday, there are no more mysteries in this sorry world. Paris, London; cities everywhere seem to be the same. What's left? Maybe cross the ocean and see how things are in the New World? Can it really be so new?

"So, sir...." Billy turns exclusively to Thomas.

Thomas purses his lips. He shoots a look at Cleland. His new friend's expression says that he is more than a little enamoured with Mr. Bing. When Thomas comes back to the head waiter, he finds Billy is studying him like he's a pressed plant in a book.

"Friend here tells me you have tastes especial. From France you are. And you found that the posture molls at The Rose were...." Billy hesitates. "Not to your taste. Prefer the touch to the look, is that it?"

Thomas does not reply. He sets his countenance so as to not betray any feeling or thought. He half expects such talk from Cleland, but he does not like the way Billy Bing is sizing him up.

"Come on, Tyrell," Cleland says. "Give the man a hint. It's all he needs. He has a *list*."

Billy Bing leans back, as if to take Thomas in from a different angle. Then he comes forward in his chair. He places his forearms on the table and cradles the rolled-up funnel of paper in his right hand just inches away from Thomas's mug. With the funnel he pushes the mug back toward Thomas just a bit. "Yes, friend, I do," Billy says. "And quite a list it is, if I do say so."

Billy unfurls the funnel of paper. Thomas follows the man's eyes as they scan whatever is written on the top sheet. Then Billy lifts that sheet and has a quick look at the sheet underneath. Then comes a cursory peek at one below that. It looks to Thomas as if there may be a dozen sheets or more. A list, yes, but a list of what?

"Your bible, is it?" Thomas asks. He knows there's mockery in his eyes.

Billy Bing looks his way. His eyes don't respond to Thomas's challenge at all. Instead, he sighs. "Something like that, yes. Friend here says you're in the mood, yet your face says you are not. Which is it? It's a busy night. I have other customers if you've only come to scoff."

Thomas blinks. He feels himself lean back against the chair. Before he can come up with a response, Cleland speaks on his behalf. "Of course Tyrell is in the mood. It's why we're here. Don't be coy, Billy. Give him a bit of what's on the list. Tyrell, you pay close attention to this."

And so begins Thomas's education about the world of availability within the Shakespeare's Head. Depending on Thomas's choice, he could have any number of pleasures at his command. A few are upstairs, but most, many pages' worth, are on Billy's extensive and detailed list. They cover willing ladies throughout the city and on both sides of the Thames. Any more than a block or two away will have to be arranged. There's Cherry, for instance, who boasts red cheeks, red lips and according to the notes on the list – and Billy Bing arches his eyebrows at this – a red something else.

"Oh my." Cleland winces at the thought. "I've seen a drawing of a monkey like that." He shakes his head.

Billy continues as if Cleland had not said a thing. There's Miss Love, who is finely furred below. She's a mulatto of dark complexion, a damned fine hairy piece if Billy does say so. Cleland chimes in that he can vouch for her. There's Miss Lorraine, a Jewess it's true. Genteel in appearance and has a fine and pretty face. Bing's list notes that she swears very little for someone in her line of work. Or if Thomas wants a bargain, Miss Robinson will go for less than a pound. But it's a bit of a hike to her place. She does it in a cabinet in her suite of rooms, not far from the Seven Dials.

"No," says Cleland on Thomas's behalf.

Or there's the Armenian, whose name Thomas does not catch. Of middling size, with coal black hair and eyes, and, according to the list, very vigorous in the sack. Or Miss Cross, a black-eyed gypsy with a curious yet delightful manner of wiggling herself. Billy says he's never had a complaint. Most find it worth the extra pennies. She'll be just a little over a pound. Much different is Kitty. She's from Ireland but a veteran in London now.

"But thirteen when she arrived and is now past thirty I think." Billy squints at Thomas to see if that triggers something. "Not a race she's not done. Jews, Papists, Turks, whatever, Kitty has had them all. Especially likes the French." Billy glances up at Thomas from his list.

"Let me see that." Thomas holds out an open hand. He's beginning to think the man is not reading but making half of this up as he goes along.

Billy shakes his head. "The list is for no eyes but my own."

"Only fair," says Cleland. He gives Thomas something of a warning look. "Cannot have been easy to compile such a list."

"It was not. Thank you, Friend. It's a knowledge and a service I gladly share. For a price."

"All right, go on," Thomas says. But he retrieves his own rejected manuscript from under his ass and puts it on the table beside his untouched mug of coffee. He figures another few minutes and he'll head off. Cleland can do what he wants.

Thomas gives a quick glance around the room. He notices, as he had not before, that there are two sets of stairs to whatever lies upstairs. He sees a file of men coming down one set, all of the well-to-do sort, with their wigs fitted and properly kept. He guesses there must be a club meeting of some sort just overhead. Yes, indeed, one of the men has what looks like a record book tucked under one arm. At the other end of the long room there's a man beginning to mount the stairs with a woman who is clearly for sale. He already has his hand up her skirt and they're not yet out of sight. So it must be at that end of the big room where the ladies on Billy Bing's list come and go.

"Still with us, friend?"

Thomas's gaze comes back to Billy Bing.

"Just getting the feel of the place," he says. "Quite a—" Thomas cannot think of what word would come next.

"That's right." Billy lifts a sheet and reads from the one below. "Here's one: wicked as a devil, it says. From the sugar islands, she is. How does that sound? Fancy a bit of brown?"

"Perhaps not tonight." Thomas digs into his pocket and pulls out his watch.

"Here's a Cleopatra. From the real Egypt too. Flays her arms like no one else."

Thomas shakes his head. Are there more Egypts than the one?

A loud wailing noise begins close by the entrance to the place. A drunken soul has just ventured in with a hurdy-gurdy and begun to crank its wheel. There are shouts of "Not in here!" and "Get out!" One of the waiters, a burly chap, sends the poor man on his way with a boot to the ass. From outside the hurdy-gurdy make a sad sound as it strikes the ground.

"Fanny then?" Billy is seemingly oblivious to the cacophony at the other end of the room. "Just arrived from the country. Pretty as a picture. Sandy hair. Breasts like peaches. Fifteen she is and not yet deflowered. Special price if you want to be the first?"

Thomas glances at Cleland with skeptical eyes. How many times do pimps sell their young ones as virgins?

Cleland slides off Thomas's mocking look. He reaches across the table to tap Billy on the arm. "What county is she from?"

Billy Bing smiles at Cleland. "I know she'll tell you if you ask. What county do you want? Gloucestershire, I bet."

Cleland appears to be thinking about that. And about the Fanny Mr. Bing has described.

Billy swivels back to Thomas. "Dolly? She's built like a Dutch boat."

Thomas laughs. "And what does that mean?"

He looks at Cleland, who is apparently surprised Thomas does not know. "A broad bottom," Cleland explains.

"That's right," Billy adds. "Keeps things comfortable, and solidly on the bed."

"Oh." Thomas clicks the lid on his watch. A quarter past midnight. A quarter hour more and he'll be off. No matter what John Cleland or this Billy says.

"Here's one of pygmy size?"

Thomas rolls his eyes.

Billy goes to the last page. "How about Miss Laycock. She lives up to her name."

It takes Thomas a moment to grasp the supposed humour in that. "Oh, I see. No."

Billy leans forward toward Thomas. Cleland leans in so he too can hear. "Our Miss Laycock has a special way to restore the spent thing."

Cleland smiles at Thomas. "Revives the stallion after its run."

Billy Bing points at Cleland. "There you go, friend. A fine way with words, you have. I should get you to help with the descriptions on the list."

Cleland shrugs but is clearly pleased. Billy turns back to Thomas. "Miss Laycock is a linguist, if you know what I mean."

Thomas knows exactly what he means, but instead of replying he brings out his watch again. Five more minutes.

"Posterior?" inquires Billy. His list is rolled up and put away, back into the funnel it was. "Costs more, but the preference of some." He flashes a quick look Cleland's way. "Friend here might agree?" Billy leans back and waits for Cleland to comment. Cleland makes a non-committal face, but he rubs his chin like there's a spot he wants to eliminate. It's enough to make Thomas laugh.

Thomas leans forward to Billy. "Des femmes françaises? I mean do you have—"

"Any French?" For the first time since he began to read names off his list, Billy finally settles back in his chair. There even comes a smile, a genuine smile. "What kind of purveyor would I be, as Friend here describes me, without the charms of the French? There just might be one waiting for you upstairs right now."

Thomas fights to keep a straight face. "Already? French? With dark eyes and dark hair?"

"Mais oui." Billy is having fun. He has worked hard to get the transaction to this point, Thomas has to admit.

Thomas glances at his new English friend, as usual dressed in his expensive green coat. If Thomas reads Cleland's open-mouthed expression correctly, his companion is surprised that after all the exotic delicacies on Billy's list, Thomas has selected a woman whose only requisite commodity is that she be French. Thomas turns back to Billy. "The name of this woman, could it be Hélène?"

"Very specific, friend, but—" Billy raises a hand and snaps his fingers. "There, Helen it is."

"Hélène," Thomas corrects. "Hé— lène."

"All right, Hay Lane it is."

Thomas smiles at this unstoppable Billy Bing. Cleland was right. "Up those stairs?" Thomas asks, using his thumb to point back over his shoulder.

"Very perceptive, the French," Billy says to John Cleland.

Thomas pushes back his chair, takes his cursed manuscript in both hands and readies to stand.

"Oh not quite yet, sir." Billy Bing is up on his feet. He places a firm hand on Thomas's shoulder and keeps him in his seat. "I must go first. That's how it works. Have to make sure Hay Lane is ready for you. Votre visite. All right, friend?"

Thomas settles back into his chair. "Of course."

"A quarter hour, not a minute more. Good pleasure, like a good meal, takes a bit of time." With a courtier's bow, like Thomas is a lord, Billy Bing is away.

John Cleland lifts his chair and comes as close to Thomas as he can. The wooden arms of the two chairs are nearly touching. The man responsible for this outing is smiling as broadly as any person can. "I'm glad it has worked out, this little exploration of ours. Do you fancy a glass of port while we wait? There are ardours ahead."

"Amours, you mean?"

"That too." Cleland rises slowly to his feet. "Oysters, I think. What do you say? Some succulent fortifiers to prolong the enjoyment ahead?"

"Des huitres with the port, bien sûr. But sit down, Cleland, I'll pay the bill. I owe you something for taking my mind off – other things." Thomas climbs to his feet.

Cleland bows from the waist. "Perhaps I will accept, dear Tyrell. It occurs to me that I might be running short. I'm going to need something to purchase my country girl from Billy's list. I too seem to have a goatish side, alas."

"Why alas?"

"Because his Fanny will come dear. Billy said as much."

Thomas hesitates then says it anyway, what's on his mind. "You know that this Fanny is not really going to be the virgin Billy claims?"

"Shhh. There's no guarantee there's a God, but people keep building churches. It's how we are." Cleland shrugs. "I prefer the fiction that she is."

Thomas heads off to get the oysters and the port. On the short walk, a growing smile becomes a laugh. John Cleland can never be the friend Jean Gallatin is or was, but Thomas finds him amusing nonetheless.

—

The quarter-hour wait that Billy Bing promised has become a full half. The emptied oyster shells and the tray they came on have long since been cleared away. Thomas and Cleland are each on their third glass.

Thomas suddenly no longer wants any more of the port. Its sweet promise of delight, like the Hélène that Billy said he could get, is a deceit. Thomas runs a finger round the top edge of his glass. He pushes the glass a short distance away and glances at Cleland on the other side of the table. "He's gone out into the city to find a whore who speaks French, hasn't he?"

"'Fraid so." Cleland takes a sip of his port, then another, a long one, to finish it off. "And a willing maiden to play my Fanny as well. Our lives are pieces of theatre, if we only knew. And it's a knave who writes the scripts."

The two men exchange harrumphs.

"Did you know that Fielding's next play is set in a brothel?" Cleland asks.

Thomas's eyes go wide.

"'Tis true. He's concocted a plot—"

"Con-cocked? What's that?"

Cleland laughs. "I think you've drunk enough. Fielding has *concocted* a plot...." He pauses and waits to see if Thomas got it this time.

"Oh," Thomas says.

"It's about two prostitutes. *A Covent-Garden Tragedy* it's called."

"How do you know so much?"

"I get around. I listen well."

"And you?" Thomas ventures. He reconsiders the glass of port. He picks it up and takes another sip after all.

"Me what?"

"Gallatin says you write about people having sex."

"Does he now?" Cleland frowns. "Well, I read a few sample pages a while back, before you started joining us. Yes, it's half true. But there is a story. And I refuse to use any vulgar terms at all. I will not talk or write like the street."

"Not easy to do, I bet. The vulgar terms are what we know."

"Well, there's no challenge in doing things the easy way, is there now?" Cleland holds out an open hand.

Thomas acknowledges that he makes a good point. Then he covers his mouth to hide a laugh.

"What is it?" Cleland asks.

"I was just thinking. Every cock must have its day." Thomas holds in his sputter of laughter until he sees Cleland laugh himself. Then the two of them nearly cry.

"You know the real saying is dog, don't you, Tyrell?"

"I do. Do I? I'm not sure." Thomas starts laughing again.

When they return to the business at hand, the waiting game, Thomas pulls out his watch. "Another few minutes is all."

Cleland nods that he agrees. "And what about you, Tyrell, any aspirations to create a fictional world?"

No." Thomas studies Cleland for a moment to see if he really wants to hear what he has to say on the subject. He decides he does. "Well, perhaps. I was thinking recently about writing a tale in which the hero is no hero at all."

"What would he be?"

"I— I'm not sure. Maybe someone forced to become a thief and spy."

"Tricky," Cleland says. "That would be like writing from the wrong end of the telescope. As long as he is hanged for his crimes in the end, I suppose."

Thomas stares at his companion to see if that is perhaps a joke. No, apparently not. Maybe he'll leave the writing of novels to someone else.

There is a hard clasp on Thomas's shoulder.

"Wondered where I was, I bet."

Thomas and John Cleland exchange blank looks. Thomas pulls out his pocket watch.

"Ah friend," says Billy to Thomas, "you can put that away."

Thomas leans back in his chair. He finds he's squinting at the man.

"That's right, just another few ticks of the clock and your Straw— no, your *Hay* Lane will be along. How about I get your glass refilled while you wait?"

Thomas does not say a thing. He chooses to be stone-faced.

"Not thirsty then?" Billy says, then switches to Cleland. "You, good sir, your Fanny is upstairs." The thin pimp lifts both hands. He wears a look that suggests perhaps some thanks are due. "She's waiting eagerly and nervously of course. Go easy. You'll be her first. Third door on the left."

"How— how much?" Cleland is quick to ask. Thomas thinks he notices his friend's left eye give a tiny twitch. It has to be the unknown cost.

"No, no," says Billy. "You're both gentlemen. Not the time to speak of that. Relax. Pleasure first. No need yet for anyone to

open his purse." Billy rubs his hands together, like he's dusting
sand. "Here, sir, let me escort you to the right room and introduce you to the fair thing."

Billy winks at the still seated Thomas as he helps the slightly
wobbly Cleland away from the table and toward the stairs. "Right
back, friend," he says to Thomas. "The French treat's on her way,
I assure you. Just another," Billy shrugs, "another little bit. More
than worth the wait, she is."

———

The soles of Billy Bing's shoes are no sooner up the stairs, out of
Thomas's sight, than Thomas is up from the table and out the
door of the Shakespeare's Head. He's come to his senses just in
time. John Cleland may let himself be fleeced by a foolish dream,
but Thomas is wiser than that. As he hurries off he taps the inside
pocket of his veston where his purse still safely lies. He only hopes
Cleland has enough on him to pay whatever figure Billy tells him
he owes after the deed is done.

His feet spin across the Covent Garden market square, lit by
a quarter moon and a field of stars. Tonight, the celestial bodies
have the sky to themselves. There's not a cloud. Thomas can see
clearly how deserted the square is. There's only him on his diagonal path straight across and a couple of stray cats running stops
and starts. One is squealing like an unoiled wheel. The two of
them dart left and right, round and round. The larger cat, cloaked
in his coat of sable, is evidently stalking the smaller, mottled one.
Thomas knows what that's about and how it will end. He wishes
the female well as she tries to escape her fate, but that's not nature's way, is it? It's a reflection that slows him down. He sucks in
a deep breath.

Oh, how he can taste sulphurous grit from burning coal. He
looks to the rooflines surrounding the square. Yes, he spies a few
plumes of spiralling smoke. Not everyone, it seems, is asleep with
their fires out. Some are still up stoking the heat.

Stoking the heat? That makes Thomas grin. Funny how words
and phrases sometimes come to mind with a double sense. It's as

if our minds are labyrinths with interconnected paths between hidden recesses. Those few words are a clear case of that. Because that's exactly what Thomas would like to be doing right now, stoking the heat. And with the woman with whom he's shared so much, up to and including this disappointment-laden English sojourn. He takes another breath. Maybe for the first time since arriving in London he doesn't mind the taste of coal soot. Maybe its burning sensation will cleanse him of wanting Hélène.

He exits the square onto a street where the houses lining both sides are all built of bricks. Head down, his fast feet lead the way. What was it he used to call his legs? His physicians. Well, physicians, heal yourselves if you would.

Thomas grimaces at the joke. It makes him glance overhead as he marches along, for he recalls exactly where the original phrase comes from. Though for more than twenty years he has rejected the faith ladled into him as a child, claiming reason and logic as his adult guides, that faith swallowed so young still surfaces from time to time.

A rattling hack and cough comes out of an alley to his right. Thomas jumps. He hears a man's voice weakly calling "Help." Thomas peers in. He can see an outstretched hand. Ah, but what if it's a ruse? If he ventures into that dark corner of the night he could well be jumped. So he does not linger at the entrance to the alley for long. Caution is better than bravery. He hurries on.

Up ahead, glowing like sculpted ivory thanks to the light of the moon and stars, the spire of Christ Church comes into view. Its sudden appearance above the rooftops surprises Thomas. He thought it would take him longer to get to Spitalfields than it did. He must have been in a rush.

A rush to where and to what? Not to home, that's for sure. He's moving out in two days. His new home will be in ... the Duchy of Utope. Yes, that's it. Nowhere. Hogarth's recent cleverness at coming up with the term almost makes him smile. Almost.

And so here he is, on Church Street so soon, standing in front of number 5. There's not a light glimmering behind the closed shutters that he can detect. They must be in bed. The question

Acknowledgements and a Note to the Reader

This suite of novels (which began with *Thomas, A Secret Life*, published in 2012) is based loosely on an historical figure named Thomas Pichon (1700-1781). The historical Thomas Pichon belongs to historians; the one I write about belongs to me and to the readers of these books. He's a fictional character living in a fictional world, though one grounded in no small amount of research. Readers interested in the key sources I relied on to help me create the world in which Thomas and the other characters move are invited to contact me via my website www.ajbjohnston. com.

Worth mentioning here, however, is that the name "Tyrell" that Thomas adopts in this novel is the same name the historical Pichon used when he came to live in England in the 1750s. Similarly, the historical Pichon became friends with John Cleland (1709-1789), as does the Thomas in this book. Whether or not he met William Hogarth, Samuel Scott or Edward Cave I do not know. Aside from the above-mentioned details, the rest of this second novel is entirely imagined rather than based on any known facts from Pichon's life.

Of the many sources I consulted to create the London described in the second half of this book, two deserve a special mention here. The first is a website called *Spitalfields Life*. Its creator, known as the Gentle Author, makes daily postings of a wide range of material. Some of that material was a great help in writing this book. The G.A. also kindly informed me via email as to which streets and parts of London date from the 1730s. One of those was Fournier Street, which in the 1730s was called Church Street. That's where I ended up placing Jean Gallatin's house, where Thomas and Hélène lodge for many months.

The second source I want to mention is Hallie Rubenhold's *Covent Garden Ladies*. It presents a period a little later than the one I depict. Marvellously written, Rubenhold's study gave me the inspiration for the scenes where Thomas goes to The Rose and to Shakespeare's Head. My Billy Bing is a precursor of the pimp Jack Harris whom Rubenhold writes about.

Special thanks go to the three people who are slowly bringing me along as a novelist: Mary T. for extremely good advice after reading the first draft; Mike Hunter for ongoing encouragement and support; and Kate Kennedy for her outstanding editorial work. Kate's initial suggestions on structural matters had a significant influence on the shape and texture of the story. So too, these pages benefitted immensely from Kate's copy-editing to tighten the whole thing up.

All flaws and weaknesses are mine alone.

AJBJ

Previous Books by A. J. B Johnston

FICTION
Thomas, A Secret Life. Sydney, NS: Cape Breton University Press, 2012.

HISTORY
Ni'n na L'nu: The Mi'kmaq of Prince Edward Island. Charlottetown, PEI: Acorn Press, 2013. Co-authored with Jesse Francis.

Louisbourg, Past, Present, Future. Halifax, NS: Nimbus, 2013.

Endgame 1758: The Promise, The Glory and the Despair of Louisbourg's Final Decade. Lincoln, NE and Sydney, NS: University of Nebraska Press and Cape Breton University Press, 2007.

1758 : La finale. Promesses, Splendeur et Désolation dans la dernière décennie de Louisbourg. Québec : Presses de l'Université Laval, 2011.

Storied Shores: St. Peter's, Isle Madame and Chapel Island in the 17th and 18th Centuries. Sydney, NS: University College of Cape Breton Press, 2004.

Grand-Pré, Heart of Acadie. Halifax, NS: Nimbus, 2004. Co-authored with W. P. Kerr.

Grand-Pré, Coeur de l'Acadie. Halifax, NS: Nimbus, 2004. Traduit par Sylvain Filion.

Control and Order: The Evolution of French Colonial Louisbourg, 1713-1758. East Lansing, MI: Michigan State University Press, 2001.

Life and Religion at Louisbourg, 1713-1758. Montreal and Kingston: McGill-Queen's University Press, 1996 [Previously *Religion in Life at Louisbourg, 1713-1758,* 1984].

La religion dans la vie à Louisbourg (1713-1758). Ottawa: Environnement Canada, 1988.

Tracks Across the Landscape: A Commemorative History of the S&L Railway Sydney, NS: UCCB Press, 1995. Co-authored with Brian Campbell.

Louisbourg, an 18th-Century Town. Halifax, NS: Nimbus, 2004 [1991]. Co-authored with Kenneth Donovan, B. A. Balcom and Alex Storm.

Louisbourg: The Phoenix Fortress. Halifax, NS: Nimbus, 1997 [1990]. Photographs by Chris Reardon.

Louisbourg, Reflets d'une époque. Halifax, NS: Nimbus, 1997. Traduit par Robert Pichette.

From the Hearth: Recipes from the World of 18th-Century Louisbourg. Sydney, NS: UCCB Press, 1986. Co-authored with Hope Dunton.

The Summer of 1744, A Portrait of Life in 18th-Century Louisbourg. Ottawa: Parks Canada, 2002 [1983].

L'Été de 1744: La vie quotidienne à Louisbourg au XVIIIe siècle. Ottawa: Parcs Canada, 2002 [1983].

Defending Halifax: Ordnance, 1825-1906. Ottawa: Parks Canada, 1981.

La défense de Halifax: artillerie, 1825-1906. Ottawa: Parcs Canada, 1981.

About the author

A. J. B. Johnston has so far published fourteen books of history and more than a hundred articles on 18th-century French colonial or Acadian history. In recognition of his prolific career as an historian and writer, John was invested by France with the title Chevalier of the Ordre des Palmes Académiques (Order of Academic Palms). Johnston has now turned his hand to fiction. Long inspired to know more about Thomas Pichon (1700-1781), in his first novel, *Th   is, A S   t Life* (CBU Press, 2012), Johnston applied his cons.   s sen   of 18th-century French history to imagine young P.   arly life in Normandy and Paris. For *The Maze*, Johnston d   sive search on 18th-century London.